Snake and Morning Star

THE STORY OF DANNY PRATT CONTINUES

BY Dave Goss

Cover art by Dave Goss

Book design by Ohno Design
    web: www.ohnodesign.com

Published by Dave Goss
    web: www.lifealongthetrail.com
    email: boggdweller@yahoo.com

ISBN: 978-1-257-84632-0

Printed in the United States of America

This book is dedicated to Harmon and Wilma Knight,
who gave life to Betty, my wife;
Granny Fowler, a continuing source of optimism;
Frank Davis, who taught me the love of sailing; and my
brother, Paul, who gave me his understanding
and a place to live when I was young and troubled.

A special thanks to Betty Southwick,
who served as Frank Davis' secretary
in the years that he was president
of the United Utility Workers Union.

Preface

It has been said many times that an author never writes a story that is total fiction. This is true in the writing that I have presented here. The book is sculpted by my own experience, as all writings are. It is a gift to myself, a mapping of influences, bad and good, that shaped my life. I do not attempt to change anyone's thinking in this endeavor.

As I am now in the "autumn" of my years, I can say that I have learned many things. The most important of those was to find peace in knowing that I am nothing special. I have asked many questions and sought answers with an open mind. I have no fear of hell, and I do not anticipate a heaven. My expectations are that I will live out my life and die with a fair amount of dignity and few regrets. And that is enough.

Dave Goss

Also by Dave Goss

Danny

Snake and Morning Star

THE STORY OF
DANNY PRATT
CONTINUES

BY Dave Goss

My greatest wish is that people that I love
Do not resign themselves to a Hell
That does not exist
But in their own minds.

~ D.A. Boggdweller ~

• 1 •

BUT YOUR MOMMA AIN'T HERE

March 28, 1967

The 707 had been cruising at 40,000 feet when the descent over Texas began. A bank of fluffy, white clouds thinned, and the city of San Antonio appeared in a colorful pattern below.

The Earth would never seem the same to Danny Pratt. After looking down upon the tiny traces of human life, he realized how minute humans are in the mix of life on the planet and how profoundly they had altered it. He had experienced what he later would call an enlightenment.

He had boarded a plane for the first time in his life and flown over part of the United States. He savored the experience and considered that he was possibly the first in his family to fly. When compared to the enormity of the universe, his world in Bay City, Mich., was but a microscopic speck of a reality vastly larger than he could comprehend.

Daniel Pratt was now a member of the U.S. Air Force. His life was controlled by the whims of people he never could hope to know. He took his military oath at the Fort Wayne induction center in Detroit. He was to be shuttled from San Antonio to Lackland Air Force Base to begin six weeks of basic training.

He had decided to enlist in the Air Force eight months earlier. He passed his draft physical, was found to be healthy and could expect to be drafted into the U.S. Army shortly after graduation from high school. He looked into the options. Since he did not have the money nor the inclination to attend college at that time, he decided to talk to a recruiter. The necessary tests were taken to determine what field of the military Danny would be most suited for at the height of the Vietnam War. It was a surprise to find out that after basic training, he would attend missile maintenance school and become a specialist. Danny had no idea that he had skills as a mechanic.

The clothes on his back, a wallet with $9 in it, a pack of Marlboro cigarettes and a Zippo lighter that smelled of English Leather were his only possessions.

He stepped into the dry, hot air of Texas for the first time. It was a foreign country to him — a place of dryness, cowboys, armadillos and tumbleweeds. The Detroit Metro Airport had been a crisp -3 degrees when he left. San Antonio, at 80 degrees, was hot in comparison.

The inductees stepped onto a blue, Bluebird bus. The ride to Lackland Air Force Base was short. The land was arid and sandy. There was some sparse vegetation only slightly green. And on the side of the road was a dead armadillo that recently had been killed, his innards still moist. The patterns of the scales on his body were fascinating, a leftover from the days of the dinosaurs. This would be an adventure, he thought. He would make the best of whatever was in store for him.

The recruits approached the gate at Lackland and were waved in by the MP at the gate. This would be his life for the next four years — olive-drab fatigues, shaved heads and colorless buildings. There were white clapboard buildings as far as the eye could see. Squads of basic airmen marched in step, up and down the streets in pith helmets and yellow T-shirts with blue satin shorts and combat boots, all looking pretty much the same. Whoever designed the uniforms did not have aesthetics in mind. Perhaps they were meant to be unattractive.

The bus stopped before a nondescript, white clapboard. There was a cocky-looking man with short blond hair and a dark tan who looked quite fit with his hands on his hips wearing neatly ironed fatigues. There were three stripes on his sleeves, making the man an airman first class.

He began barking orders as the young men stepped from the bus. He had them line up in front of what was to be their home for the next six weeks. Barracks No. 354 was now the home of Squadron 3704, Flight 392.

"My name is Airman Gavagan, and I'm going to be your new mommy for the next six weeks. From now on, whenever you address anyone who outranks you, which is everyone, the first and last word out of your mouth will be sir. You are on your way to becoming American Fighting Men. This will be the hardest six weeks of your life. I'll see to that personally. As of now, you are the lowest of the low. You could crawl under a pile of dog shit. The only rights you will have will be the ones that I give you. You'll be lookin' for your mama. But your mama ain't here."

Gavagan was around 5 feet 9 inches tall and weighed about 170 pounds. He looked the way you might expect a basic training instructor to look in his Air Force-issued sunglasses. Danny was not expecting a pleasant experience in basic training. But he knew that Marine and Army basic training was much more strenuous.

After Gavagan gave his rehearsed speech, he instructed the new flight in the art of marching. They were directed to a warehouse where they were given their military gear. Many of the young men working in the warehouse wore one stripe on the sleeves of their green fatigues, making them airmen third class.

The thought flashed through Danny's head that even after completing basic training, the men of flight 392 still would be rated third class. This was the diminishing part of the training. They were being made into insignificant, worthless beings, then they would be sculpted into soldiers — American Fighting Men.

Danny decided he would try not to draw attention to himself. He was the largest man in his flight at 6 feet 4 inches and 190 pounds. There was one other tall guy named Owens from Corpus Christi, Texas, that had the long, lean, angular look of someone accustomed to hard work. Owens had a manner of speaking that reminded him of Fess Parker, the man who played Davy Crockett in an old Walt Disney TV series. Being the biggest was a distinction he never had appreciated. Being the largest in his flight meant that he would be the one Gavagan would want to "bring down."

The workers in the warehouse seemed eager to show their superiority over the new recruits. They barked at each of them as they were told to yell out the sizes of their clothes. The new recruits would then sidestep to the next clothing station.

"WHAT'S THE FIRST WORD OUTTA YOUR MOUTH, AIRMAN?," was screamed over and over in the cavernous warehouse.

"WHAT'S YOUR PANTS SIZE, AIRMAN?"

Danny arrived at the fatigue pants department. "SIR, 32, 32, SIR!"

He didn't find out until later that the fatigue pants given to him were 3 inches too big in the waist and several inches too long. They were measured for shoes, combat boots and dress shoes, then a group of tailors measured them for the dress blue uniforms and khakis.

After a timed, five-minute lunch, the flight was herded to a barbershop.

Danny noticed a shorter man with oily, brown hair down to his shoulders, who ended up in a barber's chair next to him. The man had the look of a street tough-guy. He wore a surly expression as he gazed ahead at his own reflection in the large mirror. He had an amateur-looking tattoo on the back of both hands of words that Danny could not read. His face and forearms were scarred.

Danny remembered a story from a friend about a friend who was singled out for special abuse when he came to Marine basic training with long, blond hair. He could see a similar drama unfolding here.

There were six barbers of Mexican decent that spoke to each other as they sheered the new recruits. Hills of multicolored hair piled up on the floor. When the long-haired street tough jumped into the chair, there was an exchange of comments in Spanish and a few chuckles as the long, brown locks fell in clumps to the floor.

"You not so preety without your preety, long hair, airmon." There was a lull in the cutting activity as the other barbers laughed. Danny turned to look full in the face of the man who had just lost his lion's mane of brown hair, his face doe-eyed and humble.

"Whot? Are you stoopeed? Hold steel, airmon," said Danny's barber, as he took off Danny's Beatle locks in less than a minute.

Next, they were marched to the dispensary where they were

given multiple immunizations with one blast of pressured air. They were ordered not to move while the injection was given. But several of the young men jerked at the wrong time and came out holding a bloody compress over the ripped injection site in their right arm.

They were marched back to the barracks where they were given bunk assignments, footlockers and combination locks, an olive-drab wool blanket, a pillow, two sheets and a pillowcase. Everything that went in the footlocker had to be put in a specific place and folded precisely. Airman Gavagan demonstrated the correct way to make a white-collar bed with the two cotton sheets and the wool blanket. They were shown how to stand at attention — eyes straight ahead, shoulders back, stomach in, chest out, thumbs touching the outer seam of the trousers, heels together. Mimeographed sheets were handed out that gave them the information they would need to absorb by the end of basic training. "The Code of Conduct for the U.S. Fighting Man" had to be memorized along with the names of those in their chain of command, to name a few. They were given free time to fold their uniforms, organize footlockers and digest what was taking place.

There was much to be absorbed. Collectively, they would share information concerning the arrangement of the footlockers and repeat the memory work so that everyone heard it over and over. They had seven days before the first evaluation, when they would be expected to have everything memorized.

Danny noticed that Brian Dutcher from Reese, Mich., who was on the same flight from Detroit, was bunked directly across from him. They began talking as if they had known each other for some time. They exchanged information, finding that they had taken dates to the Tuscola Drive-In Theater on highway M-15, just outside Bay City.

The conversation was interrupted.

"Attention!"

The recruits came to attention at the foot of their bunks as they had been instructed to do earlier. A small black man appeared in the doorway accompanied by several other men who immediately fanned out through the barracks. He walked with authority — straight-necked, his face grim and fierce, head shaved, impeccably groomed down to his spit-shined service oxfords. The black man had four stripes on his khaki uniform, one more than Gavagan. He was a staff sergeant. Gavagan was giving this man a lot of respect.

They were moving up the chain of command they had just been briefed on.

"WHO YOU LOOKIN' AT, AIRMAN?" Danny was caught looking sideways at the staff sergeant. He diverted his attention. The bronze face appeared below the level of his chin. The face disappeared. He could hear a scraping sound and realized that his footlocker was being moved. The face suddenly popped up directly in his face. The sergeant moved his face forward until his nose touched Danny's. He smelled of Old Spice.

"ARE YOU IGNORING ME, AIRMAN?" Danny could feel the man's hot breath and saliva hitting his face.

"SIR, NO, SIR," Danny yelled with surprising volume.

"WHO WERE YOU LOOKIN' AT, AIRMAN?"

"SIR, NO ONE, SIR!"

"BUT I SAW YOU LOOKIN' AT ME. YOU CALLIN' ME A LIAR?"

Danny listened to the sergeant's tirade while wondering what kind of punishment he would receive. He had heard through the grapevine that there would be leading questions, designed to entrap the new recruits and illustrate that they were completely powerless. The interrogation continued. The small staff sergeant looked as if he was ready to step down from the footlocker when he suddenly turned and again poked his nose into Danny's face.

"YOU THINK YOU'RE A BIG BOY, DON'T YA?"

There was a lull in the conversation as Danny tried desperately to think of a correct response.

"I DON'T LIKE BIG BOYS!" He said so loudly that it made Danny jump. "I'M GUNNA BE ON YOUR ASS LIKE STINK ON SHIT! Do you hear me, airman?"

"SIR, YES, SIR!"

With that, the staff sergeant moved on.

After getting into the faces of several more of the new airmen, the sergeant turned and addressed the flight in general: "At ease," he said. "This is a shake-down inspection. I want all wallets and pockets emptied onto the top of your beds. Now!"

There was a flurry of activity as the men did as they were ordered. The little man walked purposefully down the length of the barracks with his hands on his hips, enjoying the fact that he was the ranking enlisted man in the room. He stopped in front of a round-headed man whose most prominent feature was his large nose. He was no taller than the staff sergeant. He stood almost nose-to-nose with him. The recruit stared straight ahead.

"God! What in hell stinks, airman?"

"Sir. My socks, sir," said the flustered airman.

"How long you been wearin' those filthy socks, airman?"

"SIR. FOUR DAYS, SIR!"

There was a pause as the sergeant took several steps. "Open your mouth, airman. Now, chew."

Most of the new recruits had been to their various induction centers around the country, then were flown here to basic training. None of the recruits had a change of clothes or a shower in several days. It was assumed that the staff sergeant had made the little recruit chew on his own crusty socks, though no one really witnessed anything since they were ordered to attention. The training methods were effective. Every new recruit now knew he was indeed the lowest of the low.

This was a moment that spoke to Danny Pratt. He was now at the mercy of many people, some quite sadistic. Gone was the carefree time of his life, riding around Bay City with his girlfriend, Kay, in his midnight-blue, 1964 Chevy Impala. He had no recourse but to follow orders and try to be as inconspicuous as possible.

———

They practiced marching daily. Gavagan was impatient. He would run up to an airman as he marched along and yell in his ear, "You're bouncing." They learned to turn in unison, left face, right face. They also tried some rhymes as they marched along to help them keep in sync. The flag bearer, a short guy with a booming voice, would lead them. He would shout out a phrase, and the rest of the flight members would repeat it. One of the rhymes was about Jody, a guy who was romancing a fictitious girlfriend.

> *"Ain't no use in goin' home.*
> *Jody's got your girl and gone.*
> *Ain't no use in feelin' blue.*
> *Jody's got your sister, too.*
>
> *Sound off.*
> *One, two.*
> *Sound off.*

Three, four.
Bring it on down.
One, two, three, four, one two.
Three four."

On longer marches they would get creative and someone else would take up leading, adding made-up verses that sometimes got a little raunchy. Gavagan cautioned the men to censor some of their words.

It was the fifth day of training. Danny had been doing well. The physical demands were strenuous but within reach of any healthy, young man.

Danny was writing a letter to Kay when Gavagan entered the room from his office.

"Let me have your attention. I have news from the base personnel office: The entire Flight 392, upon satisfactory completion of basic training, is hereby notified that they have been selected for immediate duty in the Republic of South Vietnam." Gavagan looked at the silent faces of the flight. "That's all." He then returned to his office and shut the door. The barracks was silent.

"They can't just send us over to a war zone for duty. We haven't learned anything yet," whispered Razey. Razey, as it became known, was a college graduate who had washed out of Officer's Training School. Razey had the demeanor of someone a little more settled than the younger recruits and was much more mature.

"If I had wanted to go to a war zone, I would have just waited to be drafted by the Army or the Marine Corps," said Oakley Mitchell, another guy from Michigan who had the bottom bunk, just next to Danny's. Mitchell looked a little pale, and tears were welling in his eyes.

"It wouldn't make a bit of sense to send raw recruits over to Vietnam for any reason. I don't know what is going on, but something just isn't right." Razey was not whispering any longer. He didn't seem to care that Gavagan was just behind the office door and probably listening.

That evening, during private time, Danny was busy writing a letter to Kay. Danny was not sure what to think about the announcement that Gavagan had given. He would do whatever he was required to do. But he did not want to go into combat, which was why he had enlisted in the Air Force. The romance of going to war and leaving your love behind opened a stream of feelings for Kay. He had not had this kind of longing before. He had received the first letter from Kay the day before; smelling her Arpege on the letter sent him into orbit.

So Danny poured out his feelings of longing that was overwhelming him. He sealed the letter and was placing a stamp on the envelope when Gavagan opened his office door and entered the room.

"Give me your attention." He took his practiced posture, stiff-necked, feet wide apart. "Does anyone know what today's date is?"

Someone yelled: "Sir, April 1st, sir."

"That's right. Remember the news I gave to you this morning concerning Vietnam?" He paused for a moment. "April Fool's."

There was much relief when Gavagan left the room. Danny tore up the letter that he was to send to Kay.

———

The first two weeks flew by in a flurry of activity. The flight members learned on a Friday morning that they would be given a day pass to go into San Antonio to spend a leisurely day and to spend some of the $60 they had received from the paymaster for the first two weeks of training. The mood was jubilant as everyone in the flight prepared to be seen for the first time in their khaki uniforms. There was a lot of mirror-glancing as the recruits were trying to look their best. The absence of any stripes on the shirtsleeves gave them away in San Antonio as "rainbows" because of the differing tan lines on their necks, with a light forehead from the baking Texas sun.

It was invigorating to get a break from basic training. Danny's dad had sent him a small Brownie camera. He checked to make sure there was film in it, then placed it on his bunk. He took the laundered khaki uniform from its hanger, and he turned for a moment. When he turned back to his bunk, his camera was gone. He looked around to see if someone might be playing a joke on him. Oakley Mitchell had a knowing smile on his face. "Man, you are in some deep shit."

Danny was momentarily puzzled, until he heard Gavagan's muffled voice behind his closed office door: "The airman who is missing a Kodak Brownie camera will report to me in my office. Now!"

It was a security violation to leave anything of value unattended.

"Danny banged hard on the flight office door and began the reporting procedure.

"Who is it?"

"Sir, Airman Pratt, sir."

"I knew it was you, Pratt. Get your ass in here and report.

Danny opened the office door, doing a military pivot, stopping at the front of Gavagan's desk, standing at attention.

"Sir, Airman Pratt reports as ordered. Sir."

Gavagan got up, walked behind Danny and closed the office door. He grabbed Danny by the throat and slammed him into the outer wall, knocking a framed picture from the wall as glass shattered on the cement floor. He began poking his knuckles into Danny's sternum. As he spewed his reprimand, he poked harder and harder. The pain was agonizing.

"YOU'VE COMMITTED A SERIOUS SECURITY VIOLATION: ABANDONMENT OF VALUABLE PROPERTY! YOU'RE GUNNA' PULL ALL-DAY AND ALL-NIGHT GUARD DUTY, WHILE THE REST OF THE FLIGHT TAKES A DAY PASS T0 SAN ANTONIO!"

Gavagan continued poking the sternum with more and more vehemence.

"YOU'D LIKE TO PUNCH MY FACE, WOULDN'T YOU, AIRMAN?"

"SIR. YES, SIR!" The pain was overwhelming.

"WELL, GO AHEAD, AIRMAN. HIT ME. THERE'S NO ONE HERE TO WITNESS. GO AHEAD, PRATT, KICK MY ASS!"

Gavagan grabbed a large book from his desk and threw it to the floor. It sounded almost like a shot as it landed flat on the floor. He kicked the waste can across the room, where it slammed into a metal file cabinet. Danny was beginning to understand that this was a show for the other airmen who were listening outside the office door. He continued taunting Danny while he knuckled his sternum.

The pain was getting unbearable. In desperation, he grabbed Gavagan's hand to stop the pain. He looked Gavagan in the eye, steeling himself for whatever this sadistic man had in store for him. He was ready to fight if necessary. The pain had to stop.

"Get dressed in your fatigues, pith helmet and brogans. Report to me in 10 minutes for guard duty," he said in a quiet voice. "Your ass is mine, airman." He gave one last poke in the sternum as Danny released his hand.

Danny had reached an extreme level of anger and frustration. Adrenaline was pounding through his system. He had nowhere to release the energy he was feeling. He left Gavagan's office, averting the stares from the other men as he went directly to the latrine. He became aware that tears were flowing down his cheeks. He was ashamed of his outward display of emotion. He wanted to hurt Gavagan. He had never felt such hatred toward another human. The other airmen stared at him when he returned to his bunk to get ready for guard duty.

Within the hour, the rest of Flight 392 boarded a Bluebird bus and prepared to leave for San Antonio as Danny watched from his guard position in front of the main door to the barracks.

"Owens, the tall cowboy from Corpus Christi, slapped Danny on the shoulder as he walked by on his way to the bus.

"Don't let that smart-ass son-of-a-bitch get the best of ya," he said in his own Texan way. Danny liked Owens. He looked like he was born to a cowboy hat and a spirited horse. He had a hardened look, weathered and tough for a young man in his late teens.

The day passed slowly as Danny stood guard in front of the barracks. At noon, the sun blazed upon the white of the buildings and reflected off the sand, which seemed to create even more heat. Danny's mind wandered as he paced in front of the building. Wearing his pith helmet and combat boots and his laundered, olive drab fatigues, he had great difficulty keeping his attention on what he was doing, which was nothing.

Airman Gavagan came out from the barracks to give Danny a sack lunch prepared by food service at the mess hall. It had two pints of milk, a ham sandwich on white bread with cheese and an apple. Danny ate it all, and it tasted really good. It was amazing how a little deprivation can make the simple and ordinary things seem special.

About an hour later, Gavagan returned and ordered Danny to go inside the barracks and guard the double doors from the inside. "I'm leaving. Under no circumstances are you to let anyone through those doors except me. If anyone comes by and wants to come in, you are only obliged to give him your name, rank, serial number and date of birth."

"Sir. Yes, sir." Danny watched Gavagan leave.

It was around 4 p.m. when an authoritative figure approached the barracks. The man's sleeves were covered with stripes. It was Chief Master Sgt. McManness, his non-commissioned officer in charge. Danny recognized his face from his picture that hung inside the entrance door. Danny realized he was being tested.

The sergeant tried opening the door, which was locked.

"Open this door, airman," he said, while looking through the wired safety glass of the door window.

"Sir. No, sir. You are not authorized to enter, sir."

"OPEN THIS DOOR IMMEDIATELY, AIRMAN, OR THERE WILL BE DIRE CONSEQUENCES. "The chief master sergeant was the highest-ranking person he had seen since he started basic. His face was red, and the arteries in his neck stood out. He was angry.

"Sir, I cannot allow you to enter. Sir."

"I am Chief Master Sgt. McManness, your NCOIC. Open this door. NOW."

"Sir. No, Sir."

"Give me your name, rank, serial number, airman." He pulled out a pen and a pad.

"Sir. Airman Basic Pratt, serial number 16957731, sir."

The sergeant gave Danny a nasty scowl.

"I'll give you one more chance to save yourself. Airman Pratt, open this door."

"Sir. No, sir."

The sergeant quickly turned and left.

Danny's heart was racing. He hoped that he had done the right thing, but he wasn't sure.

"Good job, Pratt." Gavagan's voice came from behind him. "If you had let him in, you'd be going back to the first day of training."

As the weeks passed, Danny could see how military training could tear you down and then attempt to build you back up. He would never see those carefree days again. His beautiful, 1964 Chevy Impala, 283-cubic inch V-8 with bench seats and 3-speed on the column and midnight-blue sparkled finish, was now owned by his dad, who took over the payments once Danny left for the service. His dad did not love that car the way Danny loved it. It was only a car to him.

Danny could not feel sorry for himself. His old drinking buddy, Dennis Hutchinson, had been in Vietnam for at least six months. Whatever he experienced in Air Force basic training was nothing in comparison to what Dennis probably was going through.

Danny wrote to his parents:

From: Airman Basic Daniel Pratt
Flight 3704
Lackland AFB, Texas

April 21, 1967

Dear Mom and Dad,
How are things at 206 24th? I am doing well. I think a may have lost a few pounds. We have PC (physical conditioning) everyday. We march to the training field before breakfast every morning in shorts, pith helmets and combat boots. It looks silly, wearing combat boots with shorts. But, we all do what we are told and try not make any waves.

Yesterday, we were running our daily mile around a quarter-mile track. I was running behind a guy named Shaw, from Tennessee. Shaw is one of those poor guys who can't seem to do anything right. He isn't stupid, he just gets nervous, then makes mistakes. In order for him to make the required mile in less than eight minutes, a couple of us usually grab Shaw's arms to help hurry him along. Most of us were already lapping Shaw by the first half-mile. I was just coming up behind Shaw when I felt something warm and moist hitting my arms and shirt. It was coming from Shaw. He had messed his pants, and it was running down his legs and hitting his boots. Once we finished, Gavagan had Shaw go back to the barracks to shower and change. The rest of us had to go to breakfast covered in muss.

Tomorrow, I'll be taking what is called a bypass specialist test. Airman Gavagan said the Air Force needs artist/illustrators. If I pass the test, I'll be an artist for the Air Force. I think I'd like that. I would be a better artist than I would be a missile maintenance man. I would go directly to my duty station for on-the-job training and skip the tech school I would have gone to. I'm keeping my fingers crossed.

It has been very hot here. They have us taking salt tablets with every meal to help us store fluids. We had a red-flag day last week, which means there is no unnecessary outside activity. It was 104 degrees that day. We pretty much stayed in the barracks all day, shined shoes and practiced the things that we needed to memorize.

I have to go for now. It's almost time for lights-out, and I have to spit-shine my boots. I miss you all. I miss your cherry-delicious pies, Mom. See you soon.

All my love,
Danny

Danny found himself needing his parents' approval. He was no longer a carefree vagabond and likely would never live at 206 24th St. again. A compassionate note from home was an indication that his parents still cared for him. He had not gotten along with his parents since he had obtained his driver's license. He had openly rebelled against them and the Wesleyan Methodist Church that he was raised in. He had been a constant anxiety to both parents. Contrary to the teachings of the church, he smoked cigarettes, drank beer nightly and spent Christmas Day in the drunk tank after passing out in a snow bank on the corner of Cass Avenue and Broadway in the South End in Bay City.

Danny's dad picked him up from the jail on Center Avenue on Christmas Day. Harold Pratt said nothing on the drive home. He was ashamed of his son, and there was just nothing to say. But Danny knew he could not be the person his parents expected him to be. He felt smothered by the rules of his parents' faith. He wanted their approval. But, if he had to do it all over again, he would do the same thing, again, and again and again. He simply could not live the life of a Wesleyan Methodist.

His mom seemed to have lost all of the joy in her life and lived in a constant state of fear. The people he grew up with in the church, except for a few, seemed morose and cynical. A self-righteous veneer covered a terrible fear and insecurity. He could not stop himself from asking the question: If you have been saved from a great lake of fire, if you are assured of eternal life, why are you so unhappy? Danny's mother, Ermine Pratt, was now afraid to leave her home, fearing that her heart might fail. She feared everything.

Danny was not aware that his mother was suffering from early Alzheimer's disease.

Danny relived the enlightenment that he had on his first plane ride to Texas and to basic training. He no longer thought of God in the same way. The feeling lasted for only an instant. But the power of the experience lingered in a sense of awe from the brilliant sun above the clouds, the tiny patterns of human life below, the clouds glowing in brightness. Goose bumps rose on his arms. Everything seemed to make sense; everything seemed to fit in its proper place. Life made sense. The feeling of ecstasy lasted only briefly. Danny found himself kneeling in his seat next to the window. His fellow passengers were staring at him as if he had lost his mind.

Danny had not shared this revelation with anyone. He didn't have the vocabulary to convey his feelings. He wrote to his girlfriend, Kay, mentioning that he had a great flight but left it there, not knowing how to express the feeling of overwhelming awe and the scale of life on the beautiful Earth.

Kay was one of the only people in his life who accepted him as he was. He received a letter from her in his third week of training that she had received her "little red visitor," that week. She was relieved. They had made love with abandon before Danny departed for basic training. He missed her scent, her touch, her long, silky, brown hair and her sweet love.

He wrote to her one evening:

May 12, 1967

Hi Honey!

I really miss you. Things are getting better here. We are getting more liberties now, and our flight will be graduating soon. We've been getting the evening to ourselves. I'm going to a movie tonight with Owens, the guy from Corpus Christi that I told you reminds me of Fess Parker.

I guess I've never seen real prejudice before. Last night, we were all showering and brushing our teeth before lights-out. A little Jewish guy named Silver, from New York City, was brushing his teeth at one of the sinks. His schwantz was touching the sink as he shaved. This normally quiet guy named Cutter went nuts. He called Silver a Jew pig and told him to get his filthy body off the public sink. The little guy seemed harmless to me, but Cutter really was ready to nail this guy for no reason.

This morning at the PT field, there was a guy in formation just in front of me named McQuarter. When we got down to do our push-ups, McQuarter landed in the middle of a fire ant hill. Thousands of the little ants were all over him in an instant. He jumped around and was yelling like he was mortally wounded. The PT instructor asked him what in hell he was doing. He says, "Sir. I'm being attacked by thousands of ants. Sir." The instructor says, "How stupid. Doing push-ups on a fire ant hill." Several of us helped brush the ants off, and he was sent to the dispensary. Later on, McQuarter showed up at the barracks with little blisters all over his body.

Jerry Mathers, the guy who plays Beaver on "Leave It to Beaver," is here at Lackland. He's going through the same training we are. I haven't seen him, but one of Gavagan's friends has him in his flight. Gavagan says that he doesn't get treated any better than anyone else.

I need to close this letter and post it. It's time for lights-out. See you soon.

I love you,

Danny xxxooo

On a Tuesday evening, Danny was returning to the barracks from a movie at the base theater. Without giving it a thought, Danny dropped the cigarette that he was smoking on the sidewalk, just outside the barracks, and crushed it with his service oxfords. He looked up to see Mitchell Oakley, the whiny guy from Midland, Mich., walking into the barracks ahead of him. He entered the barracks, then had second thoughts and returned to field-strip the cigarette that he had left on the sidewalk.

A moment later, Danny was on his knees working the combination on his footlocker, when Gavagan yelled from the flight office, "Airman Pratt, report to me in the flight office. Now!"

A moment later, Danny stood at the front of Airman Gavagan's desk in the flight office.

"Sir. Airman Pratt reports as ordered. Sir."

To the right of Gavagan stood Mitchell Oakley, at ease, with his hands behind his back, a smirk on his face.

"At ease, Pratt. Airman Oakley has something he would like us to see. Lead the way, Oakley."

Oakley walked down the hall and out the front door. He stopped and pointed to a spot on the sidewalk.

"It was right there, sir. I don't know what could have happened to it. ..."

"Airman Pratt, did you leave a crushed cigarette on the sidewalk?"

"Sir. No, sir."

"But Airman Oakley says he saw you crushing out a cigarette with your foot, then leave it. Is Airman Oakley lying?" Gavagan was enjoying the moment, with a smirk on his face.

"Sir. Yes, sir."

"Airman Pratt, why would Oakley lie about something like that?"

"Sir. He's kissin' up, sir."

Gavagan walked over and stared straight into Oakley's eyes, nose to nose. "Airman Pratt says he didn't do it, Oakley. He's much bigger than you. You callin' him a liar?" Gavagan was playing the intimidator now and was getting the reaction he wanted from Mitchell Oakley.

Oakley blinked nervously and swallowed hard before answering. "Sir. No, sir."

"Well, then you must be lying to me. Are you lying to me, Airman Oakley?"

"Sir. Yes, sir," he said, his eyes welling with tears.

"Hmmm. That's interesting. I'm going to speak with Pratt about this. We'll decide what your punishment should be for lying to a superior. Maybe I'll have you and Pratt duke it out. Would you like that, Oakley?"

"Sir. No, sir."

Gavagan dismissed Oakley. Danny stayed and talked with Gavagan for several minutes.

⸻

Danny returned to his bunk. Mitchell Oakley was pacing nervously in front of his bunk.

"What did Gavagan say to you? What's my punishment going to be?

"I can't tell you," Danny said, without looking at him. "Whatever it is, you deserve it. You just don't rat on other men in the military. In the Marine Corps, they'd give you a bloody-blanket part."

"Ya. And you still might get one, Oakley," said Owens. Several others voiced their agreement.

Oakley was allowed to mull over his plight. After a sleepless night, he approached Danny when he returned to the barracks after eating breakfast looking haggard, worried.

"I'm sorry I ratted on you," he said.

"You mean you're sorry you got caught." Danny looked at Oakley extending his right hand. It was evident that the man was frightened.

"I except your apology. But your punishment isn't up to me. Gavagan is the one who decides what happens around here. The man's a sadist. But maybe you'll get lucky."

———

That afternoon, the flight was scheduled for an inspection. Everything was to be inspected — the uniforms, the footlockers. The shoes were to be spit-shined, and everything had a proper place. It was all to get them ready for the final graduation inspection, just a week away.

Just before the inspection, Gavagan called Mitchell Oakley to the flight office. As soon as the door to the flight office closed, Danny walked over to Oakley's footlocker, picked it up and shook it vigorously.

A moment or two passed before Mitchell walked out of the flight office. He walked over to Danny and whispered: "It's not so bad. I'm pulling guard duty tonight." He smiled broadly.

" 'Ten hut." It was Gavagan, announcing that the inspection was beginning. The men stood at attention near their footlockers. One by one, each footlocker was inspected and each airman's belongings were checked meticulously for indiscretions. It was a lengthy process. They stood at attention until each man got the "at ease" order after he passed the inspection.

Finally, Airman Gavagan stood in front of Mitchell Oakley. "Open your footlocker, airman."

Oakley knelt in front of his footlocker and quickly did the combination on the lock and opened the locker as he stood to return to attention.

"What the hell is this? Is this some kind of a joke, airman?"

Gavagan yelled.

Danny chanced a glance at the locker without moving his head. The footlocker was a jumbled mess.

"Sir. Airman Pratt did it, sir," Oakley said with a shaky voice.

Gavagan walked over to Danny, stood before him looking him in the eyes. "Did you mess up Oakley's footlocker, Airman Pratt?"

"Sir. No, sir."

"Airman Pratt says he didn't shake up your footlocker. You callin' Pratt a liar?"

"Sir. No, sir."

Gavagan picked up Oakley's footlocker and dumped it on the floor. "You've got five minutes to make sure that everything in this locker is perfect. Move it!"

After four tries, Oakley finally was able to get his locker in good order.

Most of men in flight 3704 were doing well. They helped each other memorize what needed to be memorized, and they checked each other out before the final inspection to minimize mistakes. There was only one man in the flight that was doubtful as far as passing the final evaluation, Albert Lewis. He was the same guy that crapped his pants while running the mile. He saluted with his left hand on the confidence course when a cardboard picture of a first lieutenant popped up. Lewis was not dull-witted. But, he became so nervous in critical situations that he made mistakes. He was in poor physical condition. He had an irritating, high-pitched voice that sounded like he was whining constantly, his face contorting as if he was in pain. He had difficulty following directions and had not completed the mile in less than nine minutes. Minimum requirement for the mile run was eight minutes. He seemed to run out of energy running around the obstacles in the confidence course instead of over them.

Danny sympathized with Lewis. He remembered when his dad came to an intramural basketball game to see him play back in the eighth grade. He became so aware of being under his dad's critical eye that he became self-conscious and uncoordinated. He had the worst game of his life. Danny and Owens helped Lewis out whenever they could.

The day of the final evaluation arrived. Everyone was doing well except Lewis. He was lapped by everyone as he was running the required mile. Every man had finished running and was standing around congratulating each other. But Lewis had a little less than a quarter-mile to go. Owens found Danny, and they ran back out on the track behind Lewis, grabbed him by the arms and moved him along faster. The three men crossed the finish line with seconds to spare.

But, it was all to no avail. Albert Lewis had made too many mistakes. When they returned to the barracks later that afternoon, Lewis was gone and his mattress was rolled up on his bunk. Everyone assumed he had been sent back to the first day of training. No one really knew for sure. Owens speculated that he was either sent back to the first day of training or he would be booted out of the Air Force with an untrainable discharge. Danny felt bad for Lewis, yet he also thought that may have been the best that could happen to the poor guy.

———

May 17, 1967, was graduation day. Gavagan was unusually friendly and cheerful, speaking to the flight members as if they were equals. His tough-guy veneer was still in place, as he told the men he was proud of the progress they had shown.

Danny had been trying hard to please Gavagan. But he did not like the man. He had been very close to doing anything that it took to stop his knuckle from poking him in the sternum repeatedly when he had left his camera unattended on his bunk. He had felt more vehemence than ever before and could not have held on much longer. The pain was excruciating. He thought it weakened the man to take advantage of a situation where he held all of the cards. To him, Gavagan was just another glorified bully.

Only two of the men in Flight 3704 were without orders on the final day of basic training. Danny Pratt was one of them. As yet, he didn't know what his career field would be. He hoped with all of his might and even prayed that he had passed the artist/illustrator test and would go directly to his duty station for on-the-job training. But even if he didn't pass the test and was sent to missile maintenance, he would at least have some valuable training.

———

Danny was moved to the transient barracks where he would stay until he received his orders. He took his uniforms to the laundry and had a single stripe sewed onto all of them. He was now Airman Third Class Daniel Pratt. He was put on weeds and seeds detail until his orders arrived.

———

On May 24, 1967, Danny went to the personnel office as he had been doing since the end of basic training. A civilian employee in her late 30s asked him for his serial number, then handed him a Manila envelope. "Your orders have arrived," she said.

He walked to a shaded bench and sat down. He took his time opening the official-looking envelope, not wanting to hurry this important moment.

He read the orders slowly and carefully. He was ordered to take a seven-day leave. Then he was to report for duty at Eglin Air Force Base, Fla., where he would begin on-the-job training as an artist/illustrator. He could not contain his joy. Before going to basic training, he never had been more than 350 miles from his home in Bay City. Now he would be living in the Florida tropics, with sunshine and the ocean.

"Wow!" The word escaped before Danny had a chance to squelch it. He looked around to see that he was drawing unwanted attention.

Danny sat on the bench for some time just fantasizing about living near the ocean, palm trees and alligators. Miss Caris, his fifth-grade music teacher, went to Florida every year for Christmas vacation and came back dark brown from tanning in the sun. Danny thought of his brother, Peter. He knew Peter would be happy for him.

Danny felt like flying as he returned to the transient barracks. His life suddenly had taken a wonderful new direction. He was going to be an artist.

• 2 •

THE FLORIDA YEARS

"The man who views the world at 50 the same as he did at 20 has wasted 30 years of his life."

~ Muhammad Ali ~

Florida. It was a dream for Danny Pratt. Not only would he be living there, but he now was officially an artist/illustrator for the U.S. Air Force.

He arrived at night. He was then taken to the transient barracks at Hurlburt Field, an auxiliary field to Eglin Air Force Base in the Florida Panhandle.

The following morning, after breakfast at the mess hall, he reported to the personnel office, signed in and was shuttled to Air Ground Operations School (AGOS) where he presented himself to Master Sgt. Carda, his new NCOIC, who introduced him to his new commander, Col. Shelly.

Sgt. Carda took him to the second floor to the graphics shop where he would be working.

He shook hands with Technical Sgt. Ethier, his new supervisor; Airman 1st Class Berry, an illustrator; Airman 3rd Class Gary Patton, an illustrator; Staff Sgt. Lovelace, the squadron photographer; Richard Williams, a GS-9 civilian illustrator; and Ralph Henson, a GS-7 civilian illustrator.

"This must be the new rookie," said a gruff voice from behind Danny. A small airman third class entered the room carrying a cup of coffee and a cigarette.

"This is Airman Bock," said Ethier. "This young man needs some breaking in. Ray Bock has a behavior problem," Ethier smiled broadly.

Danny could tell that Airman Bock was well-liked in the graphic shop by the way the others interacted with him.

Ray Bock was around 5 feet 7 inches, with brown hair and a thin but muscular build. His parents, Danny later learned, were Lebanese. His large, brown eyes gave evidence of that. He was from Pittsfield, Mass., where his parents owned a golf course and an up-scale restaurant.

Ray was so bold and cocky that Danny had to laugh. He told Ray later that he reminded him of Chicken Hawk, the Warner Bros. cartoon character who was always trying to intimidate the much-larger Foghorn Leghorn.

Ray recently had seen the movie version of John Steinbeck's "Of Mice and Men." He began calling Danny "Lenny" after the big, slow-witted man in the novel.

Sgt. Ethier assigned Danny a cubicle, complete with a drawing table, T-squares, triangles, compasses and a set of Rapidograph technical pens. He also was given a training manual for the artist/illustrator career field.

They walked about the shop while Ethier showed him some of the work that was produced there. Richard Williams had some impressive illustrations of planes on combat missions. Ralph Henson also was an accomplished artist.

Either explained that Danny's main job, until they found out what his talents were as an artist, would be to produce viewgraphs. Viewgraphs looked like over-sized 35mm slides but were much larger with a viewing area of 810. Each color on a viewgraph was a separate sheet of transparent film. The master for the art was done on tracing velum with the Rapidograph pens. Then the master was sent through an Ozalid machine, an anhydrous ammonia process that produced a copy of the art on a clear sheet of film. Then, whatever colors were needed were added as overlays. The multicolored viewgraphs were bulky, containing as many as a dozen overlays.

This was not the type of work Danny had expected to be doing. But he would do whatever was needed to become a better artist.

It turned out that Danny moved into the same room that Gary Patton and Ray Bock were already occupying. There was one bunk bed and a single bed in the room. Since Danny was low man on the totem pole, he got the top bunk. There were three built-in wooden lockers in the room and a sink with a mirror. The communal latrine was in the middle of the hallway with a large shower room and private toilet stalls. There was a laundry on the first floor.

Ray had personalized the area around his bunk. There was a centerfold of a Playboy Playmate taped to the wall directly over his bed.

There was a day room on each floor of the barracks. On the second floor, where the single men from AGOS were housed, the day room had some durable-looking furniture, a TV that did not work and a Ping-Pong table. In the hallway next to the day room was a pay telephone booth.

Once Danny moved into the room, made his white-collar bed and stowed his clothes in his locker, Gary suggested that the three of them go on a tour of Fort Walton Beach. Danny gratefully accepted the invitation.

Patton owned a white, 1960 Corvair named Gidget with a painted cartoon on both front fenders just behind the wheel well. Danny sat in the back seat while Ray rode shotgun.

They rode down Highway 98, into the small town of Fort Walton Beach. At that time of evening, many businesses were closed. Jimmy's News Stand was open, as was the small theater next door. Down the street on the opposite side was Papa Tony's, an Italian restaurant. They stopped at Tony's and bought a Coke. The front of the place was open to the moist, warm air that carried the scent of the ocean.

As the tour continued, they crossed over to Okaloosa Island on Brooks Bridge. The Gulfarium was on the right, which boasted of having trained porpoises and beluga whales. Playground Amusement Park was to the left but was closed, since it was a weekday.

Farther along, Gary pulled in to Wayside Park where there were toilets, showers and picnic tables for public use. They took the boardwalk down to the Gulf of Mexico. It was too dark to see much, but Danny just had to kick his sandals off and wade into the small waves lapping the shore. He loved the smell of the ocean.

They continued down 98, coming to the Destin Bridge, then went into the tiny fishing village of Destin. They drove down to the wharf where there were a few boats still unloading catches for the day. They watched as a large fish, which Patton identified as a giant grouper, was lowered onto a cart on the dock. Before the fish was released from the boom hook, Danny noted that it was bigger than the man operating the hoist.

They turned and headed back to Fort Walton Beach, taking a short tour through another part of the town that Gary called Negro town. He pointed out a place called Possum Joe's as they stopped for a stop sign. There were several black men sitting in folding chairs drinking beer.

Ray stuck his head out the window and yelled to the men: "My name is Gary Patton, and I can kick anybody's ass. Remember the name — Gary Patton. Look for a white Corvair with "Gidget" painted on the sides."

Patton floored the Corvair and cussed as he nearly ran a red light while crossing Eglin Parkway.

"You son-of-a-bitch, Bock. Now my car is marked. I'll have to repaint it."

"That's OK, Patton. Just take Lenny with you when you come to town. He'll kick their asses."

Danny had sympathy for Patton. But he couldn't help but laugh at Ray, the little Chicken Hawk.

The following summer was full of new experiences. On weekends after a payday, which always came on a Thursday, Danny and Ray often would hitchhike to Pensacola, a 25-to-30-mile trip to the west on Highway 98 from Hurlburt Field. Near the center of Pensacola was a place called the Gulf Follies, which featured strippers and titillating, grade D movies. The stripper would get down to a G-string and a pair of pasties, sometimes removing the pasties if the crowd cheered loud enough.

Later that summer of 1967, Danny and Ray hitchhiked to Biloxi, Miss., and got a free room in the transient barracks at the base nearby for the weekend. The drinking age was 18 in Mississippi, and it was quite a draw for the young service men up and down the coastal states. They ate meals at the base and went out for a legal night of beer drinking at some of the numerous bars in Biloxi.

There was a strip joint called the Nevada Club that was a bit on the expensive side. Between the two of them, they had $35. They paid the $2 cover charge and went into the club.

It was like nothing either had ever seen. There was a huge, circular bar. The place was crowded with young men. But there were few young women. Danny and Ray sat at the bar and ordered a beer. A male bartender brought two draft beers in mugs. They had been buying near-beer on base for 30 cents a mug. Danny, who looked older than Ray, though they were the same age, was getting served illegally at a bar in Fort Walton Beach and a bottle of beer was 50 cents.

"Two bucks," said the bartender. They would both need to be conservative with their drinking, or it would be a short night out.

The music was loud and powerful. They met a Marine from New Jersey. He was drunk. He seemed to need to prove how macho he was. He said that he would be going to 'Nam in two weeks to kill some nips. He wanted to arm wrestle. Ray volunteered to take the guy on and did well for his size, giving the guy a struggle that lasted for at least five minutes. Danny could see that the Marine was of a different ilk than he was accustomed to. He yelled loudly, then smashed his glass on the counter. He picked up the broken pieces, folded them into a napkin and chewed the glass sandwich, then swallowed it, showing his bloodied, empty mouth. Danny and Ray decided that maybe they should find another place to sit when two bouncers escorted the man out the door.

"That guy's gunna be shitting blood tomorrow," said Ray.

Danny and Ray were talking about the lives they had left back home when Danny felt a hand touching his shoulder. He turned to see a lovely girl in her early 20s.

"Wayne. Wayne Vincent. Aren't you Wayne Vincent from Toledo, Ohio?"

Danny just stared at the girl for a moment. "No, I'm Danny Pratt from Bay City, Mich. But I'll be whoever you want me to be." She sat down on the empty stool where the Marine had been.

She no sooner sat down than the bartender appeared with a champagne glass filled with a bubbly liquid. "That'll be $2.50 for the lady's drink," he said.

Danny could not buy too many drinks at that price. So he paid for her drink, which he later found out was not champagne but Colt 45 malt liquor in a champagne glass.

"Let's go sit at a table, away from the bar," he suggested.

Danny looked to see that Ray also was talking to an attractive young girl.

They found a table with two seats, not 10 feet from the bar.

What luck, Danny thought to himself. They hadn't been in the club for more than 20 minutes, and they both had gotten the attention of some good-looking girls.

The girl's name was Lulu. She was born and raised in Ohio. She was going to school part time to become a veterinarian. He began telling Lulu about his plans to attend art school, once he was discharged from the Air Force.

Lulu suddenly stood. "Will you excuse me for a few minutes? I have something I need to do."

"Sure," Danny said. "Will you be back?"

"Yes. I won't be long." She gave him a reassuring smile, then left.

No more than a minute later, a male voice came on the speaker system: "And now, would you give a Biloxi welcome to the lovely Lulu."

The seductive music started and out strutted Lulu on top of the circular bar wearing a small halter top and bikini bottoms. She danced like she had been dancing all her life. She was a stripper. Danny felt very naive. She had been pushing drinks at the bar between acts. She began to remove her clothing — first, her halter top and then the rest. She was totally naked up there for the world to see. She stared directly at Danny and undulated her torso provocatively. His heart was racing. She pointed to her lower body and mouthed the words, "Just for you," then winked.

He was in full-blown lust, which was amplified by the beer he had been drinking.

Lulu, as promised, returned to the table where Danny sat.

"Did you like my dance?"

"Wow!" Danny did not know how to put his feelings into words.

He said he would like to see her after she got off work that evening, and that he only had $12 left and couldn't afford to buy her drinks all night.

"I don't get off until 2 in the morning." She looked at Danny and touched his face. "You're very sweet Danny. But I'm not allowed to date any of the patrons. Sorry."

With that, Lulu got up and walked off. Danny sat there with

his mouth open and watched as she introduced herself to another "patron," starting the process of pushing the expensive malt liquor in a champagne glass.

Danny looked for Ray, but he was nowhere to be seen. He went to the restroom and searched around the huge Nevada Club. He noticed there were a half-dozen booths with curtains that could be pulled for privacy. The curtain in one of the booths suddenly was pulled open abruptly. The girl that Ray had been with came out looking angry. Then Ray appeared. He saw Danny immediately and walked over to him.

"That bitch," he said. "She was only after my money."

Danny and Ray managed to run out of money on their first night in Biloxi. They spent the night in transient barracks. Danny laid in his bunk that night thinking that he almost cheated on his girlfriend, Kay. He would have if the stripper had consented. He loved Kay and did not want to be unfaithful. She was so far away, and he was so lonely. It would be another 3 1/2 years before they could continue their relationship. How could he expect her to wait for him? She planned to enter the nursing field when she graduated from high school the following summer. Kay had told Danny, on a night that they had spent together stranded along I-75 in a blizzard, that things would work themselves out if they were meant to be together.

In 1968, Danny received his second stripe. He was now an airman second class, to him, an ominous distinction, but it meant that he was a pay bracket higher. Danny called his parents to give them the news. Three days later, Danny received a letter from Kay. She had heard through Danny's dad that he had been promoted. Her letter showed her anger over not being told of his promotion first.

Danny became angry and sent her a letter the same day, saying that if she was so angry with him, perhaps they should break up. This was not the way Danny wanted to end their relationship, but the die had been cast. When he called Kay, she was distant and acted as if she never wanted to see him again. He could not blame her.

The next time Danny went home to Bay City on leave, he walked to Kay's home and picked up the black pearl ring he had given her. She was lovely. His heart ached that she would talk to him only on a superficial level. As he walked back to his parents' home, Danny threw what was to him a fairly expensive ring into someone's lawn where he never again would find it, even if he wanted to.

He had managed to alienate the girl he loved. The rest of his leave was spent in self-loathing.

———

There was a Bluebird shuttle bus that ran from Hurlburt Field to Fort Walton Beach. On paydays, Ray and Danny often would catch the shuttle to Wayside Park on Okaloosa Island, a white-sand beach that was quite popular with local young people.

One day Ray came up with an idea. He and Ray bought ice drinks in a large cup. They would walk through the hundreds of young women sunbathing on the beach, looking for an attractive girl with her bikini top unfastened. One of them would watch while the other pretended to trip, spilling a small amount of the ice drink on the sunbather's back. In most cases, the girl would scream and sit upright, exposing her bare breasts to an attentive crowd. They were delighted, after apologizing to the angry girl.

It was after only two successful attempts that Ray and Danny were approached by one of the lifeguards and were banished from Wayside Park for the remainder of the summer.

———

That the airmen who lived in the barracks had little money and a lot of time on their hands was evidenced by the many practical jokes that occurred on a daily basis. Ray was probably the most creative in his mischievousness. Gary Patton, for the most part, did not take part in the pranks. But that did not stop Ray from playing a few pranks on Gary.

One morning the three men were preparing for work. Gary, who was hairy on his body and face, was shaving. Danny was ironing a uniform, and Ray was showering, just down the hall. Gary finished shaving and rinsed his face from the tap and reached for his towel, which he always kept in the same place, folded neatly to the right of the small sink on a rack. With his eyes closed, he reached for his towel and wiped his face. He suddenly stopped and looked at his towel. Beneath the folds of the towel was a thick layer of black shoe polish.

"You son-of-a-bitch, Pratt!

Patton stood there in front of the mirror looking at his blackened face.

Ray walked back into the room with a wide smile on his face.

"What happened?" he asked, as he laughed.

"Pratt has taken things too far," said Patton.

Danny denied he did the foul deed and actually was innocent. But Gary was so angry, he would not listen. His anger continued through the day.

Two days later, the matter was pretty much forgotten. At least that's what Danny thought.

Preparing for work, Danny had just finished shaving at the sink and reached for his towel to wipe his face. Patton was preparing to leave for work. As Danny wiped his face with his eyes closed, he picked up a terrible smell, and the inside of his towel was moist and viscous.

"Shit!" Danny said the word loud enough to bring others from their rooms.

He ran out into the hall looking for Patton. Gary was just exiting the door at the end of the hall.

"Gotcha back, you bastard," he yelled.

Ray was simply delighted with himself. He perpetrated the whole scenario and suffered none of the consequences.

———

Christmas of 1967 was Danny's first away from home. He missed his ex-girlfriend, Kay, and his family. But he tried to make the most of the situation.

There was a New Year's party. The entire squadron, including officer/instructors and civilian employees, were there for a feast, mixed drinks and beer, which was supplied by the officers. Since the party was held in a community room at AGOS and on military property, the underage airmen were allowed to drink

Ray and Danny ate and drank their fill. The free mixed drinks helped to make the separation from their families and loved ones more tolerable. Gary Patton did not drink.

———

Danny failed to remember the last time he drank hard alcohol. He was 17. On Christmas Eve, Danny and Dave Piechowiak drank two pints of cheap whiskey. Danny ended up passing out in a snow bank on Cass and Broadway in the South End of Bay City. He spent all day Christmas in the drunk tank. He swore that he never would drink whiskey again.

————

Ray was mixing the drinks. He used a variety of stimulants — vodka, whiskey and gin — experimenting with different mixers. They went down easy, and Danny was enjoying himself as he slipped off his chair and passed out under the table.

————

The next morning, Danny woke up with an awful headache. He was in his bed on the top bunk, and Patton was sitting on the bottom bunk.

Suddenly, Danny felt the huge meal that he had eaten at the party the night before begin to erupt. He had no time to run to the bathroom, so he just put his head over the side of his bunk and let the contents of his stomach go. Patton was sitting on the edge of his bed, just below, shining his shoes. He caught the full impact of the purging. The vomit hit Patton on the back of the head and filled his shoes and part of his newly made bed.

Patton's tirade lasted several minutes. He ran up and down the hall of the barracks yelling at the top of his lungs. He summoned other guys from their rooms to come and look at the travesty.

Danny just laid back in his top bunk, wishing for a quick and painless death.

• 3 •

THE BIARRITZ

Spring, 1968

Danny Pratt decided that he needed a car. It would need to be inexpensive, practical and cheap to maintain. He had friends that would help with the gas. He would need insurance.

Ray and Danny took the shuttle bus into Fort Walton Beach on a Saturday and began walking around to the used car lots in town.

In the early afternoon, they came across a vehicle that Danny and Ray thought would fit Danny's requirements for a car. It was a 1960 Rambler, 6-cylinder with a stick shift. Danny knew when he saw the price that he wanted it.

The price on the car was written on the windshield, $400. The dealer accepted Danny's offer of $350, on the condition that Danny was able to obtain a loan at the Eglin Federal Credit Union.

Within three days, Danny's application for a loan of $450 was approved. He bought an insurance policy from State Farm, and he was on the road with Ray.

The Rambler was a solid, practical car. Danny intended to take good care of the investment that was going to take most of his money for one year.

Danny owned the car for less than a week when another airman ran a stop sign on base. Ray Bock was a passenger in Danny's car and was almost tossed out the door and onto the pavement. Thankfully, there were no injuries. But the collision did irreparable damage to the Rambler. It didn't look all that bad, but Ramblers had what was called unibody construction or no frame. It would have cost much more to repair the car than it was worth.

Two weeks later, Danny received a check for $350 from his insurance company as payment in full for his 1960 Rambler. On a Saturday morning, Danny and Ray caught the shuttle bus to Fort Walton and began searching for another car.

It was early afternoon, and they had walked to a half-dozen used car lots but could find nothing affordable. They were walking away from one of the lots when Ray looked to the rear of the car lot.

"Wow! What a car," said Ray.

It was a beautiful car — a convertible with leather seats, a flawless body, power seats and windows. It had long, sleek, elegant lines and small, pointed tail fins. Danny never had seen anything quite like it. It looked like a Cadillac, but it looked different, almost like a custom-built car.

"I bet they want a mint for this one," said Ray.

"Ya. Way more than a lowly airman could ever afford," said Danny.

"Isn't she a beauty?" A somewhat slick-looking salesman approached, smiling broadly and extending his right hand.

"Ya, sure is," said Danny. "How much?"

"This is a classic," said the salesman. "It's a 1958 Cadillac Eldorado Biarritz convertible. We just now got her in, not 15 minutes ago, and we have no place to park her. I can make you a really great deal."

"I couldn't begin to afford a car like that. Even if I could afford to buy the car, I still couldn't afford to put gas in it."

"I'd help you with the gas," said Ray. "So would some of the other guys in the barracks that don't own cars. Just charge people whenever you give them a ride somewhere."

"How much do you want to spend?" asked the salesman.

"How much is the car?"

"One thousand dollars," said the salesman, with a large smile that said he thought he was making an irresistible offer.

"Let me hear the engine."

The salesman produced the keys from his pocket and started the car. There was a blue plume of smoke from the exhaust. It seemed to run well enough. But the blue smoke meant that it was burning oil.

With the top down, the car was beautiful — not a dent or a rust spot anywhere. The leather seats were in good repair.

"Could you put the top up?"

"Of course. But, I'll tell you now, the top needs some repair."

He raised the top and clamped it in place. There were several cracks and one open tear in the fabric, showing the bare frame beneath. The fabric was brittle.

"I can't pay you $1,000 for this car," said Danny.

"How much do you have?"

Danny had a strong urge to just move on.

"How much do you have?" he repeated.

"I have $300," Danny said, thinking that if by some miracle he did sell him the car, he still would have money for gas and plates.

"Can you get a loan?"

"A loan right now is out of the question."

"I'm sorry, man. There's just no way that I can sell you this car for $300."

"I understand."

Danny turned and walked off, followed by Ray. He got all the way to the sidewalk before the salesman yelled.

"Do you have 350?"

Danny stopped. He couldn't believe the man was coming down that far on his price.

"The best I can do is $325."

"You just bought yourself a classic 1958 Cadillac Eldorado Biarritz."

———

Danny jumped behind the wheel of his newly purchased car. As he pulled away from the used car lot, he was aware of the stares. He stopped for gas on Highway 98 and checked out the fluids — power steering, transmission, brake and, most importantly, the engine oil. The oil was down almost a quart.

The thought that he was perpetrating a fraud did not escape Danny. Here he was, one of the lowest on the military pay scale, driving a Cadillac. The car might open a conversation with an attractive young girl, but the girl soon would find out who Danny Pratt really was. His military haircut didn't help. He and Ray automatically were identified as airmen. Civilian men had long hair. Even though Ray and Danny had up-to-date civilian clothes, there was no hiding that they were in the military.

Danny was already having doubts about buying the Biarritz. Why did he let the salesman talk him into buying this car? It was totally impractical.

He brooded over his poor decision over the weekend. He took his car out to Wayside Park and did some body surfing with Ray and Tom Balash. When they returned to the parking lot, several people stopped and stared at Danny's convertible.

On Monday, Danny told Richard Williams, the civilian illustrator, about the car he bought. He took Richard out to the parking lot to look at it.

Richard told Danny that it was an impressive car, but asked: "How can you afford to go anywhere?" He also asked Danny about the rag top and if the old car burned any oil. Danny started the engine and let the blue smoke speak for itself.

Richard just shook his head and said: "Pratt, I think you're in way over your head. I'd get rid of the damn thing if I were you."

Gary Patton liked the looks of the car but doubted Danny's judgment. "I think you screwed up, Pratt," he said.

The following weekend was a payday weekend, so, Danny, Ray and Ron Meyers took a trip down the coast to Panama City. It was a 60-mile trip and took a half-tank of gas and a quart of oil to get there. Danny bought a 5-gallon can of oil. At the rate the old car was consuming oil, he would not go for many long trips.

I was only six weeks after he bought the Biarritz that Danny decided he could not afford to keep it.

On one unusually hot summer day, Danny went to work in his fatigues. He was ordered to drive one of the Bluebird buses that took the Air Ground Operations students out to the field for some real forward air controller experience. He drove a bus full of mostly first lieutenants and majors some 10 miles out a dirt road on the Eglin Air Force Base reservation. They had just arrived when the sky darkened with threatening thunderclouds. A rogue storm emerged, totally unexpected. The storm only lasted 30 minutes, but it dumped 2 inches of rain.

As Danny watched the deluge from inside the bus, the terrible realization hit him. He had not covered his Biarritz with a tarp. He had kept close track of the weather reports, and there was no mention of rain.

When the rains finally stopped, the sun came out and created clouds of vapor. The temperature was in the high 90s.

When they returned to Hurlburt Field that afternoon, he went straight to his car. He approached it, afraid of what he was going to see. There were several inches of rain on the floor of the car. The leather seats shrunk and split at the seams where they had been rolled and pleated. The interior of his car was ruined.

Danny was convinced that the longer he owned the car, the more it would depreciate. He put a for-sale sign on it to sell for $400, knowing that whoever was interested would try to talk him down.

An Army colonel inquired about the Biarritz the next day during a break in one of the classes.

Danny told him he needed $400.

Considering the condition of the interior and the fact that it needed extensive repair, the colonel offered him $200

Danny signed the title over to the colonel and watched him drive the car away in a cloud of blue smoke.

Danny thought for a moment that it would be a good idea to put the money in a savings account and put it toward a different car. But he made the mistake of stopping by Fred's Showcase in downtown Fort Walton and ended up buying a Sony reel-to-reel tape recorder.

A month after Danny sold the car, he got a phone call in the graphics shop where he worked. It was a full-bird colonel from McDill Air Force Base in Florida. He identified himself, then asked: "Is this the Airman Pratt who owns the 1958 Cadillac Eldorado Biarritz convertible?"

"Yes, sir. I did own it."

"It is a real Biarritz?"

"Yes, sir."

"I take it you no longer own the car."

"No, sir, sold it a month ago."

He went on to tell Danny how much he wanted the car and that very few of the Biarritz model were made.

"I would have given you $1,500 without even seeing the car," said the colonel. Then he thanked the man for making his day.

• 4 •

CATCHING THE SNITCH

In 1968, the news was filled with talk of the Vietnam War, hippies and drugs. Sgt. Ethier received orders to report for duty in Vietnam and was replaced as supervisor by Richard Williams, the civilian illustrator.

A new civilian illustrator also was hired, Maurice Metrogen. Maurice was newly retired from the Air Force and had been involved in art as a hobby for many years, attending juried art shows and exhibits. He was a natural when it came to painting and drawing and became Danny's mentor. Maurice also had a great sense of humor and became involved in a three-way verbal fencing match daily, which helped to pass the time as Maurice, Danny and Ray talked over their cubical walls.

Sgt. Lovelace, the unit photographer, had little to do besides take pictures once a month at commander's call and collect money for football and other sports pools, so he was the person to spread the squadron's gossip. It was a well-known fact that Lovelace was a snitch. The snitching didn't seem to bother anyone but Danny and Ray. They were summoned to Master Sgt. Carda's office frequently concerning matters that should not have been known to the first sergeant.

One day Danny and Ray were sitting in the conference room talking, smoking cigarettes and drinking coffee on their morning break. They noticed that someone was listening on the other side of a large vent.

Ray pointed to the vent as he pursed his lips and made the quiet sign with his index finger. He mouthed the word "Lovelace."

That night Ray and Danny devised a plan. They would catch Sgt. Lovelace squealing on them. They knew that whatever they said would get back to Carda.

The next morning, they took their coffee break in the conference room next to the large vent. They waited until they could see movement on the other side of the vent and began to talk in a normal voice.

"Did you get the stuff yet?" asked Danny.

"No. I'll get it tonight if I can come up with another 25 bucks," said Ray.

"I'll get it somehow," said Danny. "Just make sure it's the good stuff. Smoke some of it first. We can't afford to get ripped off again, not with all of the people we're supplying."

"Hey. That wasn't my fault. This time I'll make sure it's good, or somebody is going to get burned," Ray vowed.

They talked for several minutes more. Danny saw Sgt. Lovelace as he passed the doorway and headed down the hall and down the stairs toward Sgt. Carda's office.

In less than five minutes, the phone rang in the graphics shop. Danny answered. It was Carda's secretary.

"Sgt. Carda would like to see you and Airman Bock in his office immediately," she said.

They reported to Carda. The sergeant looked concerned and got straight to the point.

"I've heard from a reliable source that you two have been involved in dealing drugs. What do you have to say for yourselves?"

Ray explained to the sergeant that they had set up a trap to catch Lovelace. They knew that Lovelace had been running to the NCOIC every time there was something said that would be worth any brownie points.

Master Sgt. Carda sat back in his chair and thought quietly for a moment, checking the faces of both the airmen to see if he could find any sort of indication that they were lying.

When Danny and Ray returned from the office of the first

sergeant, Richard Williams was standing near the door of the graphics shop looking toward the two men with great interest. Sgt. Lovelace obviously had told Richard what he had heard. Lovelace conspicuously was missing.

"What happened?" Richard asked.

"We set a trap for Sgt. Lovelace, and he fell for it, hook, line and sinker," said Ray.

"Do you mean that you and Pratt really aren't drug dealers?"

"Hell, no," Ray laughed.

Lovelace asked for the remainder of that day off and was not seen until the following Monday.

• 5 •

DOUBLE SPRINGS

"Bigotry may be roughly defined as the anger of men who have no opinion."

~ G.K. Chesterton ~

Gary Patton announced one day that he was going home and asked Danny if he would like to come with him on a weekend trip to his home in Double Springs, Ala. Since Danny had no means of transportation, he readily accepted the chance to see some new country.

Despite the practical jokes that Gary thought Danny had played on him, they became friends. Gary realized it was Ray who cleverly had engineered most of the practical jokes he had been involved in.

They both got permission to take that Friday afternoon off, and they left for Gary's home just after lunch. It was a six-hour trip to Double Springs from Hurlburt Field. Patton recently had bought a new car, an Austin Healy Sprite. It was a two-seater, convertible, sports car. It was a small car, but they managed to get everything they needed for the weekend in the tiny trunk. Danny was surprised that Gary could afford a new car, even though he was extremely frugal. It would be difficult for an airman second class to make payments on a new car. He didn't ask Patton if he had paid for the car by himself, but he thought he may have had some help from his parents.

They were cruising through the little town of Laural Hill when Gary said: "Don't expect to be doing any beer drinking while you're in Double Springs. Winston County, where I live, is a dry county."

It was a pleasant trip. It became a sweltering day. But the top was down on the Sprite, and it felt good to feel the air moving. Some of the homes along the two-lane road were in shambles. They would pass a house that must have been owned by someone of means next door to a rusty-roofed shack of a family that was poverty-stricken. Danny thought of the Old South of the Civil War. The area had a quaint beauty, a place with a deep history. This was nothing like his home in Bay City.

They drove through Mobile and Birmingham, Ala.

As they approached Double Springs, Gary put an Air Commando hat on and adjusted the string under his chin. The right side of the brimmed hat was pinned up. Hurlburt Field once had been the home of the Air Commandos, but they had moved. Patton bought the hat from a surplus store. Gary Patton was home from the military, and he would leave an impression on his homeland.

"Have you ever had sex with a woman?" Danny asked, as Patton slowed to enter a small town.

"I haven't had sex with anything. How 'bout you?"

"Oh, I wouldn't brag about my prowess with women, but they used to call me 'Cherry Bye-Bye' back home in Michigan." Danny meant the statement to be a joke, but Patton saw no humor in it. He later would regret this careless statement.

———

When they reached the outskirts of Double Springs, Gary pulled to the side of the road and jumped out of the car.

"I want to show you something," he said, as he picked up a sign that had been lying facedown in the grass at the side of the road. The letters were large and black with red paint willfully splattered on the white background.

Danny read the sign out loud: "Nigger, don't let the sun set on you."

"You're in Dixie, now," Gary smiled.

Danny stared in disbelief as Patton returned to the car. They moved through the tiny town.

Patton told of an incident the year before, when a neighbor left his wife home alone while he went for a trip to Jasper. While the husband was away, a black man in an old pickup truck stopped by to ask the woman if she would like her roof tarred. She said no. The man moved on. When the husband returned from Jasper, his wife told him of the black man that had stopped. The man grabbed his shotgun and went looking for him.

"He damn sure would have shot the man, but he never found him."

"I've heard about that kind of prejudice. It's hard to imagine."

"If you'd grown up in Alabama, you'd understand."

Gary, driving his yellow Austin Healy Sprite convertible down the main street, drew some attention from the folks who were out and about as he touched the brim of his Commando hat. He tooted the horn at familiar faces.

They moved onto a dirt road that snaked around homes and fell into valleys and zipped up hills. It was wonderful country. Patton was enjoying his new car as he tested it on some hairpin curves and skidded in the red, earthen road.

Patton's two sisters and his parents came out the front door to greet him as they pulled into the drive of the modest home. It was a distance from town on a winding, gravel road. They all embraced. Danny was introduced. The whole family spoke with a thick, Southern accent.

The parents were warm and friendly, extending genuine hospitality to Danny. Gary's oldest sister, Carol, would be graduating from school that year. She was attractive, with short, light-brown hair. The youngest sister, Susan, was 10, with a pretty, bright smile.

Mrs. Patton served a wonderful meal, hot and ready for them as they entered the tiny home. She poured Danny a cup of coffee from an open pot.

"Danny's never had any real, Southern coffee," Gary said, as his mother poured the drink. He explained that the water was boiled first, then the coffee grounds simply were poured into the hot water and allowed to set for a moment. There were no filters, and the coffee grounds floated free in the cup. Danny tasted the strong coffee after he added two teaspoons of sugar and some milk. It was strong and rich.

The family was warm and friendly. They sat at the table and talked for a time. Dad, Don Patton, talked of the days when they raised chickens. There was a long building behind their home where they had raised up to 100,000 chickens at a time. He told of a chicken hawk that flew into the long chicken house toward the far end, causing the chickens to run and pile up at the far end.

"A chicken stampede?" Danny laughed.

Don looked at Danny with a humorless face. "We lost 20,000 chickens. We had to load them onto a pickup truck with a pitchfork," he said. "There wasn't a thing that was funny about it."

"I'm sorry, Mr. Patton. I didn't mean any disrespect," said Danny.

They moved to the living room and watched the evening news. Walter Cronkite gave the latest on the Vietnam War.

Danny caught himself flirting with Carol, the oldest sister. She had big, expressive eyes and a charming personality. She showed Danny her record collection, which included the new Steppenwolf album. Danny stood just outside Carol's room and listened.

Later, they joined the rest of the family in the living room.

"Do ya drink beer?" Don Patton asked Danny during a commercial.

"I sure do. Winston County is a dry county though, right?"

"Being a dry county means that the politicians are the only ones who can sell beer and liquor," he laughed. "Our county sheriff sells beer out of the back door of his gas station."

———

Saturday morning was clear and sunny. Mrs. Patton learned from a telephone call that one of Carol's classmates had been killed in a car wreck the night before. The family knew the boy and his family. He had lost control of his car and hit a live oak at the side of a rural road, just a half- mile from the Patton home.

That afternoon Danny accompanied the family to a swimming hole not far up the road from their home. They brought a gasoline-powered air pump that floated on an inner tube that was connected to a long hose, a snorkel and a mask. Gary demonstrated how to use the underwater breathing device. Carol helped Danny adjust the face mask and moved the air compressor along as he explored the bottom of the pond.

They spent the hot afternoon in the coolness of the pond.

Danny felt his pulse quicken as he frolicked with Carol Patton. She was returning his flirtations. He could feel a strong attraction to this pretty Southern girl.

He loved the apparent simplicity of their lives. Not more than a half-mile down the road was a wild kind of beauty that was a delightful shock to Danny.

Gary took Danny and Carol for a drive farther out the country road where they lived. Danny and Gary sat in the seats, while Carol rode on the top, where the ragtop was stored. The winding road followed a trickling stream with deep gullies where clear water ran, cascading into small pools. Boulders jutted from the sides of cliffs where dark shady passages reminded him of a scene from Walt Disney. The hot sun was showing in small patches on the cliff side and on the red road. It was wonderfully cool here, away from the scorching sun.

Danny felt Carol's hand on his shoulder as she steadied herself on a steep slope. Danny looked up at Carol, and she smiled back.

That evening, Danny went outside to smoke. He sat on the top of a picnic table and looked at the starry sky.

He was hoping Carol would join him. Ten minutes later, she did.

They talked a long time. Danny told her about Bay City and how it differed from Double Springs.

As Carol talked, he could see he had been naive in presuming that people in the rural South were somehow isolated from what was happening in other places. She showed maturity beyond her years.

During their discussion, Danny moved closer to Carol until their shoulders touched, then put his hand on her waist. She turned, and they kissed.

Carol Patton really knew how to kiss.

The screen door spring twanged, and Gary came out the front door as it slammed. He did not see two of them in the darkness.

"Carol," he called.

They separated. Carol moved to the seat of the picnic table.

"Over here," Carol answered.

Gary walked over to them as his eyes adjusted to the dark.

"I think it's time for y'all to come in, little sister."

"OK. I was just coming in anyway," Carol said.

———

A month later, Danny went to the Patton home in Double Springs again. This time, he and Carol became more acquainted, and they exchanged addresses.

He began writing to Carol three to four times a week. He liked her a great deal. He spent his weekday mornings anticipating a letter from her. He made plans to buy another car, so he could visit her on his own.

Gary did nothing to encourage a relationship between his sister and Danny. He thought that if Gary was aware of his interest in his "little sister," he never again would invite him to his home.

———

It was around 10 months after he had met Carol Patton that Danny went again with Gary to Double Springs. Danny was getting well-acquainted with the friendly Patton family.

On a Saturday afternoon, Mrs. Patton asked Danny to get some potatoes from just across the road where they had been dug up earlier. Danny grabbed a basket and walked across the road to find a pile of large potatoes. He began moving them about, looking for the best looking of the pile. He felt a painful sting. He looked to see a white scorpion sitting atop the potatoes.

"Oh, my god!" Danny yelled as he ran into the kitchen where Mrs. Patton stood at the stove.

"I've been stung by a scorpion," Danny said, as he saw Carol come running to see what all the fuss was about.

"Ya, that stings don't it?" said Carol calmly.

"Do you mean it isn't poisonous?"

Carol and her mother laughed.

"Y'all don't have scorpions up north do ya? It'll hurt for a while, but you'll live," Carol chuckled.

———

After supper, Danny asked quietly if Carol would be interested in a walk down the road to the stream. They were less than the length of a football field down the road when Gary drove up in his Sprite, honking his horn. He pulled up next to them.

"I think you'd better get on back to the house. You're not going anywhere with Cherry Bye-Bye."

Danny then realized his relationship with Carol Patton was over until he could buy a car.

Danny could not blame Patton for reacting the way he did. He had stuck his whole foot in his mouth when he joked about his sexual prowess. Cherry Bye-Bye had, for now, ruined his chances of having a relationship with Gary Patton's sister. He was not the sexual predator that he had pictured himself to be. He really cared for Carol.

• 6 •

CHANGING GEARS

One afternoon, Ray received word that his longtime girlfriend in Massachusetts was pregnant. He made plans to marry and have his girlfriend move to Fort Walton Beach before the baby was due.

He flew to his home in Pittsfield County after Christmas and brought back his new bride. Her name was Grace, and she was a lovely, long-suffering, dark-headed woman. They rented a small apartment in Fort Walton Beach. Grace delivered a daughter they named Stacey the following spring. Ray applied for separate rations, and with the help of his parents, bought a new 1968 Volkswagen Beetle for $1,800.

After Ray moved out of the barracks, Danny got a new roommate fresh out of basic training named Terry Rush from Oklahoma. Terry was a jolly fellow, full of good humor. He worked in classroom support, running movies, viewgraphs and slides for the instructing officers.

Danny liked Terry right away. He was surprisingly athletic and agile for being a little on the heavy side. Terry didn't take life very seriously and always was ready to have a good time.

One of the favorite pastimes for those who lived in the barracks was to go to the beach, which required no money. On payday weekends, Danny and Tom Balash, who was living in the same barracks and was also from Bay City, would go to the Coral Bar in Fort Walton Beach. Tom and Danny, though underage, could get served there, but Terry could not. He looked too young. He also made even less money than anyone working at Air Ground Operations School.

It was on a payday weekend evening that Tom and Danny returned to the barracks late from the bar after running out of the money they had budgeted for the evening. Danny found Terry Rush sitting in the middle of their barracks room watching the small black-and-white TV Danny had bought second hand for only a few dollars. Terry was holding a half-empty bottle of cheap vodka.

"Are you planning on sharing that with anyone?" Danny asked.

"Hell, no. Not with you especially," Terry said. "Did you bring me back any beer? Hell, no. You and Balash go out every payday while I just sit here and do nothing. One of my real friends bought me this bottle of ..." he checked to see what it was, "...vodka. You're not getting any of it."

"Fine."

Danny kicked off his shoes and sat backward in the other available chair and watched the late-night movie that was now half over.

Terry was in a talkative mood, and his speech became more slurred with each swallow of the cheap vodka. Most of what Terry was saying was not really aimed at Danny in particular. He was just getting so drunk, he made little sense.

When the movie ended, Danny looked over at Terry. There was a puddle on the floor. His white Levis were stained.

"Terry, you're pissing your pants."

"What?"

"You're pissing your pants."

Terry looked first at his empty bottle of vodka, then at the floor, then at the wet crotch of his pants.

"Damn," he said, "I pissed my pants." He placed the empty bottle carefully on the floor, then stood, almost falling over, and walked out of the room toward the communal bathroom down the hall.

Danny followed him out into the hall just to see if Terry would make it to the bathroom. A brown stain began to grow on the seat of his pants, spreading down both legs of his white Levis.

Danny made sure Terry got into the bathroom, then went back to the room and grabbed one of Terry's towels that hung near the sink.

When he got to the bathroom, he found Terry, unconscious on the floor in front of the toilet. There was fecal material all over Terry, the toilet, his clothes and the floor.

Danny pulled Terry into the shower, turning on the water, and he rinsed him down thoroughly, finishing with cold water to revive him a little. After several minutes of cold water, Terry came around and started complaining. Danny slapped him lightly on the face.

"Get up, Terry. Get up and clean yourself up."

With great patience, Danny succeeded in getting Terry on his feet. He put a washrag in his hand that was covered with foam from the bar soap Terry had in the room. It took more than half an hour to get Terry cleaned up. Danny supported Terry's weight as they returned to their room where Terry dropped naked onto his bed. Danny covered him with a sheet and returned to the bathroom to clean up the mess in the toilet stall.

The next day was thankfully a Saturday. Everyone from the squadron was off for the weekend. Terry slept late into the day. He woke up just after Danny returned from lunch at the mess hall.

"Wow, I really got plastered last night," he said, his speech still a little slurred.

"Ha! Do you remember shitting your pants?"

"Oh, get off it, Pratt. I didn't shit my frigging pants."

"Go open the window and look out on the ledge." Danny pointed to the correct window.

Terry got up on unsteady legs and carefully walked to the window. He looked down on the concrete ledge just outside. He made a face at the terrible stench.

"Oh, my God! Somebody shit in my pants!"

Terry had the unpleasant task of retrieving his white Levis and his underwear from the ledge.

He went directly to the laundry room and washed his clothes and his towel.

• 7 •

A CHANCE MEETING

"Whoever loved that loved not at first sight?"

~ Christopher Marlowe ~

One late afternoon, Danny was coming up the stairs from the first-floor laundry room with his newly cleaned clothes. Just as he entered the door to the second floor, the hall pay phone rang. Danny answered.

"Could I speak to Gately Mitchell, please?" It was a female voice that sounded pleasant.

"Just a minute," Danny said. "I'll see if he's in."

Danny knew that Mitchell lived on the far end of the floor. He went to his room and knocked on the door. No one answered.

"I'm sorry, he's not in his room," Danny answered. "Can I leave him a message?"

"No. Maybe I'll call back later," said the voice, sounding a little stressed.

"Are you OK? Is there anything I can do?"

They talked for a few moments. She said her name was Betty Knight and that she lived in Fort Walton Beach. Danny gave his name and told the girl he lived in the barracks and that he was from Bay City, Mich. She seemed to need someone to talk to. Her relationship with Gately Mitchell was waning, and she did not know why.

When the conversation ended, Danny felt an attraction to the girl and her plight.

The next evening, Danny answered the phone again. It was Betty. He checked Mitchell's room and again got no response.

They again talked for a few moments.

This time Danny told Betty he would like to meet her. She sounded nice over the telephone, but he was prepared to not be physically attracted to her. They arranged to meet at her apartment on Mary Esther cut-off, about 3 miles from Hurlburt Field. He wrote directions and the address on a piece of paper.

Danny had no car. He walked there while thinking over what he might say to Betty. He had nothing to lose, he said to himself.

He found Betty's small apartment and rapped lightly on the door. The door opened, and there she stood.

"Betty?"

"Yes. You must be Danny."

Danny was delighted. She was lovely. His first impression was that he could marry this woman. There was something about her eyes that immediately attracted him. She was trim, to the point of being skinny. Betty invited him in.

They talked for several hours. Danny found that she was not only a lovely girl, but she was very intelligent. She was a registered nurse and had a degree in nursing from Georgia Baptist Hospital. Her dad was a chief master sergeant at Eglin Air Force Base.

They talked about common interests. She also fancied music and had been taking guitar lessons.

Betty had to work the next morning, so they parted fairly early. Before he left, Danny asked if he could see her again. She consented but told Danny she was on the rebound from a relationship with Gately Mitchell, and that he should know she still was grieving over the abrupt end to what had been a serious relationship.

Danny called Betty every evening until they met again. He walked to Betty's apartment carrying his reel-to-reel tape recorder and some tapes so that he could play some of the music he had purchased recently. They drove to Betty's parents' house in her car on a Saturday afternoon to meet her family. Betty had a younger brother, Harmon Junior; a younger sister, Mary; and another young brother, Bill.

They all sat on the floor of the family home and played cards while listening to Danny's tape recordings. One of recordings was from the musical "Hair," which Danny did not want to play because of some of the lyrics of the songs. But Betty's sister, Mary, insisted that he play the tape. Danny reluctantly played the music. No one seemed to flinch when the foul, four-letter words came out in full stereophonic sound.

Danny came from a family that believed card playing was sinful. Danny did not share those beliefs, but he was like a lamb going to slaughter when he played cards with the Knight family.

The following payday weekend, Danny took Betty to Staff Restaurant on Main Street in Fort Walton Beach, driving her 1966 Ford Fairlane. It was a moderately high-priced place and took a large bite out of Danny's resources for the next two weeks. But he was glad to spend the money. He was very attracted to Betty Knight.

On Dec. 30, 1968, Danny turned 21. He and Tom Balash went to the Coral Bar that they had been visiting frequently for the past year to celebrate. Chrissy, the barmaid there, asked Danny which birthday he was celebrating.

"My 21st," he said with a smile.

"Why you son-of-a-bitch," she yelled. "I've been serving an illegal minor for the past year. I could have gotten one hell of a fine."

Chrissy stayed angry for an hour or so but finally came over to Danny and Tom's table with a free round for Danny's birthday.

Danny and Betty spent much of their time together. Danny was invited to dinner, a wonderful meal of king mackerel, hush puppies, rice and sweetened ice tea. It was the best meal Danny had in months.

Danny took Betty to Ray and Grace's apartment, where they were all introduced, and they played cards. Ray and Grace took a liking to Betty. Ray even went so far as to predict that she and Danny would marry.

They went to Papa Don's, a nightclub in Pensacola, on a payday weekend. A good live band was playing. They all sat with their drinks and were enjoying the band. They had gone through several rounds of drinks when Ray got up to go to the restroom. Not long after he left the table, two cadets in uniform from the Naval Academy approached Grace and Betty, asking for a dance. They had been there less than a minute when Ray came back from the restroom.

He grabbed both men by the epaulets.

"That's my wife you're talking to. Get lost."

Both of the men had to look down at Ray and were so surprised at being grabbed that they backed away. They apologized and left.

Danny couldn't believe the nerve that Ray displayed.

"You're quite a piece of work, Chicken Hawk," Danny laughed.

"Nobody messes with my wife," he said.

Danny had the feeling that before the night was over, they probably would be in some sort of a conflict.

It came about an hour later. Danny had gone to the restroom. There was a line, and he had to wait for one of the urinals. When he returned to the table, Ray was not there. The girls were sitting alone.

"Where's Ray?" Danny asked.

"He went outside with some guy," said Grace.

"Did they go out to fight?"

"I think so," she said.

Danny ran out the front door. Just to the right of the entrance stood Ray, looking up into the face of a much larger man.

"Ray," Danny yelled out, as he approached the two. "Is this guy looking for trouble?"

"Maybe I am," said the stranger, turning now to face Danny.

Danny pushed the man into the shrubs directly behind him. As he bounced back, he took a swing and missed Danny's face by several inches. They moved out onto the blacktop where they circled each other, waiting for an opening. Danny shot two left jabs that hit the guy in the cheek.

As they circled, Ray could be heard shouting encouragement. The guy obviously was drunk. His movements were slow, and his wild punches were easy to avoid. Danny hit him with several more jabs before a friend of the strangers stepped in.

"I think he's had enough," he said. His partner agreed.

Danny learned that the man at first had intentions of fighting Ray. But by the time Danny arrived on the scene, they were just talking.

Ray was energized by the whole scenario when they returned to the girls at the table.

"I was just waiting for you to circle around so I could give him a few punches myself," he said.

By the time Ray retold the story of the encounter at work the following Monday, it had a little more drama in it than the actual situation.

———

One payday in early June, Danny went to Jackie's House of Diamonds in Fort Walton Beach and picked out an engagement ring. He signed the papers for credit to buy a small ring.

That evening, he and Betty went out. As soon as they got into her car, Danny handed Betty a small, wrapped package.

"I love you. Will you marry me?"

"Yes," she said.

———

They were married at the Hurlburt Field chapel on Dec. 15, 1969.

The wedding was small, and they had a reception at the Knight home on Loizos Drive in Fort Walton Beach.

The best man was Joe Litwa, a friend of Danny's. Ray was Danny's first choice for best man, but he had to go home to Massachusetts on an emergency leave for the funeral of a family member.

The couple left for a two-week honeymoon, taking their time moving north toward Danny's hometown of Bay City. They stopped at many of the tourist traps along the way like the Lost Sea, Lookout Mountain and Ruby Falls.

Danny's dad seemed happy to meet Betty, or BJ, as she was called. They got along well, better than Danny expected. Danny's mom was reserved and did not extend her hospitality.

When Danny called his mom to tell her that he was getting married, she became angry, telling him he was too young.

She remained distant throughout the visit. She became angry when BJ got a frying pan from the cupboard to cook a meal.

"That's mine," Ermine said.

It was now evident that Danny's mother was suffering from some kind of dementia.

They returned to their apartment on Cinco Bayou, where just a few weeks before their wedding, they had witnessed America's lunar landing.

————

During this period, Danny purchased a set of inexpensive drums from a mail order catalog and began playing in a small group with Betty's guitar teacher, who played lead guitar; a local school principal, Dale Vinson, who played rhythm guitar and sang; Louis Pollaro, an extremely talented artist who also was stationed at Hurlburt Field, who played trumpet, flute and electric violin. Danny had known "Louie" from the barracks.

They played at the local American Legion once a week, plus a few other gigs. Danny admitted that the group was not all that good, but the work brought in a little extra cash. Danny tried singing, but he was not a solo singer. He would stick to playing the drums.

————

Months later, Danny and BJ rented a house on Escambia Bay in Gulf Breeze, Fla., just the other side of the long bridge that stretched across the bay and into Pensacola.

The two-bedroom house rented for $100 a month and had a screened in Florida room in front overlooking Escambia Bay and a dock, where Danny could rake in oysters during the colder months.

• 8 •

I'm Feelin' It

*"In music one must think with the heart
and feel with the brain."*

~ George Szell ~

The group continued to play until Betty's guitar teacher announced that he had gotten orders and would be leaving the group. On the day that he made the announcement, he brought a friend with him, a bass player named Ed McGrath. He told the group he was having Ed take his place, something he had not discussed with anyone.

Ed was an accomplished musician with aspirations to go to a good music school once he was discharged from the Air Force. He also was demanding. He took over the group.

He stepped on a few toes in the first few rehearsals. He pointed to Danny more than once and snapped his fingers.

"You're dragging," Ed would say.

They learned new songs and started to sound good. But they needed a good lead guitar player.

Ray Bock heard the group practice one night and told Danny he knew a good guitar player through some friends who lived in his neighborhood.

Warren Sutton was a handsome man, with blond, curly hair.

Louie later would refer to him as "The Face." He had been in the Air Force, recently discharged. Warren met the group at Ray's apartment and played a few riffs on the guitar for the band members. He was good. He also could sing harmony. Ed McGrath was impressed, as were Dale, Jess, Louie and Danny. So Warren Sutton joined the group as they practiced nightly in a room adjacent to the graphic shop where Louie Pollaro worked.

The group began to sound like they had some promise, but none of them was a lead singer.

One of Ray Bock's neighbors, Jess Acuna, mentioned to Ray that he had done some singing. Ray invited Jess to come to a session.

Jess worked as a key punch operator making the cards that gave the pay rate for Air Force personnel. He was fairly short and seemed shy. Danny had met Jess and his wife, Rachel, at Ray's apartment several times. Jess came to the next practice and sang a few familiar songs. One was "Aquarius" by the Fifth Dimension. He was good. He had a well-trained voice and was able to hit the high notes and the low notes with little effort. The band members unanimously accepted Jess into the group.

They could see that a nucleus was forming for a unique group.

They practiced for several months until they were ready to play in public. They built a good repertoire of contemporary songs along with some old standards.

In January of 1970, BJ was pregnant with their first child. She and Danny began discussing the possibility of moving from their rented house on Escambia Bay to a place closer to Fort Walton Beach, where they would be closer to medical help and BJ's parents. Her due date was the middle of October.

• 9 •

JUNGLE HOUSE

*"But if a man finds himself...he has a mansion
which he can inhabit with dignity all the days of his life."*

~ James Michener ~

One night after band practice, Warren invited the group to his bungalow on the shores of Okaloosa Sound, not far from Hurlburt Field, where they practiced every night. Danny followed Warren from Hurlburt and down Highway 98, then made a left turn. It was like a tropical jungle back through the tangled vegetation, down a narrow, dirt road. The house was small and in need of some repair. They followed Warren through the screened-in porch and into the darkened cottage. Warren turned on the lights to a sparsely furnished room with a fluorescent Jimi Hendrix poster on the wall. Everyone popped a cold beer and sat in the main room of the one-bedroom bungalow.

Danny told Warren his place looked like Humphrey Bogart's house, somewhere in the jungles of Africa.

"We want you to try something that you've never tried before," Warren said, before he turned and walked into his bedroom.

Danny found through talking to Warren Sutton that they had attended the same Wesleyan Methodist Church camp in Cadillac, Mich. He also had the same strict religious upbringing.

Warren returned with a small box with a hinged top. He pulled from the box a small, glass pipe, handed it to Danny and produced a lighter.

"What is it?" asked Danny.

"It's hashish," said Ed. "It's marijuana, except that its more concentrated."

"You guys have all smoked this before?" questioned Danny.

They said they had. Louie said he had tried it, but nothing happened.

"Mr. Loop, my health teacher in high school, told us that an overdose could kill you. Then he showed us the movie 'Reefer Madness'," said Danny, as he smiled.

They laughed. They had seen the movie.

Danny took a draw from the pipe and held it as instructed by Ed. The square of hashish glowed in the small bowl. Danny passed it to Warren. The pipe was refilled and passed around twice while they sat cross-legged on the floor.

Once the pipe was put back into the box, Warren asked Danny: "How do you feel?"

"Pretty good," Danny said.

"Just sit down and give it a few minutes," said Dale.

Danny moved to the sofa and sat between Warren and Ed.

Warren walked over to the Jimi Hendrix poster and flicked the black light on, lit some candles, then turned the only lamp off in the room.

There was a sudden change as if Danny was moving from one place to another, a place that Danny Pratt never had visited. Everything seemed to take on a new perspective and a new look. He looked at his fellow band members. They were grinning broadly.

Danny suddenly was extremely thirsty.

"You wouldn't have a Coke in the house would you, Warren? My mouth is so dry it feels like it's full of sand."

"Danny's got cotton mouth," laughed Jess.

Warren brought him a cold, 16-ounce bottle of Coke. Danny looked at the bottle, which was illuminated by several black lights around the room. It looked to him like a bottle full of sand.

"OK, Warren, what are you trying to give me? You didn't think I would notice that it's a bottle full of sand?" Danny looked at Warren. He was laughing. So was everyone else. Danny began to laugh hysterically, having a hard time catching his breath. He then realized his perception of virtually everything had changed.

"It's not sand," Warren said. "Here, I'll drink some of it." He grabbed the bottle from Danny's hand and took a swallow. He smiled broadly, then handed it back to Danny.

"I don't believe you." Danny took the bottle from him and went to the kitchen, poured half the bottle into the sink and felt it.

When he returned to the group, he was fully aware of how altered his mind was.

"Holy shit, I'm really stoned," he said.

By then, the band members were trying to draw air and grabbing their stomachs from laughing. Danny walked around the room and looked at everything in detail. The poster on the wall, the weave of the carpet. He walked out onto the screened-in porch. He heard a disturbing noise from the jungle of growth around the house. It sounded almost like a baby crying.

"What is that?"

"It's a peacock. One of the neighbors lets it run loose in his yard," said Warren, with a grin. Danny did not know if he should believe him or not.

He had a sudden sense of paranoia. He never had contact with marijuana. In his high school years, he wasn't aware of anyone who smoked pot. It was something that people did in California on Haight-Ashbury where the hippies hung out or in drug houses, where they also injected heroin into their ravaged bodies. There were extreme penalties for possession of any sort of cannabis product, including hashish. People who repeatedly were arrested for pot use spent decades in prison in some states, like Texas and Alabama.

He saw headlights coming up the dirt driveway. He suddenly was afraid it was the police. "There's a car coming up the road. Are you expecting anyone, Warren?" Danny wanted to knock a hole in the wall to escape.

"There are other people who live back here. It's probably just one of my neighbors," Warren suggested.

The car moved slowly by the cottage.

Warren moved to his Pioneer stereo system and put "The Jimi Hendrix Experience" on the turntable. Danny listened to the music as never before. He was in a trance. He was able to detach himself from the room and move into the music.

When the first song ended, Danny opened his eyes. The others, who sat on the floor with him, closed their eyes. Louie laid his head back on the sofa and looked like he was asleep.

"Holy shit," Danny yelled out suddenly.

They all jumped simultaneously. A round of guffaws followed.

Next, Warren put on "Disraeli Gears" by Cream.

Ed McGrath slid over next to Danny.

"Listen to how tight these guys are. Ginger Baker is a great drummer. Not a fancy drummer. Listen to how he accents the beat and puts in the foundation along with the bass guitar," said Ed.

This was the beginning of the mentoring Danny received from Ed. Ed truly loved music and taught Danny an appreciation that he never could have attained on his own.

Everything they listened to that night took on a new meaning and intensity Danny never had experienced.

Warren got up after the album finished and said he had the munchies. Ed had picked up some lunchmeat and some bread. They moved into the kitchen and made sandwiches.

Dale and Danny were in the kitchen after the others moved back into the living room. Dale was at the counter, and Danny stood behind him waiting to use the mayonnaise. It suddenly was quiet.

"The world's greatest sandwich maker," Dale yelled at the top of his lungs.

Danny was startled. He jumped and dropped his sandwich on the floor. Dale and Danny laughed so hard they fell to the floor, holding their aching stomachs. The others joined them in the kitchen and soon were laughing with them.

Danny began to look at the world around him with new intensity. Ed and Danny got together frequently to smoke some pot and listen to music. Ed continued the mentor sessions, pointing out the dynamics of different songs and following a particular instrument to show its contribution to the music.

Danny took an old set of mid-range speakers and hooked them to his 8-track in his van. The sound was amazing. They would sit in the parking lot at Wayside Park with their heads between the two large speakers, the volume on full and listen to anything available. Ed brought the sound track from "2001: A Space Odyssey." They listened to the fanfare where the ship emerges from the space station, then goes to the "Blue Danube Waltz" by Strauss. It was easy to get totally lost in the music.

———

One evening Danny invited Ray to his rented home on Escambia Bay. BJ was working the night shift at the hospital in Pensacola.

Ed rolled a joint and the Beatles' double white album was on Danny's stereo. The volume was cranked up as they listened to the first record in the album, then the second. "Helter Skelter" was playing when Ray suddenly yelled and ran from the room, holding his hands over his ears.

Danny turned the music down and went to see what was wrong.

"Did you hear that?" Ray yelled. "They were yelling my name in the background — Ray, Ray, Ray, over and over. I'm going to die."

Ed played the song again to try to see if that was true.

They listened to "Helter Skelter" again. It was toward the end of the song.

"Right there. Listen," Ray said, his eyes as big as saucers.

Danny thought he heard what Ray was hearing. "I can hear what you might be talking about. But it could sound like just about any one-syllable word."

"God damn it, he's calling my name." Ray would not be consoled. He left shortly after, still upset.

———

The group needed a name. One night at rehearsal they all gave suggestions. Danny remembered the name of a hardware store on the west side of Bay City called Unclaimed Freight. The group liked the name, and it stuck.

Ray Bock came to one of the group's rehearsals. He was taken with the sound of Jess' voice and the tightness of the group.

"Look," he said, pointing to his arm. "Goose bumps. That means you guys are good. He began coming to band practice whenever possible. He told everyone to come and hear Unclaimed Freight.

One night, just before their first paying gig, Ray showed up with a colorful, round sign that fit on the front of Danny's bass drum. It read: Unclaimed Freight. The letters formed to fit the round space and had a contemporary look. The group was impressed. Ray was adopted as their unpaid road manager.

The first paying engagement was in a small town, about 30 miles from Fort Walton Beach. It was at a small high school dance. Everyone was anxious as they set up the equipment.

They assembled on the stage in the gym and waited for the principal to introduce them.

"Allow me to introduce a new group from Fort Walton Beach, Unclaimed Freight."

They started out with "Aquarius," a Fifth Dimension song that was popular at the time.

When Jess began to sing, he was much more animated than he had been in practice. His stage presence was incredible. It inspired the group to play the best ever.

Ed gave the signal to end the song, and the crowd erupted with applause.

As they prepared for the next song, the principal approached Jess.

"Can y'all play any country songs? We have some requests for Johnny Cash or Merle Haggard."

Jess politely told the man that they did not have any such songs in their repertoire, but that they would be working on some new material.

They were satisfied with their first public performance but realized that they needed to add to the music if they wanted steady work. They began to expand their repertoire. "Honkey Tonk Women" by the Rolling Stones, "Green River" and "Lodi" by Creedence Clearwater Revival, "Black Magic Woman" by Santana and Joe Cocker's version of "With a Little Help My Friends" joined the lineup.

Louie Pollaro married shortly after Danny and BJ. He married a lovely girl named Brenda with a great sense of humor. She was from his hometown in Denison, Texas. Louie showed Danny some of the cartoon strips he had drawn and sent to Brenda before they married. The name of the cartoon strip was "Brenda Jean the Latrine Queen and Lou DeSade." Every time he wrote to Brenda, he included a new strip the same size you would see in the Sunday funny paper. They were masterfully drawn in pencil by Louie. It was the most creative work Danny had seen. The story took place in the sewers of Paris. There were turd men dressed for combat while patrolling the sewers. Louie didn't seem to think his work was anything special. But the artists Danny worked with, including the civilian illustrators, saw Louie Pollaro as a prodigy.

Danny and BJ took to Brenda right away. They began getting together. Brenda seemed to have a way of keeping Louie's feet on the ground. They bickered humorously back and forth. She called Louie a pompous ass. That was the first time Danny ever heard the term. He chuckled at her ability to keep up with the inventive repartee.

Louie began working for a company in Fort Walton that made molded, plastic products. Louie would make the master mold from plaster of Paris then make a plastic impression of the casting. One day Danny stopped to visit Louie. He showed Danny some of his work. There was no limit to Louie's creativity.

"Let me show you my favorite piece," he said. He walked to the back of the studio where he worked and produced a black, plastic plaque. When he turned it around, Danny could see that it was a female's butt, beautifully shaped.

"Wow! Nice plaque," said Danny.

"It's Brenda," said Louie. "I covered Brenda's ass with Vaseline, then applied the plaster of Paris. Everything went fine until I tried to take the plaster off her ass. It stuck to her pubic hair. She really screamed when I was removing it. It took over an hour to get it off."

"Is she still talking to you?"

"Oh, yeah. Do you want a copy? I can make you one."

"I don't think BJ would appreciate it like I would. Tell Brenda that I love her moldings.

In the following months, Unclaimed Freight began to get more bookings. Jess bought a conga drum and was proficient at playing it, especially on some of the Latin tunes.

They played at Playground Amusement Park on Okaloosa Island across from the Gulfarium. It was a comfortably warm night. Danny had bought an old VW van, which turned out to be underpowered for the equipment they moved from place to place. They set up on a high stage and looked down at a fairly large, gathering crowd.

They were getting a good response from the crowd when they started playing "Honkey Tonk Women" by the Rolling Stones. Danny's drum chair suddenly collapsed and he fell, 10 feet from the back of the stage onto the sand and gravel.

He laid there, regaining his senses as the group continued playing. The wind was knocked out of his lungs, but he did not seem to be injured. So he climbed back up on the stage and continued playing without missing a beat. The crowd applauded.

After the performance, Danny went to get his old VW van to load the equipment. He turned the ignition key and the whole rear end of the van went up in flames. Louie rushed over and dumped sand onto the top of the engine, effectively stopping the fire. Louie found that the ignition wire popped loose and when he started the engine, it sparked directly into the carburetor.

That night, Danny was given a ride home by Louie. BJ was working at the hospital in Pensacola. Danny was bushed, so he went straight to bed. Around 2 a.m. the phone rang at the other end of the house. Danny got up, ran through the kitchen and into the living room, stepping first into the bowl of moist dog food and then into some fresh, warm dog droppings. When he got to the phone, it was BJ.

"Hi. What kind of night did you have?" she asked.

"You wouldn't believe it," Danny said.

Married life was a drastic adjustment for Danny. It also was an adjustment for his new wife, BJ. Danny was happy to live a spontaneous life. He felt a continuous, nervous energy. There was always something that made him feel uneasy if he sat too long. It was a nagging deep inside that surely came from guilt that he was not who he should be. It was the "I'm damned" syndrome that came from religious teachings that modified behavior through stark fear of eternal damnation.

BJ was strong-minded and steady. Danny knew she was a devoted wife and that she would be a devoted mother. She was honest to a fault. Danny learned not to ask BJ a question if you didn't want a blunt answer. She was in many ways like her dad, Harmon Knight, a chief master sergeant, who after a 30-year career, was preparing to retire at the young age of 47.

In 1970, the same year Danny began playing drums in the band that was to become Unclaimed Freight, Harmon bought a used cabin cruiser with a 6-cylinder engine. It was a seaworthy boat of around 24 feet. Harmon talked to Danny before buying the boat, asking if he would be interested in going fishing on weekend mornings. Danny was enthused about going deep-sea fishing on a regular basis. He also wanted to get to know his new father-in-law.

They began getting up before the sun on Saturday mornings and heading out into the Gulf of Mexico as the sun rose in the west. It was a grand feeling with the smell of the ocean and the charter boats all heading out Destin Pass, with seagulls in chase and the never-ending panorama of the sea.

They would pick up conversation from commercial fishermen on the CB radio and find where the fish were on any given day.

Danny was mesmerized by the Gulf of Mexico when he first saw the power of the waves and had the feeling that you were in a tiny boat, trusting the whims of the oceans to take kindly to you. He once drove to Destin Pass during a close brush with a tropical storm just weeks after his wedding. Mighty waves exploded on the enormous boulders of the jetty as a Coast Guard cutter entered the turbulent pass. The cutter was tilting to the power of the waves and was in danger of crashing on the unforgiving massive boulders. A sea anchor was deployed in an effort to retard the will of the wind. Danny could feel the adrenaline pulsing in his veins. He could feel the excitement and the fear of the danger that the men of the Coast Guard were feeling. Danny could not take his eyes from the massive energy he was witnessing.

He brought his camera along, knowing that whatever pictures he took would be ruined by the moisture in the air generated by the crashing of the enormous waves and the stiff wind.

The cutter moved into the relative calm of the inner-coastal waterway. It was an inspiring adrenaline rush.

———

About 3 miles off the coast of Santa Rosa Island, to the east of Destin Pass and near Fort Walton Beach, they found a man-made reef, made from the shells of old cars that were first stripped of all but the metal shell, then piled atop each other to give red snapper, grouper and other sea life, a haven.

Harmon anchored his boat over the reef one late morning, with Danny manning the anchor. It was a calm day with small waves rippling over the surface. It was hot and humid. They had caught several red snapper when Harmon said to Danny: "Pull up that anchor yonder, we're moving,"

Danny took a grip on the heavy anchor rope and began pulling. He was able to pull the anchor in a foot or so when he hit the weight of the anchor. The anchor would not budge. He stood and put his back and legs into lifting it. With great difficulty, it began to move slowly.

"I'm waitin' on ya," Harmon said impatiently.

"I don't remember the anchor being this heavy," said Danny, as he slowly pulled the weight up from the bottom of the gulf.

After a minute or two, Danny stopped to take a breath. This was hard work.

"Dad gumit! You still don't have that anchor up yet?" Danny looked into the clear depths of the water. "Look at this," he said to his father-in-law.

Harmon walked over to the stern of the boat and looked into the water. "A Volkswagen," he said incredulously.

"Let go a that anchor," he said.

Danny released the anchor and let the Volkswagen shell settle back to the bottom, leaving some slack in the rope. Harmon moved the boat to different angles until the anchor loosened from the door strut of the old, rusted, barnacled shell of the car.

One Saturday morning, they began trolling with cigar minnows before they reached Destin Pass, and they were still in Choctawhatchee Bay, where they had launched. Harmon was navigating the boat while Danny was enjoying the early-morning newness of the day. Two lines of 100-pound test fishing line were trailing the bait 50 yards from the stern of the boat, the sturdy deep-sea rods in pole holders where the heavy fish line was spooled. The gulf ahead was moderately calm.

The high-pitched whine of one of the reels brought Danny from his morning drowsiness.

"Fish on!" Danny yelled.

Harmon cut the engine as Danny grabbed the active rod. He set the hook with a determined yank of the rod. "Whatever it is, it's huge," Danny yelled with excitement.

The line moved through the water forcefully, from left to right.

All of Danny's strength couldn't slow the exit of the line from the reel. The tip of a large tail broke the surface, causing a big eddy. Then the high-pitched whining of the reel became even louder. With a snap, the reel gave up the last of the heavy line.

Harmon guessed that it was either a shark or a manta ray that was trailing 100 yards of line he had stripped from the reel with seemingly no effort.

Danny really enjoyed the fishing trips with his new father-in-law. But, there was a problem. He always had bookings with Unclaimed Freight on the weekends. When they played at the clubs, they would not finish until 2 in the morning. Harmon would call on Saturday morning around 5:30 to see if Danny was ready to go fishing.

One morning when they played at the Faux Pas, a trendy club on Okaloosa Island, Danny didn't get home until after 3:30. At 5:30, the phone rang. Danny answered while still half asleep. It was Harmon. Danny was really tired and told Harmon he had just gotten to bed and asked his dad-in-law if they could go fishing later in the day.

"It's too darn hot later in the day. That's OK. If I can't get anyone to go fishing with me, I'll just sell that dad-gum boat."

That same day, Harmon made a few phone calls and by the afternoon, the boat was sold.

———

Unclaimed Freight began to get more lucrative bookings. One was at the Hurlburt Field, Officer's Club where they played some new material, such as "Misty" and some Three Dog Night tunes and more tunes by Joe Cocker, and Santana. They played at the NCO Club at Eglin Air Force Base.

Around this time, they were approached by a man from Panama City who offered his services as a booking agent.

They signed with the agent and began to get some good bookings. The group's favorite new booking was Papa Don's in Pensacola. They played to a packed house. The band members were getting tight, and Jess was an accomplished performer. Danny and other members of the group had been to Papa Don's to listen to other live groups. It was one of the best clubs in Pensacola. They were booked there for three weeks. Things were looking up for Unclaimed Freight.

In September, they got a booking for a sorority house in Tallahassee. It was a 2 ½-hour trip to Tallahassee from Fort Walton Beach.

The morning of the sorority gig, Danny and Ray Bock loaded up some of the gear in a 1961 Chevy station wagon Danny had borrowed from his dad-in-law. After loading some column speakers in back, they left early to work out the logistics before the evening's performance. They stopped along the way at their agent's office in Panama City to sign some contract papers and get the bookings for the month. Ray had become a part of the group, helping set up and balance the sound system, and he was now the voice of the band to the new agent.

It took only a few minutes to take care of business at the agent's office, and they were on their way to Tallahassee. Ray had talked to Danny about attending Pratt Institute after they were discharged. They were filled with optimism about the future and agreed that whatever happened, they would remain friends and stay in contact.

Danny and Ray were filled with the anticipation of playing to a college crowd. Danny noticed quite a change in Ray. He was still Ray, spontaneous and uncensored. Ray really saw something in the group. He was capable of incredible focus. His large eyes got larger. He even threw off the macho way he talked in normal conversation. He was energized whenever he listened to the music of Unclaimed Freight. The first time he had seen Jess sing on stage in front of a crowd, vitalized and full of the confidence that comes from being really good at something, he got goose pimples. Telling Danny that this was his gauge for good music, he pointed to his arm.

It was just before Danny became involved with the band that Danny and Ray were looking for a particular color of paint in the room where the oil-based paint was stored, downstairs from the graphic shop. Ray had been surly most of the day. He tended to take the strife he felt in other areas of his life and put it on someone else, namely Danny. He had been mean-spirited all morning, calling Danny "Lenny" and "stupid shit-head" among other things. At first, Danny thought that Ray was joking, as he usually did. But verbal barrage continued. Once they were in the paint room, Ray ended one of his sentences with "stupid shit," and Danny, for the first time since knowing Ray Bock, lost it. He grabbed Ray by the neck and set him on the paint table.

Danny saw the first sign of fear on Ray's face.

"You'd better let go. I know some people who can beat the hell out of you," Ray said, lacking the certainty normally in his voice.

"If you don't knock it off, Ray, I don't care who you know, I'll crush you like a bug. I've had it! You're not going to be talking to me like that again." Danny stared into Ray's eyes, seeing the fear they held. He immediately began to feel sorry he had attacked his best friend. But he also knew he could not tolerate that kind of disrespect from anyone.

Ray avoided Danny for the rest of the day, then the rest of the week. Danny felt the guilt he had been taught to feel in his religious upbringing. He wanted Ray's friendship and had the habit of picking up whatever guilt was available. He began to wonder if there could have been another way to end the disrespect. He saw Ray as a loud-mouthed little brother.

On a Saturday, after not talking to Ray for almost a week, Danny decided to go to Ray's apartment. Ray answered the door, uneasy at seeing Danny there. Danny held up a six-pack of Busch. Ray opened the door for him to enter.

Ray was polite but reserved, totally different from the real Ray.

"What's eating you?" Danny finally asked.

"What do you think? You attacked me," Ray said, incredulously.

"I couldn't do anything else. You sounded like you had no respect at all for me. You and I have been friends, and I want that to continue, but I can't put up with that kind of bullshit. Not from a friend."

After that encounter, Ray became involved with Unclaimed Freight. Now they had a quiet understanding that did not require further comment.

They were rounding a curve near the small city of Blountstown, east of Panama City, when Danny noticed a cloud of dust just up the road. On the right shoulder was a car, wheels spinning in the loose gravel, raising a high cloud of dust. The car was heading in their direction on the wrong side of the road at a high speed. The car moved onto the highway and headed straight at them in their lane.

Danny swerved to the left to avoid the car. The other car followed and hit the Chevy head-on.

Danny awakened to a female holding an umbrella, shielding him from the baking sun. Danny was dazed. It took him a moment to piece together his thoughts. The smoldering wreckage of the Chevy wagon was several feet away.

"How's Ray?" he asked.

"He's OK, said a male voice from behind him. The ambulance is here. We're taking you to the hospital at Tyndall Air Force Base."

Danny started to get up, but was told to lie still. He turned his head to check on his friend but could see nothing but a pile of crumpled metal.

The ambulance attendants were impersonal. They talked about social matters as they moved, with the siren blaring, at a high speed toward the hospital.

He was taken from the emergency room directly to X-ray where he was put through some torturous posturing to check for broken bones. He had a puncture wound in his left shoulder, his ribs were extremely painful, and both wrists were painful to move. His right wrist was put into a splint and a drain was installed in the deep puncture wound in his shoulder. The attendant said his ribs were not broken but severely bruised.

"How's my friend, Ray? Is he OK?"

"They told me you and your friend are OK, but two people in the other car were killed."

"Oh, no," said Danny.

"Can I see my friend, Ray?"

"The doctor will be in to see you once we get you to your room. You'll be staying here for a while."

They took Danny to intensive care and told him he would be staying long enough to insure that he did not have internal injuries.

They hooked Danny up to a heart monitor and put an IV in his arm. There was an older man in a bed across from him who appeared unconscious. He had an oxygen mask on and tubes in both arms.

Danny was in a stupor. Nothing seemed real. He had no sense of passing time.

A doctor appeared at the end of his bed. He checked Danny's chart, then approached.

"How are you feeling?"

"I'm alright. Just a little sore. How's my friend, Ray?"

"I'm sorry to tell you this, but we got our information from two sources. We finally got it right. Your friend was killed instantly in the wreck. One of the men in the other car also was killed. The driver survived."

The doctor continued talking, but Danny did not hear. How could Ray Bock be dead? They had been talking about going back to school one second, and the next second, he was gone. He felt numb. He was given pain medication, and it helped him to sleep much of the remaining time he spent at the hospital.

When Danny awakened on the second day after the accident, the unconscious man that had been directly across from him was being carried out on a gurney. His body was covered with a sheet.

BJ and her dad picked up Danny that afternoon. BJ told Danny that the base chaplain and his commander, Col. Shelly, had paid a visit to her parents' house, where she had stayed while Danny was out of town. She was told that Danny and Ray both had been killed. She told the men that she knew that it was not true. This was different misinformation than Danny had received just after the accident.

The next few days were a blurry memory. The band members came to visit Danny at his home on Escambia Bay. The other members of the band arrived at the sorority house in Tallahassee late that afternoon, only to find that Danny and Ray had not arrived. Since they had left much later, they worried that something might have happened. They bought a secondhand set of drums for Danny and had set them up in the area where they were to play that evening.

They finally contacted the State Police and soon found out what had happened. They were also given the same misinformation. They learned from the State Trooper that the impact speed, the combined speed of the two cars as they collided, was 135 miles per hour.

Jess contacted Ray's parents in Massachusetts and asked about funeral plans. Ray's parents, who owned a golf course and a restaurant in Pittsfield, would pay for all of the band members to fly there for Ray's funeral. An uncle, who lived nearby, owned a motel. They would provide everything that they would need to attend Ray's funeral at absolutely no expense.

They all went except Dale Vinson, who could not leave his job as principal of a local school.

Just before their departure, Danny found that his left arm also was fractured. He had a splint on his left arm and a cast on his right arm.

BJ instructed the band members that they were to give Danny a bath once they arrived at the motel. Danny would have none of it.

Their plane landed in Hartford, Conn., where they were picked up by one of Ray's older brothers and taken to the Bock home. They were treated like members of a royal family. Virtually all their needs were seen to. They ate dinner at the up-scale restaurant at the golf club and had the use of a rental car for the time that they spent there. They were given whatever they wanted to drink from the bar.

That evening while visiting with Ray's family, Ray's mother called the family's priest to arrange for the funeral service. The priest refused to give the last rites because Ray had not attended confession for several years. After much tearful pleading by Ray's mother and a substantial gift to the parish, the priest finally agreed to come to the funeral home and give Ray his last rites.

The priest arrived. He put on his priestly garb and knelt by the casket.

"Hail, Mary, full of grace. The Lord is with thee. Blessed art thou among women. And blessed is the fruit of Thy womb, Jesus."

The phrase was repeated for an eternity. Each time it was repeated, Danny became a little angrier. The fact that a priest could take the Bible and twist its words into some self-serving purpose was disgusting.

The members of the group talked among themselves. The hypocrisy of the whole situation was just unbelievable. Ray's mother was pleased that her son had received his last rites.

The next morning, after an incredible breakfast, Mrs. Bock asked if the band would play a few songs so the family could get an idea of why Ray was so enamored with the group.

There was a party room at the golf club where drinks were served, and a set of drums sat near a small stage. Ray's parents were able to come up with several guitars and a bass. Since Danny's fingers were exposed, he played the drums as best he could, and Jess sang through the audio system. The group played several of their favorite tunes to an appreciative audience.

"I see now why Ray liked your group so much," said Mrs. Bock.

A small, local group came in and played for the family and friends of Ray Bock. They played well. As the night went on, they played "Green, Green Grass of Home," bringing tears to the eyes of many who knew Ray. Ray's older brother, visibly shaken, gave instructions to the band not to play that song again that night.

The funeral service was held at the cemetery with full military honor guard. As they fired the 21-gun salute, Danny finally broke and let all of the grief out for his friend. Tears flowed freely down his face and onto his dress uniform.

Grace Bock was presented a folded American flag. She was stoic as she accepted it.

The group thanked the Bock family for their overwhelming generosity and flew back to Fort Walton Beach that afternoon.

Within a two-week period following the accident, Danny and BJ, with the help of the band members and BJ's parents, moved their belongings from Escambia Bay to Mary Esther, just on the fringes of Fort Walton Beach. The house they moved into was not near the quality of the place on Escambia Bay. It was elevated on cinder blocks and was more expensive than the other house. But it offered more room, and it was close to friends and medical facilities. BJ took a new job in Crestview, Fla.

There was a memorial service for Ray Bock at the base chapel on Hurlburt Field. Danny made it through the service in a dazed state. As he walked out the front door of the chapel, he broke down and began to cry, his face distorted as he tried to hold back. His mother-in-law stood outside the chapel waiting for Danny and BJ. When she saw Danny, she said, "What a face," then chuckled. Danny's need to vent his grief stopped. He could not believe his mother-in-law could be so insensitive to his feelings for his friend.

In mid-October, BJ neared the due date for their baby. Danny still had a cast on his right arm and a splint on his left. He had Ed McGrath come over to drive them to the hospital in case the baby arrived. Danny and Ed were sitting in the living room drinking a beer when BJ's parents arrived.

When Wilma Knight, BJ's mother, walked into the house, she immediately noticed that Danny and Ed were drinking beer.

"We're taking your friend home," she said. "You're not going to sit here drinking beer while my daughter is getting ready to deliver your baby."

"You're not taking my friend anywhere. This is my house, and I make my own rules. I want you to leave and don't ever come back." Danny was as angry as he ever had been.

BJ's dad tried to get them to calm down. But it wasn't going to happen. This was the beginning of a power struggle in the Danny Pratt home that would continue for many years.

For some time after, BJ's mother would not come into the house when they visited. Danny refused to apologize. If he gave in, the situation would only get worse.

• 10 •

MOVING ON

On Oct. 29, Derick Martin Pratt was born in the wee hours of the morning. He was a fine, healthy baby.

When BJ came home, her Grandmother Fowler was there to assist BJ and Danny with the new baby. Danny's involvement with the care of his wife was limited. Granny Fowler was a great help.

BJ was a wonderful mother and wife. As the weeks went by, she helped Danny bathe as well as take care of Derick.

Danny eventually healed and began practicing with the group again. They all felt the absence of Ray Bock.

Danny received $5,000 as a settlement from his insurance company. His lawyer asked him repeatedly if he had any pain in his back or anywhere else that might give him trouble later in life. He didn't want to take more than the $5,000 offered. He did not want to profit from the accident that had killed his friend.

He bought a pristine, 1964 Ford window van and a new set of Ludwig drums with a double bass drum, three tom-toms and Zildjian cymbals.

The agent who had been booking their gigs before the accident called Jess one day. He wanted them to practice until they felt ready to play again. Then he strongly suggested they enter a battle of the bands scheduled at the municipal auditorium in Panama City. The winner of the contest would receive $1,500, a tidy sum at the time. The group agreed to the challenge.

There was a brilliant flash then a deafening clap of thunder you could feel in your chest. The members of Unclaimed Freight stared out the door of Danny and BJ Pratt home. The group had won two preliminary battles and was now going to the finals in Panama City.

They would compete with six other bands from three states. It began raining hard as they finished loading the equipment into Danny's 1964 van. It rained as hard as any of them had ever seen it rain, coming down sideways, carried by the wind and punctuated by the heavy, booming bass of the thunder.

The group decided the rain would not stop them from getting to the Panama City Civic Arena. They would be there for this contest, come hell or high water.

Danny jumped into the van and was prepared to follow Warren and Dale in Warren's VW. When he turned the key, the starter kicked in, but the engine would not start. They all tried a hand at getting the engine to work but only managed to run down the battery.

They were in a state of depression as they stared out the screen door of the humble bungalow. The Pratts had moved to this new location just before Derick was born. Everyone was staring at the monsoon rain coming down so heavily that you could not see the road 20 feet away. They could think of no way out of their predicament.

"I think we could have won," said Jess.

They ran out of options and stopped seeking new ones. They were resigned to the fact that there was no way to get to Panama City.

They were all feeling morbid when BJ's dad, Harmon Knight, pulled into the driveway and dashed into the house.

Harmon could tell immediately that something was wrong. Danny explained the problem. Harmon went out into the driving rain to find out why the van would not start. Danny held an umbrella, offering minimal protection from the deluge, as he checked under the hood.

"I think you have a bad fuel pump," Harmon yelled above the storm.

Danny explained that they might just as well wait until the rain stopped, since it was unlikely they would arrive at the civic center in time to play, especially in this weather.

Harmon jumped into his car and headed down highway 98. Within 15 minutes, he returned with a new fuel pump and set about installing it.

The faces of the band members began to brighten a bit. But the rain continued to pour, and it was 60 miles through bad weather to get to the arena.

Harmon enjoyed a challenge. He proceeded to install the pump in the worst downpour imaginable. He finished the installation, then pulled his car up to the front of the van and hooked up the jumper cables.

It started. The group was ecstatic. Everyone thanked Harmon for his courage and his determination.

Danny checked the time. They had 45 minutes to get to the contest. Depending on the order that the groups were to appear, they still possibly could perform despite being late.

They set off into the storm. The wipers would not go fast enough. Visibility was extremely poor. For the most part, Danny could not drive faster than 25 or 30 miles per hour. He kept losing Warren in his Beetle in the blinding rain.

They arrived at the arena 30 minutes late. They were anxious as they unloaded.

As they put the last of the equipment backstage, the first two bands already had performed and the third group was then on. They were really good. It was a five-piece band from Alabama. They played "Suite: Judy Blue Eyes" by Crosby, Stills & Nash. Their harmony was good and their timing was really tight.

It seemed an eternity for the next two bands to finish. Each group had a similar amount of experience. Jess concentrated as he paced nervously backstage. Ed gave the group some last-moment timing instructions.

The last group finally finished, and the huge curtain dropped. It was time. They hurriedly set the equipment in place, plugged into the amps and got into position. They listened as the announcer, (who was also their agent,) gave a short history of the group. He told of the accident that killed their manager, Ray Bock, and that the drummer, Danny Pratt had broken both arms. Now they were back to play for the group assembled there.

"And now, give a rousing welcome for Unclaimed Freight."

The curtain lifted slowly, and they could see for the first time the large crowd in the coliseum behind the bright spotlights.

Ed counted off the beat to "Black Magic Woman." Louie started the song with the flute, Warren hit the first lick on lead guitar, and Jess picked up the beat on the congas.

Suddenly, all of the nervousness was gone. It was the groove that good groups sometimes find. The movement of the music, the internal swaying of the beat to a common heart beat, a common breath.

Danny was not an onlooker any more. He and Ed, Warren, Jess, Dale and Louie were a cohesive source of energy named Unclaimed Freight. They were now a tight group that had been playing long enough to know exactly what to expect from each player. Ed had stressed the dynamics of different songs so the music ebbed and flowed, feeling the force, the intensity of Joe Cocker, with Warren's lead guitar wailing a lament in the high, treble strings.

Danny really enjoyed the talent and the friendship of Louie. Louie only could be described as an artistic prodigy. In addition to being by far the most talented draftsman you could ever hope to meet, Louie played the trumpet, the flute and the electric fiddle. Despite his abundant talent, Louie Polaro was a nice guy.

One of Danny's bass drums began to creep away from him. The bass pedal soon would be out of reach. He caught Louie's eye, and Louie danced over while playing his trumpet and pushed the bass drum back.

Jess was a quiet, unassuming person in private. But, when he stepped onto the stage, he took on a totally different persona. He sang his best, and when they played "Aquarius," the crowd reacted with jubilant applause.

They finished with what was perhaps their signature song, their rendition of Joe Cocker's "A Little Help From My Friends." The dynamics were key to this song, and it seemed to come flawlessly. Louie played the trumpet, which gave the group the sound of a full orchestra.

The curtain dropped. The group members gathered backstage and congratulated each other on what was possibly their best public performance yet.

As they began to pack away the equipment, the announcer stepped to the microphone.

"We now have the decision of the judges," he said.

He revealed the third-place winners first, the first group they heard when they arrived that sang "Suite: Judy Blue Eyes." The second-place money was given to a group from Apalachicola.

"And the first place money goes to ...," he paused for dramatic effect, "Unclaimed Freight."

• 11 •

SEPARATE PATHS

It was only a month after the victory at the battle of the bands that Unclaimed Freight received some bad news. Ed McGrath got orders for Vietnam.

This really should have been expected, since the only members in the group who weren't in the Air Force were Dale Vinson and Warren Sutton. And Warren recently had been discharged.

Through the many times that they had played together, each performance was better than the last. The band was like family.

Ed McGrath, who was sultry at times, taught them all a lot. But, when Ed and Danny became friends, it was the beginning of a transformation. Ed did not abide by any religious ideals. He also had gone through the questioning of religion, the questioning of virtually everything. He said he had opened his mind to other possibilities. He had been raised by the Catholic Church, and he held bitter feelings of his experiences in the church.

Danny told Ed about a time when he sat in his Sunday School class. The lesson was about Samson. The teacher, Ed Bedell, who was a layman of the church, was talking about the part of the Bible story when Samson began slaughtering the Philistines. Ten thousand were killed by one man, with the jawbone of an ass.

Danny had raised his hand to ask a question. He asked his teacher why the Philistines didn't quit attacking the guy and just stand back and shoot arrows or throw rocks at Samson.

Ed Bedell went straight to Harold Pratt after church and told him what a pain in the ass his son had been in class that morning. He called Danny a smart alec.

Danny got his spanking when they came home from church.

But "this time," Danny said, "I was not going to cry." He told his dad that he had only asked a simple question, that he was not being a smart alec.

Danny's dad spanked him anyway, saying that he had given his word to Ed Bedell that he would.

"I can't go back on my word," Harold Pratt said.

"There seemed to be no justice in my dad's decision." Danny said. "Why was it bad to ask questions? Why was Ed Bedell so pissed about my question?"

"Fear." Ed said. "They are all afraid. In their minds, they have nothing to look forward to if they don't abide strictly to the dictates of the religion. They are afraid if they do anything "bad," they will burn in a lake of fire. And that is how the church can keep people in line and keep them coming back, keep them paying 10 percent of their income to the church. They have to, or their mortal soul is going to fry."

Danny and Ed had many of these discussions. They learned from the experience. Ed was an intelligent man. But Ed had self-esteem problems that would pop up now and again, and he would become surly.

The whole band was behind Ed, even when he became reclusive. Ed decided to seclude himself in his room at the barracks one night after practice. The group went to his room and would not leave until Ed came with them to a bar in Fort Walton.

Jess and Warren tried hard to hold the group together. But after a few months, Danny decided that he needed to go on with his life. He wanted to study art at the Art Students League of New York in Brooklyn.

In March of 1971, Sgt. Daniel Pratt was honorably discharged from the Air Force.

• 12 •

THE CIA

After Danny's discharge from the Air Force, Danny, BJ and Derick spent the following summer at his sister, Maggie's, home in Lincoln Park, just out side of Detroit. Maggie set them up in the basement. BJ found a job at a local hospital, and Danny drew unemployment and watched Derick.

Danny, along with BJ's brother, Bill Knight, took a trip to New York City to explore the possibility of Danny going to school at the Art Students League in Brooklyn. Danny was flying high with the expectations of living in New York City and being schooled by classical artists who studied the Old Masters.

The cost of living in the Big Apple was prohibitive. It cost the two men $30 a night for a small room in the Woodward Hotel, $1 for a hamburger and $6.50 just to park their van overnight. This was a time when a half-dollar would buy a full meal at McDonald's or Mr. Hot Dog on Broadway in Bay City.

Danny bought The New York Times and scoured over the apartments for rent section, which was bigger than many hometown newspapers. Danny and Bill went to look at the most inexpensive place they could find. When they went to see the place, they found a tiny, one-room efficiency apartment with a double bed that pulled down out of the wall. The tiny apartment was not even minimally adequate for their needs. The rent was $220 per month. It would not fit into their budget, even for a larger room.

They returned to Detroit the next day. Danny had his thoughts on the Art Students League, but there just wasn't a way he could envision BJ and Derick living in a one-room studio apartment. The year that he and BJ were married, they rented a small house on Escambia Bay in Florida with a dock and a screened-in sun porch overlooking the saltwater bay for $100 a month. Danny began looking at other school options.

Danny's sister, Maggie, her husband and their three kids were preparing to move to Colorado Springs, Colo., that summer. Maggie suggested Danny look into going to art school there. Danny did some research and found that the Art Institute of Colorado was located in downtown Denver. It was a reputable school and had the curriculum Danny was looking for.

With the optimism of early pioneers, Danny, BJ and Derick left Detroit with all of their meager possessions loaded into a U-Haul and a 1964 Ford van and drove head-long into the unknown, with no jobs and no assurance that Danny would be accepted at the Art Institute of Colorado.

This was Danny's first trip out West by car. Everything was a new experience. It was an exciting adventure seeing the majestic mountains for the first time. They spent their first night in Colorado at a motel, where Pikes Peak stood overlooking Denver, 70-some miles to the west. BJ and Danny stood on the balcony of their third-story room and looked at the mountains in the distance. The scene was metaphoric with the high mountain in the distance and the labyrinth of the streets of Denver somehow leading to that peak. Danny was giddy with excitement over the possibilities.

The first order of business the next day was to apply for admission to the art institute. BJ waited with Derick in their van as Danny grabbed his portfolio and went into the school for an interview with John Jellico, one of the owners. His portfolio consisted of some of the illustration art he had done in the Air Force. After being questioned by one of the administrators, Danny was given word of his immediate acceptance. When Danny returned to BJ and Derick, he was walking on air. He was accepted and would begin classes in just four weeks.

BJ was hired as an RN at a local hospital the next day. Since they were living in a motel, they began to look in earnest for an apartment.

In the following days, they found a basement apartment on Vrain Street near West Colfax in a Jewish community. The owner of the apartment was Jewish and spoke of sending money to Israel every month whenever Danny stopped by to pay the monthly rent. The man was not friendly. He was a businessman and did not pretend to be anything else. The neighbors were also Jewish and stayed to themselves. It was not a hostile neighborhood, but it definitely was not a friendly one.

From the apartment, it was a 3-mile walk to the school on 13th Street. It was an experience walking the streets of Denver for the first time. There was a brown haze over the city each morning as Danny walked over a bridge that took him over a busy four-lane. He was excited to be a part of this energetic city.

The art school environment was fertile and exciting for Danny in his first year. After being in the military for four years and being raised as a Wesleyan Methodist, the freedom of literally letting your hair grow and letting your creativity go was a cathartic experience. Danny never experienced such freedom. It seemed that virtually everything and everyone was accepted without judgment.

On the first day of school, Danny met a young guy, fresh out of high school named Rich Mazour. Rich had been a football player, and he needed to find a place to live. Danny talked to BJ, and they offered Rich a room in their apartment for $50 a month. He accepted.

There were drug addicts, homosexuals and ex-cons in the school. There was also a recently retired Army colonel named Jim Kelaher. Jim seemed to really enjoy being alive and reveled in the freedom of the school after 30 years in the military.

There was a rich rancher's son from Texas who wore expensive Western clothes and echoed his dad's dress as well as his values. There were also kids directly out of high school who showed great promise artistically.

It was early summer of 1972 that Ed McGrath phoned Danny. Ed, who was still in the military, had returned from Vietnam after a year and was stationed in Cheyenne, Wyo. He began to visit Danny on weekends since Cheyenne was only 70 miles from Denver. BJ said very little, but she did not like the influence that Ed had on Danny. They drank beer and smoked pot most of the time when Ed came to visit.

Danny felt somewhat obligated to Ed. He had turned Danny into a better drummer and had greatly increased his knowledge and love of music.

Ed McGrath introduced Danny to the Doobie Brothers. He brought the eight-track album, "Toulouse Street" with him on a visit. Danny was taken by the group, their energy and precision. He rarely had been so inspired by any musical group. He bought the album and played it on his Webcor, portable, battery-powered, eight-track player in his car or wherever he went. The player was round and looked like a motorcycle helmet.

Danny introduced the Doobie Brothers to a school friend, Bruce Williams. Bruce also loved the group and found out they would be giving a concert at Tology's in Boulder, Colo., a small, college town just down the road from Denver. They drove to Boulder and purchased tickets to the concert. Bruce, Danny and BJ, who was pregnant with their daughter, went to see the Doobie Brothers in a small, renovated theater. It was a magical experience. Danny never had experienced music like this. The small theater was crowded to capacity. The air was heavy with cigarette and marijuana smoke. Joints the size of cigars were being passed throughout the shoulder-to-shoulder crowd. Danny was one of the tallest people in the room. After a dozen or so tokes on the joints and several beers, Danny began to get really light-headed. He told BJ he needed some fresh air. They headed for the exit, but Danny didn't quite make it. He collapsed on the floor of the lobby as they headed out, almost knocking a young girl off her feet.

Once outside, the fresh air cleared his head. He was embarrassed by the incident. BJ was a foot shorter than Danny and pregnant, but she helped him out of the nightclub.

Danny and Ed saw the Doobie Brothers again at a small bar in Denver called The Beer Keg.

Danny noticed that after not seeing Ed for several weeks, he was losing weight rapidly. He asked Ed why he was losing so much weight.

"I've been taking speed," he said. "I can get by with little sleep. When I start coming down, I just take a couple more."

Danny looked at him for a moment. "You look terrible," he said. "You look like someone who's losing a battle with cancer. I know you're smarter than that, Ed."

Ed had been dating a girl from Danny's art class named Robin. Robin also showed concern over the drastic change in Ed's appearance.

———

One weekend, Ed brought a couple of his friends who also had served in Vietnam to stay at the Pratt home for the weekend. One of the young men recently had been discharged from the Air Force and now had longish blond hair. They went to a nearby park in Denver and threw the Frisbee. They were taking a break and smoking a joint when a couple of young and attractive girls walked by, obviously interested in Ed and his friends. The blond guy smiled at one of the girls. She returned his bright smile.

"Would you like to ball?" the blond guy asked.

"Yes," the young, pretty girl said.

He rose from the grass, took her hand, and they walked off into a large stand of dense bushes and disappeared in the center of the growth.

Danny looked at Ed. "A sign of the times," he laughed.

———

On one particular Thursday, Mike McCracken was teaching his figure class when they broke for lunch. Steve Seib, a Vietnam veteran, invited Danny up on the roof of the old, three-story building for a smoke. They climbed the steel fire escape ladder to the tarred roof. Steve rolled a joint of Thai stick, and they smoked as he told of his experiences with the native highland people of Vietnam. He spoke of their peaceful existence in the mountains of Vietnam and how he had befriended them.

The Thai stick took effect, and Danny really got into Steve's experience. They talked for what could have been hours but was only a few minutes, then returned to Mike McCracken's figure drawing class.

Danny had been working on a timed, 20-minute pencil drawing of the blond model that happened to be there that day. The girl was young, maybe 20. The nudity was no longer a novelty.

Art students seem to revel in their liberal attitudes. This was a place where anything and everything is scrutinized, analyzed, digested, then accepted.

Danny was stoned when he descended the steel ladder and entered the classroom. He spent another hour rendering the breasts of the model, being sure to capture the roundness. Mike McCracken walked slowly around the class, checking on the current drawings and giving suggestions.

"Ah ... those breasts look about as good as they're going to look." Danny looked up at Mike, whom he had befriended, and Mike got a look at his bloodshot eyes. "You went up on the roof for lunch, I see."

"Ya. Do you think I'm over-working the breasts?"

"Maybe just a bit," he said.

Mike was giving him a subtle hint. Danny listened to the man.

The Art Institute of Colorado conveniently was located in downtown Denver. It was within view of the capitol building and a stones throw from the Museum of Modern Art. Mininger's Artist Supply was just a few blocks away.

Danny would walk by the Denver Mint on his way to and from school each day.

During lunch break, many of the male students from CIA would gather in the large, open field that led to the capitol building. The contest would get quite physical with many of the students returning to school in the afternoon bloodied and bruised.

One afternoon, McCracken approached Danny at his drawing table, asking him if he would mind helping him screen potential models.

"Why, I'd be more than delighted," Danny smiled. Mike asked

the school secretary to send the applicants in one at a time to the life-drawing studio. Two attractive girls in their mid-20s came in.

"Ah … I'd like to see the models one at a time, please."

One of the girls spoke, "Do you mind if we audition together? We're both a little nervous about this."

"What kind of job do you think you're applying for? I'm looking for nude figure models. If you are hired, you'll be naked in front of 30 artists at a time." Mike said.

He looked at Danny, who gave Mike a smile as he wiggled his eyebrows.

The girls turned and headed back toward the entrance door.

"Wait. Mike, these girls are probably new at this. Let's give them a chance at modeling together. They both have nicely shaped faces, and the bodies look pretty well-formed," Danny said, trying not to sound too enthusiastic.

"Ah … OK. Let's give them a try. Remove your clothing and strike a few poses."

The girls were nervous but did not hesitate to do as Mike had asked. It was awkward for them. The poses were stiff and unsure.

Mike did not rush. He eyed the two girls carefully then asked them some standard questions, ending up with, "Do you still want to be a figure model?"

One nodded her head and said yes. The other shook her head while saying no. They both shivered in the cavernous, cool room.

"OK. Ahh …. be sure to leave your number, and I will call you if we would like to see you again."

The girls dressed and left in a hurry.

Three other women and one man were interviewed that afternoon. The man was in his 30s and was quite fit. His musculature was good. Mike told him that if the CIA were to hire him as a figure model, he would need to wear briefs or an athletic supporter. He said he didn't wear underwear, and he didn't own a jock strap.

"Those are the terms," Mike said. "We can't have a male model getting a hard-on in a figure-drawing class. It's just too distracting."

Two female models were hired. Neither of them was the first two interviewed. The male also was hired.

Danny had a tremendous amount of respect for Mike McCracken. Mike recently had left his secure job at Disney Studios, where he participated in the creation of Tigger from "Winnie the Pooh." He sculpted the cartoon characters, making them three-dimensional so they could be drawn by other artists. He showed Danny some of his drawings. Danny had his first glimpse of what a true professional artist looked and acted like.

Mike was not a handsome man. He had longish blond hair, which he combed back in wings on both sides of his head. He looked as if he could have been from several generations, '50s and '70s, primarily. His demeanor said he didn't care about that sort of thing anyway. He was direct in his opinions and gave no apologies. To Danny, McCracken exemplified all the qualities that he wanted to emulate as an artist. He was highly intelligent and seemed to be interested and knowledgeable about everything.

Mike didn't come to CIA until Danny's first year of studies was half over. He became the figure drawing instructor. Mike picked up where John Jellico left off. The class studied and drew all of the bones of the body, then drew the muscles and their attachments on tracing vellum and then added another overlay of the skin. Danny thought he was really learning something. He had wanted to first hone his skills as an artist, then let his art take him where it would.

It was only a month after Mike McCracken arrived that John Jellico retired, and a new school administrator arrived. His name was Bill Travis, a former Central Intelligence Agency agent. The irony that a CIA agent should become the administrator of an art school called Colorado Institute of Art escaped no one.

The students had been used to having freedom to experiment and to be themselves. This was to be expected in a creative environment. They smoked cigarettes whenever and wherever they pleased. Some of the students would throw their cigarette butts on the floor of the snack area, where there were several vending machines.

Bill Travis wasted no time. He began implementing the same kind of strict discipline that he had become accustomed to while working for the government agency. He started an investigation when he found a Winston cigarette butt crushed on the floor of the vending area. He began questioning each student, asking if he smoked and if so, what brand of cigarette. He also questioned one of the female students about being seen in the company of a black male student, asking if they lived together. The girl was outraged that she should be questioned about her private life.

This was the start of an undercurrent of discontent flowing through the school.

One of the second-year students drew a caricature of Bill Travis, who had a comb-over. It was a pen-and-ink drawing of the administrator with a wisp of hair hanging down his forehead in the shape of a penis. It was a really good likeness of the man. It was pinned to the bulletin board. Travis found out after questioning several students, that this was the work of Jerry Anderson, a talented draftsman with a distinctive style. Anderson was called into the administrator's office and told that if anything like this ever happened again, he would be expelled. Anderson, who already had spent the better part of two years at the school, would be graduating soon and did not want to start over. He was humbled by the tongue-lashing.

That same day, McCracken pulled Danny aside: "You know you don't have to put up with that bull shit," he said. "Travis has no business prying into your lives. He works for you. You pay the bills. You need to start a student government. Elect a president, then decide to work together to stop him. If you were to have a student strike, where you collectively withheld your monthly school payments, Travis would quit that bull shit in a real hurry."

During the afternoon that same day, Danny asked for the attention of his fellow students. He explained what McCracken had said but was careful not to use his name. He asked for a vote on whether they should have a student government so they could have a collective voice. The vote passed unanimously. Danny announced that he would like to be a candidate for president of the student union. One other student vied for the office. They campaigned in the classroom. Danny's platform was based on the fact that he would make no promises but would do his best to see to it that the students had their say in running the school. Danny won the election.

During the first-ever student union meeting, Danny brought up the subject of Bill Travis and his investigations into the private lives of students. He asked how many students would support a student walkout or strike, withholding the monthly tuition if Travis continued. Several students were skeptical and feared being expelled if the walkout wasn't a success.

Before Danny closed the meeting, he summarized his take on the situation: "I'm very much in favor of not allowing Bill Travis to continue his attempts at intimidating us. We have the power to stop him. But since you elected me to represent you, I will do whatever the will of the majority wishes. Let's think this over. Talk to each other about it, and we'll discuss it again in our meeting next week."

As it turned out, Travis got wind of the first meeting of the new student union, including the topic of discussion. He never again intruded into the privacy of the students. Danny also noticed that the crushing of cigarettes on the floor of the snack area stopped.

It was early spring when Danny threw a party at his small home on South Julian on a Friday night. They had been evicted from the apartment on Vrain when the landlord discovered that they had a dog. Everyone from the school was invited. He put notices up all around the school, then invited each one individually, including the teaching staff and the office people. There were more than 100 students attending the school at that time. Danny told everyone that he would buy a case of beer and supply some snacks. If they wanted anything else, they were to bring it.

Danny and BJ were not prepared for the people that showed up that Friday. The house was filled to only standing room in the small house, and there was a continuous line to use the toilet. The backyard and the garage also were filled with people. When Danny went after more beer just up the street a half-mile, the street was filled with parked cars.

McCracken came a little later than everyone else. As the evening moved on, the crowd thinned, and Danny found himself sitting next to Mike on the floor of the living room. Mike and his wife were buzzed and so was Danny. BJ and Derick had gone to bed for the night.

They talked until nearly sunrise. Mike would talk, then Danny. Each of them was being candid about life in general and what was important in life. Danny revealed his hang-ups with religion and with the trials of life: "I just don't have the time to dedicate myself to art. I am too busy mowing grass and feeding kids in the evening to do much of anything," Danny complained.

"What are you looking for? Sympathy? We all have our crosses to bear. Get rid of the victim bull shit. If you really want to be an artist, you will find a way."

———

If Danny were to try to find fault with Mike, it would be in his delivery. When he was verbally instructing the class, he was almost torturous to hear. His mind raced ahead of what he was attempting to say. Until he really got going with his train of thought, he would say "ah" between words and phrases: "Always ... ah ... be aware ... ah ... of where ... your light source, ah ... originates." It was distracting.

One day Danny was talking to Bruce Williams about Mike's vocal delivery in class. They decided they would approach Mike and ask him if they could instruct him in a speech therapy class. Mike, being a good-natured man, agreed that they would all eat lunch in the administration office that day. They ate their lunches, and then the class began. Danny explained what was expected of Mike McCracken. They would narrate a fairy tale from memory. Every time there was a hesitation of any sort, a bell would ring. After the stories were told, the number of rings was counted. The following day, the process would be repeated. They would compare the number of rings from each day. The results were hilarious. All three were creative in telling whatever fairy tale they had chosen.

At first, Mike would just pause without the "ah," and there would be a blank space in his dialog. By the finish of the second session, he had made an improvement.

Bruce Williams brought the tap bell to Mike's next lecture. Bruce held up the bell for Mike to see. "Ah ... I see I'm being, ah, graded on my lecture today," he said, pointing to Bruce who was ringing the bell and smiling broadly.

Danny, Bruce Williams and several other students from CIA, took an extra sculpture class from Mike McCracken in the basement of his home outside of Denver. The classes were held in the evening, they were given no credit and there was a per-hour charge. Danny arranged to have Derick taken care of by the lady that normally watched him during the day.

———

It was around this time that Danny began having problems. Self-esteem always had been in short supply in the Pratt family. Danny found himself scrutinizing his life and did not like what he saw. He felt guilt over not being a better father to Derick, a better husband to BJ.

He would take his son for long hikes on Lookout Mountain, where a trail near Buffalo Bill's grave coursed around the mountainside into an area that was unspoiled. This became his church in a spiritual sense. Derick would ride quietly on his shoulders and never seemed to complain. Not yet 2 years old, Derick was laid-back and had a peaceful demeanor. He seemed to enjoy the grand scale of the mountains as much as his dad did.

One late afternoon, the sky was gray when Danny and Derick reached the trail head on Lookout Mountain. Danny brought a large plastic bag just in case it rained while they were on the trail. He also carried a small canteen of water and Snickers candy bars for both of them. On some portions of the trail, there was less than a foot of ledge between the mountain and a lethal drop. When they reached the top of one of the peaks, a panorama opened up and Pikes Peak would be visible in the distance. But on this day, it was obscured by a hazy sky. They sat down in a small meadow where several bristle cone pines showed their twisted trunks and sparse foliage, the only evidence that they had lived off this rocky soil for several thousands of years. They drank from the canteen and shared one of the Snickers while taking it all in.

Danny was taken suddenly with the deepest melancholy. He could not explain why his mood became morbid. He sat there quietly with his son for an undetermined amount of time, and tears ran down his face. He looked at the innocent life he had helped create, a wide-eyed little man, whose life he would help to mold. He had not been the dad he had wanted to be. He gave his son another piece of the Snickers bar.

His mood was broken when a thunder squall moved in, further darkening the skies. Thunder echoed and re-echoed through the mountains. They started back toward the trail head. They were close to the narrow portion of the trail when the rains came, all but blinding them. He found a small outcropping of rock, which created a small shelter in the mountainside. Danny took the plastic bag from the side pack he was wearing and covered them both. Derick's eyes were bright with excitement as a torrent of rain poured from the sky making small streams that emptied onto the trail. A horrendous bang from a close lightening strike frightened Derick. He looked at Danny to see that everything was OK. "It's OK, little guy," Danny said with a big smile. Derick started to laugh, but his laughter turned into a cry when another close strike flashed nearby along with an earth-shaking report of thunder. Danny held him close until the rain suddenly stopped.

• 13 •

Unprepared

Spring came after a long winter. Danny, Bruce Williams and three other first-year students at CIA made plans for a hike into the high trails of Rocky Mountain National Park.

On a Friday afternoon in late spring, the party of four students packed their gear and headed to the park. It had been a warm 80 degrees in Denver. They brought clothing that reflected the warmth of the day. Some brought light jackets and sweaters.

Danny had been to the park earlier in the fall with BJ and Derick and literally fell in love with the vastness of the rugged mountains. They arrived at the entrance near Estes Park, a picture-postcard of a place of unbelievable beauty. There was no one at the gate in the entrance. Danny drove into the park and up the winding mountain roads into the higher elevations. There were scant clouds with a brilliant backdrop of stars in the crystal clarity of the thin air.

A herd of at least 20 elk blocked the road that curled through a wide meadow. Danny stopped the car and stepped outside. The huge animals stood all around him snorting and shifting about. He was excited about being this close to wildness. When Danny slipped into the car and slowly inched forward, the herd slowly moved off the road. Bruce Williams rolled a joint and passed it around as they moved up a steep grade.

———

They found the trail head while it was still dark, secured backpacks and gear, then headed up the narrow foot trail. Using a lantern-style flashlight, they moved several miles up the trail before the sun began to rise. They arrived at a pristine, glacial lake of incredible beauty. A beaver was the only disturbance on the lake as they sat for a rest and watched in awe as the sun rose. They ate a portable breakfast of granola bars and water, silenced by the grand panorama.

Danny grabbed a small set of bongo drums from his pack and climbed to an outcropping of rocks some 50 feet above the trail. He sat crossed-legged and began to beat a slow rhythm on the two drums. The rhythm seemed to flow on its own, and it echoed through the canyons and came back in rhythm to the beat he was tapping lightly on the drums. It would have been impossible to locate the source of the drums, as the sound echoed and re-echoed. Danny felt somehow empowered by the sound. He played for a time, creating new patterns and new moods with the ancient, universal sound of the drum. Once he stopped, the echoes continued for several seconds

They moved on and were delighted with the beautiful surroundings. The going was getting rough, with steep grades and sore muscles. But no one complained.

The student artists hiked until Bruce suggested they eat some lunch. They busied themselves with collecting firewood.

Bruce and Danny worked at getting the fire going. Once it was blazing and had created some glowing coals, coffee was made with an old percolator. Everyone was famished. They ate whatever they had brought with them. It was Fanny, a girl from St. Louis, who first noticed the drop in temperature.

The temperature continued to drop for the next few hours. Then, it began to snow. At first, the snow was wet and uncomfortable. They moved inside the shelter of the small tent. Then the wind began to whip, causing the tent to shudder. The temperature continued to drop. They would need to make a decision to either stay for the night and risk getting snowed in, or they could pack up and head home before the situation became worse. They voted. Since no one was prepared for the cold temperatures they were now facing, they decided it would be best to leave. Fanny was the only one who voted against leaving. She had rolled up in her sleeping bag and was content to stay there until the storm passed. But no one knew how long that would be and how much snow would accumulate if they stayed the night. The food supplies they had brought were already half gone. They took down the tent, cleaned up the camp and left.

The trail, which was clearly marked on the way in, was almost impossible to find without careful scrutiny. It was covered with blowing snow and the tracks quickly disappeared. Once exposed to the open trail, the full force of the wind and the snow could be felt. They were in the midst of a Rocky Mountain blizzard.

Those who hadn't brought warm jackets covered exposed flesh with blankets, towels or whatever they could find to hold in the precious body heat.

Danny said it was fortunate the group left when they did. The snow was drifting, and Danny found himself kicking through some of the drifts that had completely obscured the path to the car. His hands and feet were now numb from the biting cold. His only focus was to get to his Ford Fairlane and its sheltering heat.

Fanny, who was directly behind Danny on the trail, slipped and almost fell to what would have been a certain death. She became hysterical. "Oh, my God! We're going to all die out here," she screamed.

"No. We're not going to die. Don't even think about that. We're not that far from our car. Just keep going, Fanny," Danny said. He tied a small length of rope around his belt and handed the other end to Fanny, hoping she might feel a little more secure. He hoped she didn't slip again and pull them both into the chasm below.

It was getting difficult to see more than 10 feet in any direction. The going was getting tougher by the minute. Any bare skin exposed to the blowing wind was raw soon.

They moved slowly along the path until Danny came across a small, man-made object. He picked up the rectangular shape and brushed the snow from it.

"Sardines in mustard sauce," he announced, yelling over the wind.

"Those are mine," said Bruce Williams. "I had them out when we stopped at the lake this morning. We must be near the glacial lake, not more than 2 miles from the trail head."

This seemed to brighten the spirits of the group. It was possible that we would make it out of this adventure alive.

Danny did not see his Ford Fairlane until he almost ran into it. Suddenly, it was there in front of him like a welcome mirage in the desert.

Danny tried to get his car keys out of his jeans pocket, but his hands would not work. They were like useless pieces of frozen meat. It took great effort for him to finally wrestle them from his pockets.

Then he had to manipulate the key to open the car door and then turn the key in the ignition. But after an enormous expenditure of energy and great anxiety, the 6-cylinder engine started, giving life-saving heat to five cold and exhausted art students.

Danny drove the Ford out of the small lot at the trail head. Parts of the parking area were wind-blown, and the snow was not as deep where the wind had whipped through in a straight line, exposing dirt and rock beneath. They reached the main park road. It looked passable in areas, and then there were high drifts that he knew were not.

"We can't make it out yet. We'll need to wait until the road is plowed," Danny said.

"They have some enormous plows here in the park. They keep the main road in and out plowed because of the hotel and restaurant. It shouldn't be long before the plow comes through," said Bruce.

They hadn't waited long before a large plow with a V blade approached, spewing great clouds of snow. The driver pulled to a stop in front of the Ford and climbed out of the huge plow. Danny stepped out of his car.

"You'll never make it out on your own. Follow me. I'll get you at least to Estes Park," said the kind man.

They related their story to the other students on the following Monday. Danny told himself he never again would underestimate the severity of the Rocky Mountains.

Danny did not really know what he believed in as far as religion went. He was unsettled over the fact that when he prayed, which he did not do frequently, he had no comfort in knowing his prayers were heard. Prayer seemed just like every other ritual of the Wesleyan Methodist Church unless you really believed it was just a futile gesture. But how do you come to really believe any doctrine without asking some probing questions?

Danny and BJ explored several churches in the area. One could be described as New Age by present standards. The minister's message was lost to Danny. The church doctrine was unclear. It seemed that anything you wanted to do somehow could be rationalized by the pastor's way of thinking and that what really mattered was whether you felt good about yourself. Of course, there were funds needed for helping to spread the word. It was quite a departure from Danny's growing years in the Wesleyan Methodist Church and BJ's roots in the Southern Baptist Church. The pastor gave the benediction, then hurriedly moved to the exit doors, where he shook hands with the members of the congregation as they left. He wore heavy makeup with eye shadow. Danny really didn't know what his belief was, but he was not ready for the liberal interpretation of the Bible this church was representing. BJ found the place somewhat humorous.

Danny called his dad in Bay City one evening. Derick was asleep, and BJ was working. He wanted to give his dad the impression that all was well. But his dad did not seem to be interested in what he had to say. He found himself fabricating and lying about how well he was doing in school and how good life was in beautiful Colorado. He felt empty after the talk. His parents had not attended his wedding to BJ in Florida in 1969. They never called him for any reason. His Grandma Warren, his mother's mother, died and was buried before Danny even knew she was gone. These things piled up in his mind. The marijuana seemed to give him a hiatus from the self-loathing. His thoughts of inadequacy festered like an abscessed boil, building up pressure and yearning to break open.

It was later that same year that Mike McCracken took leave for a week. The figure drawing class temporarily was replaced with "creative drawing." A visiting instructor and a successful commercial illustrator taught the two-session class on consecutive Thursdays while Mike and his family traveled. The instructor explained the difference between good illustration and self-indulgence. He showed the class some of his own work in the form of a slide show. Danny noticed a distinctive style. His angled figures looked too well drawn, as if they were traced.

"Excuse me. Is your artwork traced?" Danny asked the instructor.

"It takes a good amount of skill to trace artfully to capture movement and fluidity."

"Do you mean to tell me that after spending the past four years of my life trying to perfect my drawing skills, I'm going to be in competition with people who trace? What's the point in learning to draw? Why not just teach creative tracing? I'm sorry, but I don't see anything honorable about tracing instead of drawing."

All of the unreachable ideals that Danny had been taught to strive for in his religious up-bringing had surfaced, and he was angry. Angry that none of it, none of it was real. He was angered that he could make no sense of his life. Everyone was divisive by nature. Absolutely anything could be sold to the highest bidder.

"Damn you," said Danny as he stood and left the drawing studio, went to his drawing table and began packing his things. His frustration had been building up for months. This visiting "artist" and his traced photographs had put him over the edge. He was leaving Colorado Institute of Art.

As he was packing his things, John Jellico, the founder of the school walked in. Jellico had retired but continued to keep in touch with the school, not wanting to lose one of the joys in his life.

"Mr. Pratt, I really need to talk to you for just a moment. Could you come to my office for a minute?"

He reluctantly followed the man to his office. Another of the owners of the school was waiting there and stood when Danny walked in.

As it turned out, word had gotten to Jellico that Danny was angry and had stormed out of the tracing class.

Mr. Jellico began talking, referring to the other owner now and again for agreement. He seemed to understand that Danny was ready to leave. They both put their hands on one of his shoulders. Danny burst into tears and could not stop crying.

BJ was disturbed that her husband had dropped out of school. But she remained supportive. She was pregnant with their second child. Since he had dropped out of school, he no longer would be receiving monthly income from his GI Bill. He needed a full-time job to keep the family going.

• 14 •

RIDGE HOME

Danny began looking for a job that would fill the financial gap, now that he no longer would be receiving a monthly check from his GI Bill. He had been working weekends for Arthur Timmerman, a local contract painter in Denver. But that would not be enough income with BJ pregnant for their second child coming in early December.

BJ was working the 3 to 11 shift at Ridge Home and Training Center, a state-owned facility for mentally handicapped. The facility was about the size of a small college campus. She worked in the hospital center there.

One night Danny arrived at Ridge Home Hospital to pick up his wife at 11 p.m. Derick was sleeping in his car seat in the back of their new 1973 Datsun. BJ came out of the door and beckoned for Danny to come in. "I want to show you something," she said. Danny took his sleeping son from his car seat and followed his wife into the building.

BJ disappeared for a moment, then returned holding a tiny bundle. It was a baby. The body of the baby looked normal, but, the baby's head was extremely small, about the size of a golf ball.

The baby's eyes were open permanently. BJ explained that the baby was a microcephalic. Danny was startled by this caricature of a baby, who looked with unseeing eyes. There was no brain, only a brain stem. The baby stopped breathing while BJ held him. She squeezed his tiny chest, and he breathed again. She explained that the baby would not survive the evening. The parents had the baby delivered to Ridge Home and wished never to hear about it again. This scenario was repeated over and over at Ridge Home. Danny had to wonder how he would react should he and BJ have such an experience. The shocking sight of the newborn baby had opened up a world he never knew existed.

That night as they drove home, BJ suggested that Danny apply for employment at Ridge Home. The next day, she brought home a job application explaining that they had been looking for new retardation technicians for several of the male halls.

The next morning, the application was delivered to the Ridge Home personnel office. Within the week, Danny was called to come in for an interview. He was only one of around 30 applicants for four job openings.

A pleasant, middle-aged lady met them outside the personnel office. She addressed the men and women: "I would like you to follow me as I lead you on a tour of our campus. I want you to see what will be required of you should you decide to work here and are hired."

The tour started at an old building in the older section of the campus. Willow Hall was a facility for higher-functioning females with the physical and mental capabilities of an average 6- to 8-year-old. They were shown how the floor was organized, how the residents were fed and cared for. These girls, who represented ages 10 to 40 years, were capable of feeding and dressing themselves. They had minimal communication skills. Many of the girls had Mongoloid features — the open mouth, the thick tongue, the fleshy tissue around the eyes, the small ears.

The next stop was one of the two halls on campus for profoundly retarded males, Birch Hall. The guide had a key and unlocked the steel doors. Birch Hall was a much newer, round building with a central nursing/observation station. Very little activity escaped the technicians who worked there.

There had been nothing in Danny's young life that could have prepared him for his first visit to Birch Hall that day. As the touring group entered the building, there was a resident with his face pressed against the safety glass of a window overlooking the day room. A river of drool flowed from his mouth and down the window.

There were many residents lying on mats or sitting on the tile floor, many of them rocking. Several looked to be in their 30s and 40s. Each was in constant movement, seemingly unaware of the world around him. One of the younger boys sat in a wheelchair. The guide said the boy was a hydrocephalic. His head, which rested on a large pillow, was so enormous, he could not support the weight. He wore a specially made helmet to protect him from injury. The guide then led us to a room where she picked up a small form from a playpen.

"This is Jeffy," she said. "Jeffy is one of our favorites. He's a microcephalic. His brain is very tiny, not much more than a brain stem. He will have a long life if he makes it to 6 years.

Jeffy was 4 years old and tiny. His head was about the size of a tennis ball that had been squeezed from the sides, making his head long and narrow. The eyes were vacant and tiny. He was fed from a nursing bottle. Danny could not help but wonder how much those tiny eyes could see, or if they could see at all. The guide said the male residents of Birch Hall were from 4 to 42 years old.

Despite the smell of fecal matter, the place was relatively clean. Many of the residents in Birch Hall had to be hand-fed, and many wore diapers.

They were led back to the day room where the guide suggested they mingle with the residents and help out whenever they could with their care.

Danny walked about the day room and found an older man, possibly in his 40s, lying on his back on a mat. His diaper was soiled and leaking beneath his trousers. Danny located the clean diapers, plastic pants and several clean towels and washcloths and changed the man's diaper.

The guide came by as Danny was finishing up. She told Danny he would have no trouble getting hired. If you can change a grown man's diaper, we'll find a place for you, she said.

Danny was hired. He went through two weeks of orientation, then went to work in Red Oak Hall, a place for the profoundly retarded, as a retardation technician trainee. He, along with four other staff members, would be responsible for the feeding, bathing, clothing and general behavior of the 32 residents in Red Oak Hall.

He also was responsible for the daily behavior-modification training of two of the higher functioning boys, Jeff Upkes and Gerald Steel.

Jeff was severely autistic. He paced the day room constantly. When he couldn't pace, he would fiddle with his fingers. He was tall and thin. To communicate with Jeff in any way, you had to get his attention by interrupting the movement of his hands. He was capable of dressing himself with prompting from a staff member. He needed to be redirected frequently when performing any task, or he would immediately return to his compulsive behavior of finger-fiddling or pacing.

Gerald was severely retarded, but he was one of the higher functioning boys in Red Oak. Gerald had a limited vocabulary and was able to perform small chores such as sweeping the floor, brushing his teeth or washing his face. He was able to focus his attention on the task at hand. His behavior modification stimulus was a small tray of french fries or "fench fies," as he called them. Gerald loved his french fries and became completely delighted when he was given his fries upon completion of a task. He would shout "fench fie" and clap his hands. Danny couldn't help thinking that Gerald was not that bad off if he could get such delight from something so insignificant to others as a french fry. Gerald was 16. He had the characteristic excess of gum tissue that comes with a lifetime of drug therapy, making his teeth look small. He had a severe case of acne and tended to drool a lot when he thought of his favorite food..

As the weeks went by and then the months, Danny grew to like his job. The day he first had a glimpse of Ridge Home and the residents who lived there had an impact on Danny Pratt. It had been easy to feel sorry for these people, to reflect upon what they didn't have. Compassion and empathy is good, but sympathy has no place here. Danny found that when he spoke to the boys in an authoritative voice with no hostility, the boys were more inclined to cooperate and respond.

There was a 15-year-old microcephalic everyone called Mousy. Mousy had no gag reflex. Danny was warned to keep an eye on Mousey because of his habit of swallowing towels and washcloths or any kind of textile he could get his hands on. Danny soon realized this when he was giving Mousey a shower one evening. He noticed something protruding from Mousy's rectum. He had swallowed a washcloth, and it had made its way through Mousy's digestive system. He seemed to suffer no ill effects from the washcloth, but the staff feared that if he swallowed too much it might cause a blockage in his intestines.

"He's a living towel dispenser," Danny told his supervisor. Mousy spent most of his day just sitting on the floor of the day room striking the right side of his face with his forefinger where a permanent welt was raised. As he was striking his face, he repeated what sounded like a mantra, a deep guttural noise similar to a hum. Mousy was able to walk short distances in a stooped posture but was not capable of speech.

The oldest resident in Red Oak was Alan at 40. You could see Alan any time pacing the day room frantically. Alan did not like to wear clothing and would tear it off as soon as he had the opportunity, then he would begin to masturbate. He now had a nylon rope that had been tied in a knot around his waist and threaded through the belt loops in his denims. His waist had a raised welt that was bleeding as he tried with all of his strength to remove the rope. Danny asked why this was being done since the only people Alan would come in contact with would be other male residents and the staff. "Isn't the cure worse than the crime?" he asked. His supervisor, Pearl, a black woman in her mid-40s explained that one day a local politician was touring Red Oak, along with several other visitors. They came upon a naked Alan masturbating in the day room. The visitors were shocked. Shortly after this visit, they were instructed by the director of Ridge Home to find a way to stop this behavior. Pearl explained that this was the only way to keep pants on Alan.

Gary Hastings, at 14, was the boy who kept most of the other residents stimulated. Gary was ambulatory and much more coordinated than most. He always was up to mischief. He would steal a dessert from one of the other boys or swat one of them in the head, making them yell, then run away giggling. Though Gary liked to tease, he really never hurt anyone.

Tony was a tall, aggressive boy. At 15, he was the most aggressive resident. The boy may have been handsome, but he had no teeth. Tony had bitten off the ear of one of the residents a year earlier. All of his teeth were removed, and he was given a pureed diet. He was kept heavily sedated and by the time Danny met him, all he did most of the day was sit cross-legged on the day room floor, rocking, his eyes unseeing.

During the following winter, a new RTT was hired. His name was Rob. Rob was around 5 feet 10 inches tall, with long, blond hair. He had just finished a long rehabilitation after losing his right leg to a Viet Cong land mine. He was one year younger than Danny, and they were instant friends. Rob was not one to feel sorry for himself. Despite a slight limp, you would not know that Rob had a prosthesis. He had a similar temperament to Danny's — the ability to take life pretty much as it came, complaining very little and to enjoy himself in the moment. Rob had the self-assurance of someone who had been tested and came out of the experience a better man.

Whenever they worked together, the two men intermingled with the boys in the day room, just trying to stimulate them a little. They would turn on some music that had a good beat and start clapping their hands in rhythm. This got Gerald Steel excited. He would giggle and clap his hands and salivate. They would toss a Frisbee or throw a ball back and forth or roll a large ball. Gerald always wanted to play. There was a definite stimulation there, something that several of them could be involved in at the same time. The energy seemed to flow through the room.

Roland, one of the lower functioning residents, screamed out when Gary stole the ball from another boy and hit Roland in the head with the it. Whenever the Frisbee came close to Mousy, he would test to see if there was a way for him to swallow it.

When spring arrived after a heavy Colorado winter, Danny and Rob started to take some of the higher functioning boys outside in a fenced-in area where they could sit in the warm sun for a few hours. Roland was blind and never seemed to notice the world around him unless he was touched. He reacted to the warm sun on his face. He would stop his perpetual rocking briefly and seemed to be luxuriating in the sun's energy. Gary Hastings even stopped his impish behavior when he was out in the sun, if only for a moment.

Since Gerald was higher functioning, he let Rob and Danny know when it was time to go in on the cooler days. He would come to Danny and say "I code," while hugging himself, and they would take the boys inside.

On a warm morning in early summer, Danny had parked his car in the Ridge Home lot and was just unlocking the door to Red

Oak Hall when he noticed a bus pulling up to one of the dorms for higher functioning girls. It had Ridge Home and Training Center written on the side. Danny talked to Pearl, the morning supervisor, later that day.

"Would it be possible for us to use the Ridge Home bus for an outside trip with the higher functioning boys? I drove a bus when I was in the Air Force. I could drive, and we could take them on a trip up into the mountains. I think some of them would really enjoy a trip."

"Good thought," Pearl said. "I don't know if we can do it or not, but I'll sure find out."

The following week, Rob and Danny took nine boys on their first trip into the mountains. Some of the hyperactive and aggressive residents like Gary Hastings were given a boost in medications to subdue active behavior during the trip. Bag lunches were prepared in the dietary department and sent over to Red Oak. The trip was to last maybe two hours or so, but Pearl thought it would be a good idea to take food. The morning medications were dispensed, and everyone was encouraged to use the toilet. Rob and Danny took off around 9 in the morning. Rob was really good with the boys and had all or them behaving as they headed down West Colfax Avenue and into the foothills and mountains. With the exception of Gerald Steel, none of the boys had ever been off Red Oak Hall. Danny drove the yellow bus out highway I-70. He took this highway mainly because there was a tunnel along the route, and he wanted to get the boys' reaction when the lights went out. When they entered the quarter-mile tunnel, Danny went "oooo" as a reaction to the sudden darkness. There was a chorus of "oooo" from Rob and the boys. Gerald clapped his hands with glee. The first-ever bus trip into the mountains was considered successful.

That spring, Rob and Danny took four of the boys to a rodeo in downtown Denver. The trip went well. After a little more than an hour, the boys began to show signs of restlessness. Danny, Joe Dunn, a well-behaved resident in his 30s, and Gerald walked down to the steel rails that looked down on the arena. During the calf-roping competition, they watched the speeding horse and rider whiz by. Danny happened to look past Joe on his right and saw Gerald urinating through the rails onto the arena floor. Gerald had just finished when Danny noticed. He old him that only the horses and cattle were allowed to pee on the arena floor.

"Men have to use the bathroom," he said.

"Otay," said Gerald. No one in the crowded arena seemed to even notice.

———

As the winter waned, Danny wanted to look for a job in the art field. He talked it over with BJ. He would leave Ridge Home and look for work as a commercial artist.

———

He handed in his resignation, stating that he would be leaving Ridge Home and Training Center. Two weeks later, he said good-bye to the staff and the residents.

Danny approached Gerald Steel and told him that he was leaving. Gerald watched as he said good-bye to the others on his last few moments. He followed him to the door. "Bye Da'e," he was unable to pronounce the letter "n." Danny reached over and gave Gerald a hug. Gerald clapped his hands together. "Fench fie," he said.

• 15 •

A HOT TIME IN TEXAS

Spring, 1973

Denver was warming up. The high-mountain snows melted early, and the Colorado streams, some of them overflowing, were flowing rapidly but receding. Pikes Peak could be seen with its lofty peak void of snow.

Colorado had held many dreams for Danny and BJ Pratt. But now, they were preparing to leave.

The idealism that he acquired in his childhood in the Wesleyan Methodist Church was translated into naivete in the real world. Danny had learned to question all things and was in a constant state of mental turmoil. He was too young, too idealistic and too bull-headed.

Danny knew this but was powerless to change. He told BJ he was compelled to move on. He had worked at Ridge Home for a year after leaving school in a distraught state of mind.

———

On a warm spring morning, Danny, BJ, Derick and the new baby, Marcy, left their home at 160 South Julian in Denver and again moved into an unsure future. Danny had not found employment when he went to Atlanta looking for a job. He also searched in Fort Walton Beach, where they were married. Employers wanted to see a diploma that stated officially: "This man knows what he is doing. He is qualified."

Danny knew nothing about sales. In fact, he did not like salesmen. On the third afternoon of his visit to Fort Walton Beach, Danny spotted a help-wanted sign for a sales manager. Danny showed the owner, Chuck Smith, his portfolio. Chuck hired him that afternoon and wanted him to get to work the next morning. Danny explained that he never had managed anything or sold anything but shoes. Chuck thought that if Danny could draw a picture of a proposed construction job, it might be a great selling point. And he liked Danny's attitude and enthusiasm. Chuck agreed to let Danny return to Denver to move his family to Fort Walton Beach. He gave him 10 days to wrap up his business in Denver then drive back to Fort Walton with all of their possessions.

Danny flew to Denver, packed up a U-Haul trailer and a 1966 Ford and left. It was quite a sight as the Pratts left their home. Ed McGrath, his girlfriend Robin and Bruce Williams helped them load belongings and clean the house.

The overflowing trunk of the Ford had to be tied with a rope. Their queen-size mattress and Danny's 10-speed bike were tied to the front of the U-Haul. It reminded Danny of the Joad family in "Grapes of Wrath."

Danny was not in the best of spirits. He made an effort to be optimistic as they drove away.

It was unseasonably hot as they left Denver in late May. Colorado Springs, then Pueblo passed by the open windows of the Fairlane. Marcy had a fever but fussed little.

Derick was content to just sit and watch the world passing, his face cooled by the warm breeze. BJ was the navigator. She plotted the route and told Danny where to turn and what highways to take. She made sandwiches and drinks and passed them out from a Styrofoam cooler that also served as a table in the crowded car. They had intended to drive as far as possible to conserve money. BJ and the kids slept while Danny continued to drive into the evening. It was near 2 in the morning when they pulled into a filling station in Santa Fe, N.M. BJ volunteered to drive while Danny and the kids slept. The heavy air cooled to a more comfortable level as they drove into the foothills.

Danny was awakened as BJ hit the brakes to avoid running over a coyote. He watched his wife briefly as she drove through the night. BJ rarely complained. And when she did, she would state her opinion, then let the subject drop. The bright morning sun made the vast panorama seem beautiful and lonely. Socorro and Truth or Consequences were places that did not exist in their lives until then.

El Paso came into view around suppertime. They traveled along the Mexican border and couldn't help noting that Mexico looked just like Texas. Danny recalled a song he liked from 1959 — Marty Robbins' "El Paso," which told of a passionate gunfighter who took the life of a young cowboy for the love of a girl named Felina.

There was rich history in this area. It was hard country that spawned many stories and songs.

Heading east from El Paso, the vastness of Texas unfolded before them in a grand panorama that was vast, varied and very hot.

A small, crowded, mom-and-pop restaurant seemed like a good place to stop for supper. The people of Texas seemed different. Many of the customers in the place had a quiet resolve that was suited to the temperament of the land. Many men wore the ever-present Western hat. One old man sat near the window in the sun with three other elderly folks. He removed his hat to reveal a distinct ring. The skin on the back of his neck went from milky white at the top to dark copper at the bottom. The women in the cafe were sturdy and looked unpretentious. The waitress was the only woman in the place who appeared to be wearing makeup.

On the back wall, over trays of drinking glasses, was a Lone Star flag mounted to the wall and the horns of a longhorn steer. Danny felt somewhat conspicuous, being the only male in the place with shoulder-length hair and a beard. But the people of this rural community gave Danny and his family little notice. They ate an inexpensive lunch, then moved on.

The flat, arid landscape stretched on and on. There was a deserted ranch with rusted cars and farm machinery strewn about in the fields, a rusty windmill and outbuildings that had gone to pot. Danny couldn't help wondering what history the old ruins could tell.

Betty and the kids took catnaps in the heat and complained little.

Several hours later, they reached a hilly area with thick, dried vegetation growing among gnarled, short trees. It was a welcome relief from the monotony of the flat, sandy desert.

They were just 15 miles from Fredericksburg, Texas, when they crested a hill. Just the other side of the hill was a large construction fire. A area had been cleared of brush and trees. A great pile of stumps and dried bushes was ablaze. Danny swerved to the left as far as he could, but he still felt the intense heat of the flames. He cussed at the ignorance of anyone who would build a fire so close to a state road then drove on.

They traveled another 5 miles before Danny heard a noise, and the trailer rode over something causing a loud, metallic crash. He pulled to the shoulder and stopped to investigate. When he stepped from the car, the mattress that was tied to the front of the trailer was in flames. The rope that held the mattress and his 10-speed bike burned through, and his bike had fallen under the trailer. The blazing mattress then fell onto the open trunk of the car, igniting the contents.

Danny grabbed Derick and yelled for BJ to get out and run into the woods. She grabbed the baby and the diaper bag and fled. The gas tank of the old Ford was in the rear, under the trunk. There was real danger that the tank might explode at any moment. They watched as everything they owned began to go up in flames.

"The cat's still in the car," BJ yelled. "We have to save the cat." Danny ran back to the car just as the Fredericksburg volunteer fire department arrived. He snatched the cat from the back seat. As he left the car, he reached into the glove box and removed the half-ounce bag of pot he just remembered was there. This was the conservative part of the country, and the fines for possession of marijuana were high, and spending years in prison for the offense was not uncommon. He reached BJ and the kids, telling them he needed to relieve himself in the thicket nearby. He walked until he was out of sight, then turned the plastic bag containing the pot upside down and scattered it about the brush.

The firemen soon had the fire under control. The U-Haul was a total loss. The contents were either smoke-, fire- or water-damaged. The inside of the trunk of the Ford was burned along with the contents. The firemen towed the car and the burned-out trailer to a nearby garage to see if the car could be repaired. Danny found an inexpensive motel nearby and booked a room.

BJ called her parents, Harmon and Wilma Knight, and told them the news, as they were expecting the arrival of the Pratts the next day. They wired some money through Western Union to help with expenses.

The garage determined that the wiring in the rear of the car would need to be redone. It would take at least two days to get the parts for the taillights. Danny told the garage owner to just rig the taillights to work. He would get the rest of the work done when they arrived in Fort Walton Beach.

Danny and BJ went through the charred ruins of the trailer to see if anything could be salvaged. The most valuable thing they lost turned out to be the thousands of photos Danny had taken. Some of them he had developed and printed himself. They could not be replaced. They managed to save very few.

It was a disturbing development. They were stranded in a strange town in Texas with no transportation, few clothes and virtually no material goods. But they were alive.

They were watching TV in the motel room that night, when there was a knock on the door. It was Bob from the garage. Handing Danny an estimate of the cost of repair, he told Danny that the wiring in his Ford should be finished by late morning of the next day. He expressed sympathy for their plight then asked Danny if he could buy him a beer. Danny checked with BJ to see if she was OK with him leaving for a few hours. Danny made sure the kids were in bed for the evening.

They drove less than 5 miles and came to what looked like an old country store. Bob led the way through the dimly lit place, then out the back door to an open terrace with bare electric lights and candles at a dozen or so tables arranged in a semicircle. The clear, starry Texas sky was the canopy.

It wasn't long after they had drank their first beer that four men in dusty Western hats appeared. Two of them pulled acoustic guitars from their cases, another pulled out an acoustic bass guitar, while the fourth tooted on a trumpet.

"Now you're goin' to hear some real music," said Bob.

The four men tuned their instruments, then began to play. It was the first time Danny had heard a mariachi band. Some of the songs were in Spanish, and he could not understand the lyrics. But the sound that these four improbable musicians made was astounding. The musicians changed throughout the evening, and some of the people in the audience would take a turn playing and singing songs like "San Antonio Rose" and "Tumbling Tumbleweeds." It was like an open-air jam session with some of the most talented musicians Danny ever had heard. They stayed until the music stopped.

Bob drove Danny back to his motel room, and Danny thanked him profusely for the incredible evening.

The car was ready around 10 the next morning. Danny paid Bob for the repairs, and they were again on the road, this time with just their clothing and a few meager possessions.

They were a sight as they drove through the streets of Fort Walton Beach with the burned-out 1966 Ford with the makeshift taillights below the charred trunk.

Danny said that things could be much worse. BJ had been stoic through the ordeal that had been their marriage. He was fortunate to have her. She was not only a good wife and a good mother, she was a best friend.

The Pratt family lived in Fort Walton Beach for a little more than a year. Danny started an advertising business there, then contacted his old art school friend, Bruce Williams, who still lived in Denver. Bruce joined him in the fledgling business. They called their enterprise the Triad Art and Design Studio.

They started to make money. Bruce sent for his girlfriend, Vicky, who joined them in the business. She was an excellent artist and graphic designer.

They rented office space in a new building and had the owner add extra windows for more natural light.

Things went well for a time. They did design work for a planned community called Sandestin, which was backed by Chase Manhattan Bank of New York City. They designed menus and advertising or the new community, which boasted several golf courses and high-end restaurants. Everything about Sandestin was the highest quality.

Triad put a lot of time and effort into giving Sandestin owners what they wanted. It looked as if they were going to do well in their association with the new community.

But by late summer, Sandestin began to have problems. Triad Art and Design Studio received a registered letter stating that Sandestin was in bankruptcy.

Within weeks after that disclosure, Danny, Bruce and Vicky paid their bills and closed the business.

• 16 •

THE HOSPITAL YEARS

1974 to 1983

These were difficult times for Danny and BJ Pratt.

In December of 1974, Danny lost his dad. Danny found him on the floor of his boyhood home, dead of a massive heart attack.

It was a numbing shock for Danny. He had not been ready for his dad's death. He was still in the process of proving his worth to his dad.

Danny's oldest sister and her family moved into the old homestead. Peter, the oldest male, became the executor of his dad's estate.

Ermine Pratt, Danny's mother, had been suffering from early Alzheimer's since the young age of 40. She no longer knew her name or the names of her children.

Danny and BJ attempted to care for Ermine in their mobile home in Alpine Village on Two-Mile Road near Bay City. It became an impossible task. At night, Ermine would walk restlessly through the confining trailer, waking the kids and trying to open the locked door in the rear of the home where there was no porch. She would mistake the bathtub for the toilet.

Danny was a light sleeper. He trained himself to be aware of any unusual noises during his sleeping hours. The slightest disturbance would awaken him.

He was not sleeping at night. He was becoming ill-tempered. It simply was not going to work. Danny wanted to fulfill his dad's request that he care of his mother. He had tried. BJ was doing her best, taking care to bathe and care for her mother-in-law. But Danny and BJ both worked.

Long after Danny was married, he realized that his mother's negative behavior was largely due to her dementia, which slowly had been destroying her brain. Though Danny then realized that the behavior was not really her fault, the open hostility she showed his sister, Maggie, still was fresh in his memory.

Danny called Peter and explained the anxiety he was feeling. Peter decided to take over the care of his mother in his home. She stayed with him for several months. It became too much for his wife, Evelyn, and his daughter, Cindy.

Ermine was moved to a foster care home on Lauria Road in Bangor Township. She did well there. Danny picked his mother up from the home and took her to church on Sunday mornings, but he could not escape the guilt feelings over not fulfilling his dad's wishes.

————

Danny had been "let go" from his job as a salesman at Goodwin Printing Co. on Bay City Road in Midland.

He searched diligently for a job, checking the want ads and going to every business he could think of and filling out applications.

One day he received a call from General Hospital in Bay City. Administrators had reviewed his application and asked that he come in for a job interview as a nurse aide.

He was hired and began his orientation two days later, where he learned the proper way to care for patients — taking temperatures and blood pressures, making a bed, easing a patient into a wheelchair, using the bed pan properly, giving CPR.

After the two-week orientation, Danny went to work on 1-F, a floor for men. He began work on the day shift to learn the floor routine, then, after another two weeks, he was moved to the second shift.

The supervisor on the second shift was Elgie Zerod. She introduced him to the other workers. Linda Rotarius was the ward clerk, Elody Van Depute was the LPN, Linda Shroer and Pearl Weidner were nurse aides. Danny was the only male working on the floor.

Elgie was a gutsy, outspoken, straight-to-the-point, in-your-face, registered nurse who could cuss with the best of them. She was also an excellent nurse who could empathize with those patients who were seriously or terminally ill.

One day, only a few days after Danny started work on the second shift, Elgie was talking with a man who was in the final stages of terminal cancer. He was in great pain and had asked for a pain shot. Elgie told the man that she could not give him an injection for another half-hour. She sat at his bedside as he talked of his plans for the coming year. When he finished what he had to say, he looked at Elgie as if he wanted her approval.

"Now Jim, you know you are dying. Don't be making any long-term plans," Elgie said.

As Danny listened to the conversation, he was taken by the bluntness of her words. He was at first concerned that she was being insensitive. But, as she explained later, she had spoken to the man many times and had developed a rapport that eventually seemed to brighten his spirits.

"I know I won't be around much longer. But, it is good to be optimistic, even in the worst of times. Isn't it?" asked Jim.

"You're damn right it is," Elgie said, as she patted his hand.

Part of Danny's daily routine was to play games or just talk with the patients once his early jobs were complete.

There were two orderlies who were on call for the entire hospital. Vern Jeske was a pleasant, long-suffering guy with abundant energy and a good sense of humor. Dave Thompson was a short, balding man with gray hair and a sharp wit. Dave did little to hide the fact that he was gay. He always had something humorous to say. Danny liked to do some verbal fencing whenever they ran into each other. The two orderlies often would come to 1-F to play spades with Danny and some of the patients. They wore pagers and were never far from a phone. Danny was responsible for answering any buzzers that might go off on 1-F. The patients enjoyed the break from the monotony of long-term care, and it was said to be therapeutic for them to get their minds off their illness.

—————

Danny had always been good at remembering jokes, so he would come up with a new one as often as he could while he was taking vital signs or giving special care.

Pearl Weidner was a pleasure to work with. She always was upbeat and full of energy. She had worked with Danny's mother, Ermine, at the old Samaritan Hospital and had fond memories of her. Pearl was known for her vigorous back rubs.

There was a long room at the southern end of 1-F that they called the porch. There were six beds in the room. One of the patients on the porch was a sculptor, Alan Paulsen. Alan worked in metal sculpture, mostly bronze. He had been having respiratory problems and was a patient there when Danny first started work.

Danny told Alan he would be interested in seeing some of his work. He spoke of his own art career, which was now in limbo. He said he went to the Colorado Institute of Art. They talked about art whenever they met. Alan said that he currently had some of his work hanging in the Brass Lantern on Third and Water Streets across the street from St. Laurence Brother's House of Nuts.

Danny went to the Brass Lantern the next day to see Alan's work. He was impressed with his ability to bend and cut sheets of copper and brass and shape them to express his inspiration. The brass sculptures of sailboats filled the place. Some were abstractions while others were more literal interpretations. It was pleasing to see that Alan's art wasn't just trendy art. Each piece had a personality. The man was an artist.

When returning to work the next day, he told Alan that he was impressed with his work. Alan said he was just getting to the point where his work was selling well. The works at the Brass Lantern were all done on commission. He was getting more commissions by the day and was eager to get back to work.

Danny brought some of his work in for Alan to see. They were pen-and-ink drawings. Alan said that he liked the work, so Danny gave him a signed print of a horse drawing called "Rascal."

Danny and BJ were off that weekend. They took Derick and Marcy to Frankenmuth, where they ate a chicken dinner at Zehnder's. They took a leisurely walk down the main street to check out art galleries. Danny was proud of the way his kids behaved in public. Marcy was a toddler and was given a ride in a stroller, while Derick held on to his dad's hand as they moved down the crowded street. The sun was setting, and the colorful city of Frankenmuth turned on its show lights to a beautiful Bavarian village, right in Michigan.

Three of the galleries the Pratt family visited featured works by Alan Paulsen. Danny told BJ and the kids that Alan was one of his patients.

———

When Danny returned to work the following Monday, he went directly to the porch to tell Alan he had seen his work at several galleries in Frankenmuth. Alan's bed was empty. He found Elgie in the kitchen getting a cup of coffee and asked her if Alan Paulsen had been discharged.

"That's right, you weren't here yesterday. He was transferred. He has cancer of the esophagus. When they scoped the inside of his throat, it was coated with green from the copper in his sculptures. He's full of cancer."

Within a month, Alan Paulsen's obituary was in the Bay City Times. He was 29 years old.

• 17 •

HAPPY MOTHER'S DAY

On Mother's Day of his first year of employment at General Hospital, Danny was busy at work when Elgie asked him what he had gotten BJ for Mother's Day. He said he had not purchased a gift yet and had little money to buy one.

One of the terminally ill patients had died the week before. The family sent a bouquet of flowers to the staff in appreciation of good care the man had received. Danny looked at the bouquet of colorful flowers and noticed that some had started to wilt.

Danny asked Elgie what she planned to do with the flowers.

"They're starting to wilt," he said.

"OK, Pratt. What you are really telling me is that you forgot to get your wife a Mother's Day present. Correct?"

"Correct," he said sheepishly.

"You'd better run down to the gift shop before they close and get her a card to go with the bouquet. You don't think for a minute that BJ is going to buy this do you? That's a $50 bouquet."

Danny thanked Elgie, then ran down and purchased a card for $1.

Before going home that night, he removed all of the wilted flowers and put fresh water in the large vase that held them.

When Danny reached home, BJ was already in bed. He placed the beautiful bouquet on the dining room table and went to bed.

When the alarm went off in the morning at 5, BJ got a few extra winks while Danny got up and made coffee. As BJ walked down the hall of their mobile home, she saw the elegant bouquet sitting on the dining room table.

"Did someone die at work?" she asked.

One day when Danny was taking his supper break in the cafeteria, he met an RN named Tom Doerr. Tom had an out-going personality and was interested in a vast amount of topics that they talked about over their meal. He was incredible at remembering names and details of things he had experienced. They began to seek each other out at dinner breaks. Tom worked in ICU, and word around the hospital was that he was very proficient at his work.

Danny was called to ICU one day when a large patient, who was in a coma, needed to be rolled over. Tom was manning the unit alone. Vern Jeske also was there to help. It was no easy task, rolling over the 500-pound man. There was nothing to grab on the man except the fat.

When the task was completed, Danny stayed behind and talked to Tom for a few minutes. He went about his duties as he talked. One man, who was in a coma, had halo traction applied to his head. Screws were embedded in his scull around his shaved head. Tom explained that the man had broken his neck in a car accident as he checked the IV fluids and his urine output. Danny was amazed at Tom's casual efficiency.

It was during this time that Danny and BJ moved from their mobile home in Alpine Village to a big, old house at 1808 Ninth St., just three blocks from General Hospital. Elgie Zerod gave Danny and his family a place to stay in her enormous Victorian home on Van Buren Street while they waited for the former owners to evacuate their newly purchased home.

The house was in need of extensive repair. It once was owned by the Trahan family, who owned Trahan's Funeral Chapel on

Madison Avenue in Bay City. They bought the huge, four-bedroom home for $15,000. It had a big coal-burning octopus furnace in the basement that had been converted to natural gas. There was an ancient fireplace in the living room, which had been a big selling point for Danny. BJ had a hard time adjusting to the draftiness of the old house, with 9-foot ceilings and very little insulation.

There was an old carriage house in the back of the property. Danny could see his new art studio when he looked at the old, run-down building. There were three apple trees in the back of the double lot and a grape arbor along the fence.

It became common for Danny to float to other floors whenever another floor was short-staffed. He worked on ground floor 1-C and the orthopedic floor. He got to know some of the other workers in the hospital.

One of the nurses, Lucy Grills, was known for her lavish parties that she and her husband, Ray, threw several times a year. She lived in Essexville in a medium-sized house on Main Street.

Lucy would cook up meatballs, escalloped potatoes and other casserole dishes, then freeze them several weeks ahead of time in preparation for one of her gatherings. Ray would record dance music on reel-to-reel tape so the music was non-stop. Their large basement always was decorated for the appropriate season or theme. She provided a keg of beer and a variety of booze and mixes. Her parties were popular, and cars would fill both sides of the street until the early morning hours.

BJ did not attend any of the parties since she worked in the morning, and she did not drink alcohol or enjoy the party atmosphere.

Life was good. Interacting with patients was fulfilling for Danny. He enjoyed the times when he could help people smile when they were at the mercy of some illness or disease that could take their life. The people he knew in his private life were either religious to the point of exclusion of others who did not share their faith, or they were so involved in making large amounts of money that nothing else was important to them.

He began to see patterns of behavior when a person was close to death. There was an intense fear, an all-consuming fear that compelled the person to look for some meaning to his existence. The material things that one may accumulate in a lifetime, suddenly had no meaning. He could offer these people who were coming to the end of life an ear. He could listen without judgment as someone unloaded his emotional baggage. He was a nurse's aide. His earning potential was small. Yet he could offer a lonely man on his deathbed someone to talk to. The simple act of listening was priceless.

The workday would begin when he left his house on Ninth Street and walk the short, three blocks to General Hospital. He would talk himself into a positive mood. It always worked. No matter what was going on in the rest of his life, the patients were having a more difficult time. When he got to work, he was ready for the day.

Danny worked almost a year on 1-F when he noticed a posting for a mental health job on the bulletin board. It was an orderly position and would mean a small hike in pay.

He talked with Tom Doerr that day about signing for the job. Tom encouraged him to get his foot in the door, and if he liked the work, go back to school. Tom also encouraged him to go to nursing school. He signed for the job, and a week later was summoned for an interview.

• 18 •

PSYCH

The old elevator squeaked, then groaned to a halt on the fourth floor of Mercy Hospital. Danny Pratt stepped off the elevator with two registered nurses.

Lillian was in her early 50s. Blond and confident, she had the bearing of a professional and was pretty for her age.

Jan was shorter, with a bright smile and good sense of humor. She also carried the confidence of someone who had experienced quite a bit of life for a woman in her mid- to late 20s.

Jan walked to a steel door with a small reinforced window, pushing a buzzer to summon someone to open the door. A young male head popped into view in the tiny window. His eyes widened. He stared at Danny for a moment then moved on.

Seconds later, the click of a key opened the door to a short, middle-aged woman. Julie Richardson was the floor supervisor and also a registered nurse. She greeted Danny with a friendly smile and welcomed him to 4-South, the psychiatric unit. Julie also carried herself with a great amount of confidence. She gave Danny a tour of the unit.

There was one long, central hall. To the right of the entrance was the day room, where a half-dozen people sat smoking and watching TV.

Directly across from the entrance was a seclusion room. The door was opened to show a steel bed, bolted to the floor. There were two leather straps to secure the feet and two more for the wrists. A thick, wide belt held the waist. Julie explained that the room was used for agitated patients as a protection for themselves as well as others. The patient would be strapped to the table then sedated. The sedation, she explained, would induce sleep and calm in the patient, they would sleep from eight to 10 hours.

There were several patient rooms on each side of the hall, then a dining room on the left with a locked door that opened to the kitchen. The meals were brought from the hospital cafeteria on a hot cart, which plugged into the wall.

They moved down the hall, past more patient rooms on both sides, to the nurses' station, which was bustling with activity. The ward clerk was Colleen, who waved and smiled as she held a phone to her ear with her shoulder and leafed through a chart. Margaret, an RN, sat behind a table making notations in a chart.

There was a Zippo lighter attached to a steel chain. A shy female patient walked quietly to the shelf where the lighter was chained, lit her cigarette, then retreated.

"You can probably guess why the cigarette lighter is chained to the wall," said Julie.

Danny nodded and smiled.

Across the hall from the nurses' station was Julie's office, which also served as a room for the doctors to consult with patients privately.

Danny's first week was spent in orientation, learning the routines and responsibilities. He would not be required to wear any kind of uniform as he did on the medical floors. The dress code was casual and loose. He learned to observe behavior and document his observations.

At that time, 4-South was facilitating a methadone program for heroin addicts. They were given methadone to replace the heroin and gradually withdraw from the methadone.

Part of Danny's orientation was given by Maria, the unit psychologist. She had moved to Bay City from Santiago, Chile. She

130

spoke with a heavy accent as she explained to Danny that heroin addicts seldom were cured. She said they tended to be divisive and manipulative and that they would do practically anything to get a "fix."

Several months later, Danny got to put his new knowledge to work. One of the patients he was assigned to follow on his shift was an addict in his mid-20s. He introduced himself to the man as they watched "Roots," Alex Haley's story of his slave ancestors. His hair was gnarled and greasy. His teeth had not been brushed for a time. He did not seem concerned about his lack of hygiene.

At first, the young man would talk very little and seemed dazed and vague in his response. It took a week for him to take an active part in the conversation.

He spoke to Danny of his troubles and his life in general. He voiced a lot of remorse over his addiction and what it had done to ruin his life. His eyes dampened as he talked about his 2-year-old daughter that he had with his former girlfriend and how he had to "clean up his act" and raise her to be a good person. He thanked Danny for the talk and shook his hand.

The patient continued to improve over several weeks, playing cards with the staff and a few other lucid patients. His hygiene was no longer a problem. He showered daily and shaved. His teeth had been flossed and brushed. Danny charted that his patient seemed a little nervous at times but also said that the nervousness could be caused by the excessive amount of coffee he drank.

One day, Dr. Tanal, the head psychiatrist for 4-South, called Danny into Julie's office. He asked if he thought his patient, the heroin addict, was ready for a weekend pass. Danny cited the improvements that had been made and told of his feelings of remorse over having the addiction and his plans to make a better life for his daughter. His hygiene improved, he was much brighter and more sociable. He also said he was not keeping company with the other three addicts in the methadone program.

Dr. Tanal signed the order, allowing the patient to go home on a pass for the weekend.

Danny talked with the patient about his hopes for the visit

before he left on his pass. He said he would stay away from other addicts and spend some time with his daughter. He offered his hand to Danny and thanked him for his efforts.

Danny was off that weekend.

He returned to work on the following Monday to find the patient shirtless and disheveled and watching TV in the day room.

"How did the weekend go?" he asked.

"Just peachy," said the addict, diverting his eyes, which were bloodshot and half closed.

Danny found out in the morning report that his patient had gone from the hospital directly to his parents' home where he stole everything of value that he could find and sold it to buy heroin.

He was taken in by the man completely, and he felt foolish.

After a six-week orientation on first shift, Danny began working on the second shift. Lynn was the shift RN. She was in her mid-20s, as were Liz and Cathy, who were LPNs. Mark was the ward clerk who was about the same age. They were all young, energetic and competent.

The second shift was a change from the first shift. Doctors' visits and medical procedures kept the first shift busy. Visitors were more frequent in the evening and were allowed to visit, under most circumstances, until 8 p.m. The staff did its best to keep the lucid patients active. There were video tapes, some therapeutic and some for entertainment.

One of the therapeutic video tapes was "What Is Essential" by Leo Buscaglia. The tape was of a talk that Dr. Buscaglia gave at a university. He was a great motivational speaker. The essence of the talk was uplifting. He examined human life and what was important and nurturing to the human spirit. He also talked of accepting your own death and the power of giving of yourself to feel more complete. He ended his talk with the phrase: "Life is God's gift to you. The way you live your life is your gift to God. Make it a fantastic one."

The tape always inspired conversation. Buscaglia was called "the love doctor" by the media. It was a fitting moniker, Danny thought. Over time he would see the same video once a week, but he never tired of seeing it and always enjoyed the ensuing conversation.

Dr. Wayne Dyer's "Your Erroneous Zones" was another video that always got the patients talking. In the future, Danny was to see this tape many times.

Beth DeWyse was the occupational therapist who was hired just after Danny. He worked with Beth as she conducted craft sessions, held cooking classes or took some of the patients for walks on pleasant days.

On one warm, spring afternoon, they took four patients for a walk through downtown Bay City. There were three women and one man, Bob.

Danny talked with Bob as they walked north on Water Street, past the Wenonah Hotel and the Mill End Store, up Center Avenue, then down Washington Street and back to Mercy Hospital. It was a good day.

Bob was a handsome young man in his late 20s. He was recovering from an attempted suicide. He had slit both wrists in a serious attempt to end his life. He would have irreversible ligament damage.

He had been unresponsive for weeks but now was smiling and talking as if nothing was wrong with his life. It was good to see so much improvement in the man. His wrists still were bandaged from the razor slashes.

"Do you think you will ever try to kill yourself again?" Danny asked.

"All I can say is that I'm feeling fine right now," Bob said, with a broad smile. "I thank you and the mental health staff for all of your help."

Danny would regret that he or the mental health staff did not see the warning signs. Bob was content, because he had figured out what he was going to do. Two days later, Bob was discharged. He went to his parents' home, crawled under the house and shot himself in the head.

One night Mark, the ward clerk, received a call from the Bay City Police. They were bringing in a white man in his mid-30s who was known by the 4-South staff. He was in a full-blown schizophrenic break. Lynn briefed the staff on the orders and told Mark to stand by to see if more male personnel was needed to get the man into seclusion.

Danny and Liz prepared the seclusion room for the man, who on previous admissions, had been quite violent. Dr. Tanal had called in the orders for the patient's admission. He was considered to be a danger to himself and others. He would be taken to the seclusion room, restrained, then sedated.

About 15 minutes after the call, the buzzer at the entrance door went off. Lynn stepped out the door to evaluate the patient's condition. Three policemen were there with the patient, who was in handcuffs. His name was Thad, and he stood around 5 feet 8 inches and weighed around 160 pounds. His eyes were wide, and his hair was wet with sweat.

In Danny's opinion, more male personnel would not be needed.

One of the police officers removed Thad's handcuffs. The instant his wrists were free, he lunged at Lynn, his hands going for her neck. One of the officers grabbed him before he was able to get to Lynn. Lynn turned to Mark, who was standing at the open door. "Call for help," she yelled.

Thad screamed obscenities and kicked as he struggled with surprising strength.

Your attention please: All available male personnel to mental health, stat," said a female voice over the intercom.

A moment later, the doors of the elevator opened, and six burly men from different areas of the hospital stepped out. Thad fought as if he was in mortal combat, biting, kicking and screaming.

To avoid injury, there were two people per limb as he was moved to the seclusion room. They wrestled him to the steel restraint bed. Thad jerked and knocked Danny off balance. It took seven men and women to restrain the small man. Danny was amazed at his strength and determination.

Thad continued screaming and fighting against the immovable leather straps, spit flying from his mouth as Lynn gave him an injection of sodium amytal. In another 10 minutes, Thad was still. Liz entered the room and took Thad's blood pressure.

When Danny came to work the next day, Thad was sitting in the day room smoking a cigarette and drinking a cup of coffee. He looked up at Danny, but there was no recognition in his eyes. He didn't remember anything about his break from reality.

The 3 to 11 shift staff in mental health was a lively bunch. They all were younger than Danny, and he was the only married person on that shift. He enjoyed their level of energy, the way they all worked together. There was no arguing over whose job it was to do different tasks. It was satisfying work for him. He liked the way they all came together in a moment of crisis.

Liz, an LPN, was a strong woman. She stood around 5 feet 10 inches with a sturdy build. She wore heavy, meticulously applied makeup with long, black lashes and a heavy mask of facial rouge. Her hair was bleached blond and sprayed so that every hair had its place. By her own admission, she was never seen without makeup. When it came to any physical conflict, Liz could hold her own.

Mark recently had left active duty in the Marine Corps Reserve. He was not tall but wide, with broad shoulders and a strong build. He enjoyed the macho part of his job when he was required to help restrain a patient and was an excellent ward clerk.

Lynn, the RN, was soft-spoken and efficient. Danny didn't think she could raise her voice, even if she wanted to. But Lynn led the unit with an assurance that he had to admire. She was in her early 20s, with long, curly, brown hair and a serene countenance.

On Dec. 7, 1977, BJ gave birth to a boy, Lucas Daniel Pratt. Lucas was among the first babies to be born in the new Bay Regional Medical Center after the merger of General Hospital and Mercy Hospital finally took place, and everyone moved into the new building on Columbus Avenue.

Julie, the head nurse, and Maria, the unit psychologist, worked together, with input from the staff, to design the new unit. Once a few flaws were corrected, it became a functioning unit.

One of the flaws wasn't discovered until several months after the opening of the new facility. One particularly violent patient was locked in the seclusion room without being restrained. He kicked at the concrete-core door until it crumbled. He was placed in an adjoining room where he was put in restraints.

Two weeks later, an agitated patient punched holes in the three layers of sheet rock in one of the seclusion rooms, then began to pull out the wiring, forcing the staff to turn off the electrical service to the room.

It was a modern, comfortable unit. The day room was huge and furnished with comfortable, durable furniture and an enormous picture window at the southern end of the room. The windows were made of safety glass. On either side of the day room were the patient rooms. There were cafe tables and chairs near a central nursing station. The nursing station had a modern tube system for the quick and efficient delivery of medications. There was a well-appointed kitchen and a large TV room with comfortable furnishings. The staff had a break room with lockers, toilets, a table and chairs and a sofa.

Danny, Mark and a new orderly named Jud started getting together after work at Denny's Green Hut on Columbus Avenue, just down the street from Bay Med. Denny Hayes was the owner and had been a teacher at Central High School when Danny graduated in 1966. Denny was an energetic, outspoken, sports-minded man. He always was promoting the Green Hut, hiring players from the Detroit Lions football team to come and spend an evening at the bar. Denny also founded Green Hut Charities and the Bay County Sports Hall of Fame. He sold green beer on St. Patrick's Day and hired some quality Irish entertainers to come in during a week of celebration.

Tom Doerr was now working at the new ICU at Bay Medical Center. Tom, who was four years older than Danny, was a bachelor. Tom also became a regular at the Green Hut, along with many of Tom's friends. The Green Hut became a favorite oasis for the 3 to 11 crew at Bay Medical Center. Some nights the hospital gang would party until closing time, then get together in the old carriage house at Danny's home, which he had turned into an art studio. During the cold, winter months, Danny would start a fire in a small wood-burner. It was a cozy, well-lighted place to play cards or just talk, and the fairly loud music from Danny's stereo would not disturb the neighbors. Many of the world's problems were solved there.

BJ worked the day shift and was asleep by the time Danny got off work. On the nights when Danny stayed up late, he would wake up in the morning to feed the kids and get them off to school, then go back to bed..

Danny was aware that he was partying and drinking too much. But the lure of the social interaction with his friends was strong, and he had no wish to change the course of his life. BJ was strong in her religious beliefs. Danny, on the other hand, had not been capable of making any real commitment to any religion. Yet he kept attending church, hoping one day he would feel what others had professed, that he had some value, that his life had meaning.

———

It was several months after the move into the new Mental Health Center that Maria, the psychologist, announced she would be leaving her job and returning to Santiago, Chile, where her husband lived and where she needed to be.

Dave Rawlings replaced Maria. Dave was tall with dark hair and a thick mustache that reminded Danny of Gene Shalit, the movie critic on "The Today Show" on TV. Dave did not appreciate the comparison. He recently had received his master's degree in psychology. He brought new life to the new mental health unit.

Dave conducted group therapy sessions, which Danny would attend and contribute to when he deemed it prudent. Dave was personable and could even get some of the more introverted patients to express their feelings.

One woman in particular would talk about how her family constantly was taking advantage of her. She could not understand why they demanded so much and why they seemed to have no respect for her.

Dave Rawlings interrupted her: "Excuse me, but can I borrow a cigarette from you?"

She handed him her full pack of Winstons. Dave took two cigarettes from the pack, then handed it back to her.

She continued explaining the disrespect that she suffered.

"Excuse me again. Could I borrow a few more? It will be at least three hours before I can get out to buy some." This time, Dave took what remained of the pack, except for one cigarette. "Thank you," he said.

"Sure, anytime," she said, wanting to get back to the conversation.

"Did you notice what I just did?" asked Dave.

"Yes. You borrowed some cigarettes."

"I took your whole pack except for one cigarette."

"That's OK. I don't mind, I've been without cigarettes before."

"When would you get to the to point where you said no, you

can't have any more cigarettes?"

"I don't know. I'm just a giving sort of person. I like to help others." She was getting teary-eyed.

"So, I probably could just keep asking for cigarettes or money or anything else until you had nothing left to give."

"Probably," she sniffed and daubed her eyes with a Kleenex.

"Do you see what you are telling me?"

"What?"

"You are showing me that you don't care about yourself. You are showing me that I am more important than you are. You are almost screaming: 'Please take advantage of me.' "

Over time, it became apparent to Danny that there were patients who came to mental health who did not want to be cured or even relieved of whatever problem they had been admitted for. There were those who worked for General Motors who found that a complaint of depression could get them an expense-paid vacation in the mental health unit. All it took for a six-week vacation was an order from the GM psychiatrist. The patient then would tell the mental health staff that all they really needed was a long rest from the rigors of the production line. If the patient was urged to get involved in unit activities — crafts, exercise, outside activities — all the patient needed to do was complain to the GM doctor, and he would write an order excusing them from all activities.

There were times when Danny easily drew the conclusion that there was much room in the mental health business for those who cared less for the well-being of patients and more for easy money.

Bill Dawson was hired as administrator of the mental health Unit. He was an organizer. He would bring the Mental Health Center up to contemporary standards.

He hired a recreational therapist named Janice. She was 23 and had freshly graduated with her master's degree. She had a calm demeanor and was efficient and conscientious.

Danny was assigned to work with the new therapist on the day shift, setting up and implementing new programs for the inpatients.

One afternoon as Danny was leading a discussion following a

Wayne Dyer video, Dawson, Janice and Julie, the head nurse, came into the room, took a seat and observed as the patients became involved in the talk. Danny had a feeling that he was being evaluated for something.

A week later, Dawson called Danny and two other workers to his office. He told them there was now a new position in the mental health field, mental health worker. Each was to find a specialty that he would become proficient in. The job required some educational background in psychology. He offered the three a chance to become a mental health worker. He told Danny he would need to take a class in basic psychology, which was offered just across the street in the Bay Medical Center complex. The other two already had received their bachelor's degrees in psych. The one female of the group said she would like to work in the sex therapy field, while Danny chose recreational therapy.

After taking the required psych class, Danny became a mental health worker/recreational therapist.

They played bingo with the more lucid patients. They cooked in the small, unit kitchen making pizza, spaghetti, fried chicken, etc. Janice contacted the owners of Alert Bowling Lanes in Bay City, and they began to take several patients at a time to bowl once a week. They also took a van load of patients to the YWCA for a weekly swim. They purchased four bicycles and began biking in good weather. They went for hikes on the Tobico Marsh Trail.

Danny enjoyed working with Janice. She put a lot of energy into her job and completely revamped the activity therapy program.

Danny and Tom Doerr were getting together at least once a week now. Danny decided to introduce Tom to Janice.

She met Tom Doerr at a euchre tournament at Danny's house within a year after she began working in mental health. Tom, who was on the rebound from a bad relationship, really took to Janice. Though there was a 17-year difference in their ages, it proved to be a good match. Both were intelligent and ambitious.

After a year, Janice took a job in the new Substance Abuse Treatment Center in what had been the Samaritan Hospital where Danny's mother worked in the '50s and '60s.

The following year, Tom Doerr married Janice in St. Mary's Church, where Tom had been attending church his whole life.

Danny enjoyed interacting with the patients. He started a music appreciation session where the only thing that the patients were required to do was listen to music. He would play music he really liked by Mozart, Willie Nelson, Abba, Chet Atkins, Crosby, Stills, Nash & Young and Steely Dan, among many others.

Before playing some of the songs, he would ask the patients to concentrate on different sounds in a particular song and how tight the timing was. He would illustrate how different melodies portrayed feelings. The group listened to Leonard Bernstein's rendition with the New York Philharmonic Orchestra of "Peter and the Wolf." Or they would follow the bass guitar through a classic rock-and-roll song and notice how much it added. He would pick up the beat of a song and keep time by slapping his thighs to help relate the rhythm.

As time went on, there was also an art appreciation session that was given once or twice a month, depending on the patient turnover. The sessions varied. Danny bought six art posters and mounted them on illustration board. Several were of paintings of people in different situations. Danny would put the poster on a tripod, ask each patient to look closely, then try to determine what was happening by the expressions on the painted faces. The patient would interpret according to his life experience. An open discussion usually followed.

In another art appreciation session, Danny would tape a piece of newsprint, 5 feet high and perhaps 10 to 12 feet long, on the day room wall. He would then draw a picture of the interior of a bus, showing one side with seats and windows. He would ask one of the staff to draw himself sitting on one of the seats. The patients would usually laugh, once they found that proficiency at art was not required. Then patients would be asked to draw themselves into the picture. Just the social aspect of each person drawing a picture was entertaining and many times therapeutic. The drawings were sometimes revealing. One of the patients had suffered a closed-head injury, resulting in extensive brain damage. He drew himself so tall in the bus, that there was no room for his head within the confines of the paper, as if he was incapable of comprehending what to draw.

Danny also found that he had an avenue for his own art. He created a slide program about a man and his dog. He made drawings of the dog and the man as a cartoon with a narrative. Bob Carr, an RN that now worked with the nursing staff, had a good speaking voice and did the audio. The idea was to have the character express some feelings about his life in a way that could relate to the listener's experience.

It was a joy for Danny to see patients leave their private torment and appreciate life.

There were a few patients Danny came in contact with that he had a special empathy for. One such patient was Jacob. Jacob was a Vietnam War veteran. Whether he was a survivor of the war is up for interpretation. He was a paranoid schizophrenic, with fear showing in his eyes most of his waking moments. He was a man who could, at times, be quite lucid. But Jacob would not let anyone get behind him. A loud noise could set off his paranoia. He was kept amicable by large doses of psychotropic medications.

There was a man named Chester, who had been in the Marine Corps during the Korean War. He was well known as a combatant. He would be admitted by the Bay City Police whenever he stopped taking his psychotropics.

Lillian, the middle-aged RN from the first shift, evaluated him when he was in a full-blown schizophrenic break. Lillian had a haughty arrogance about her that Chester didn't like. He struck her with a closed fist with harmful intent. Lillian was hit on the side of her head, but the greater force of the blow was deflected by an alert staff member.

A large Mexican man named Juan was admitted under orders of the General Motors psychiatrist. In the morning report, some of the charting from the previous night when Juan was admitted was read.

There was a suspicion that the man might just be play-acting to get some time off from his job on the assembly line at the Chevy Plant in Bay City. As Danny listened to the report, he assumed the new patient would, under doctor's orders, not be attending any of the activity therapy sessions.

Later that morning, Lillian was giving a group of nursing students a tour of the Mental Health Center. She was showing the large day room when the group came upon Juan, who was lying facedown on the floor, banging his fists, repeating: "Lordy, Lordy, I want to die."

Lillian looked down at the large man, who was taking up the space between two chairs, and said: "Juan, why don't you go over by the television and do that?"

"OK," Juan said. He got up, walked to the designated spot, laid facedown on the carpet and continued where he had left off: "Lordy, Lordy, I want to die."

Lillian was quite vocal when she met with the GM psychiatrist that afternoon. She told the doctor that the man did not belong in mental health. But it was to no avail. Juan stayed for two weeks in psych, then had orders from the doctor to rest at home for another four weeks.

Some of the patients were repeaters. The best they could hope to do was come in several times a year and get an adjustment on their medications. Then they would be back out in public after a few weeks.

This was the case with Dina, who was well known by the staff. She would come in during a psychotic beak, get her meds adjusted, then enjoy the comforts of the unit. She rarely got involved in any of the activity therapy sessions.

During morning report, it was brought to light that Dina had not taken a bath since she had been admitted and that she had a strong, offensive odor. Dina would ignore the staff when she was approached with towels and a washcloth. This went on for a week.

It was mentioned in one morning report that Dina had a history of getting messages from God over the radio. Danny decided to try a new approach.

He made a cassette tape of a radio program then added a message in his voice. He went to the day room and placed the edited tape in the stereo system. The radio program he had recorded began to play. Dina, who walked constantly, happened to go by the stereo at the most appropriate time. The radio program suddenly stopped. Danny's voice said: "Dina, take a shower."

Dina went directly into the linen room, grabbed a towel and washcloth, went to her room and took a shower.

———

Since Danny was now working days, he rarely saw the people he once worked with on the second shift except for an hour before shift change when they overlapped and they gave the daily report to the second shift.

There was some hostility he had not been aware of until one day when the patients made pizza for the afternoon activity. The second shift came in and shared the 10 or so pizzas made by the patients. Danny went to the occupational therapy office for a moment to make a note. There was a loud rap on the door.

Liz stuck her head in the door. "Come with me." She had a scowl on her face that would curdle milk. Her face was red with anger.

Danny followed her to the kitchen where Jud stood by the sink.

"We are not going to clean up your patients' mess," she pointed a several dirty pans in the sink.

Liz was livid, as was Jud.

"Do you remember that not long ago, we worked together? What the hell happened? Why are you so damned hostile? Those aren't my patients, they are our patients. Does this have anything to do with my getting the activity therapy job?" Danny also was livid. He looked directly at Liz. "This is petty bull shit!" She averted her eyes.

Danny walked to the sink and cleaned and dried the pizza pans. When he finished, he turned to see that Liz and Jud had left.

This was the beginning of the passive aggression. Mark also felt some hostility about the fact that he also wanted the job and felt he had not been in the loop when the job was opened. But Mark had talked about his feelings of not getting a "fair chance" at the job. There seemed to be a consensus of opinion. Danny had the least amount of medical education and should have been the last person to get the position. Jud had a bachelor's degree in psych, Liz was a LPN, and the other two mental health workers also had degrees.

But Danny knew why he had gotten the job. It was because he really liked the work, and he was good at it. He put a lot of thought and energy into his job, even before the mental health worker position opened.

Even Lillian showed signs of passive aggression. She had complained to Bill Dawson when Danny left for the new position, that Danny was needed on the floor. She also said that Danny should not have the word "therapist" attached to his name.

One Friday afternoon, Danny returned from Czuba's variety store. He had picked up some bingo prizes for the game that Danny was putting on for the patients on the following Monday. Bingo was a favorite. The winners, which eventually included everyone who played, received prizes such as jigsaw puzzles and other inexpensive gifts.

Danny sat at the nursing station and showed Lillian the prizes he had gotten for the game. Then he took the prizes and stored them in an unlocked drawer in the activity therapy office.

On Monday, Danny was setting the tables in the day room for bingo. He went to the activity therapy office to get the prizes from the file cabinet. The drawer was empty. He thought for a moment, but he was sure he had put them in the unlocked file drawer.

Lillian had worked the weekend. He went to her at the nurses' station and asked if she knew anything about the missing prizes.

"Oh, yes," she said, with a self-satisfied expression. "We gave them out with our own bingo game on Sunday."

Danny couldn't believe what he had just heard, "You gave away the prizes for the bingo game that I am about to start?"

"Yes, I did. Am I wrong in thinking that the prizes were for the patients?"

"Of course, they are for the patients. But you did that deliberately. I didn't realize you had that kind of meanness in you." He looked at her for a moment, then left. He never again left the file cabinet unlocked.

It was late spring in 1983. Danny was losing his zest for his job. His self-esteem had hit an all-time low. He had loved this job. But now, the job no longer was his focus. He was feeling a lot of hostility toward those he thought had turned against him.

After talking it over with BJ, Danny announced to the new mental health supervisor that he was leaving. He would give all of his energies to his art career.

• 19 •

MOM COULDN'T HELP IT

On Thanksgiving in 1983, Danny's mother, Ermine Pratt, died. Danny and his siblings breathed a sigh of relief. She had been dying for many years. Her Alzheimer's was not diagnosed until after her death.

Danny remembered his mother in earlier years. She was loving, she was smart, she was vibrant. He could not remember his mother displaying the mean-spirited behavior that she had exhibited in her later years. She had been strong-minded when she had his dad get rid of Taffy, the cocker spaniel that was Danny's constant companion when he was young. She had stepped in a pile of fresh "dog muss" as she called it and told her husband to get rid of the dog.

Even at a young age, he remembered the mean things people did to him. Every negative interaction that he experienced registered even stronger than the kindness he had learned to expect. The slow and steady progress of her disease could not be seen except in retrospect.

By the time Danny received his first driver's license, his mother had alienated everyone she knew. She became seclusive, not wanting to see her children when they came home for a visit. She was openly hostile to Maggie, Danny's older sister. He hated her for it.

She began to show signs of mental deterioration in her early 40s. By the time Danny came home in 1973, she did not know her youngest son. She looked into Danny's face and seemed to have some sort of recognition. But all she could say was "oooh," as she touched his face.

In 1974, Danny's dad, Harold Pratt, died. Ermine had been stepping over his lifeless body for more than a day before Danny and his brother, Peter, found him lying cold on the kitchen floor of their home. The blood had pooled in his neck. The moment they turned the kitchen light on in the dark house, they knew he was dead.

There had been a forewarning of his dad's death. He had dreams where his dad died, and he would awaken with a feeling of dread that did not leave him through the day. Danny could now recognize, after working in mental health and observing patients as they showed signs of depression, that he was depressed. He needed his dad's approval. He would now need to learn to live without it.

Danny and BJ cared for Ermine in their home in Bangor Township. Derick was 5 and Marcy was 3.

Ermine paced the floor at night, waking the kids as well as BJ and Danny. She used the bathtub for a toilet, or she would fail to lift the lid before she used the toilet. She would try to open the rear door of the mobile home, which had been locked because there were no stairs there. The 3-foot drop surely would break a bone. With both of them working different shifts, the situation was dire.

Danny spoke to Peter, telling him that they needed help. Perhaps the siblings could share Ermine's care.

Maggie was living in Colorado Springs. Louise, Danny's youngest sister, lived with her husband and children in Bay City. Lucile, Danny's oldest sister, also lived in Bay City with her husband and kids. Ermine had stirred some strong emotions with the advance of her disease. It was a burden that none of the siblings wanted to bear.

Peter took his mother into his home for several months. He soon became aware that it was an impossible situation. Since Peter was the oldest son, he became executor of Harold Pratt's estate. He found a foster care home on Lauria Road in Bangor Township, where Ermine would have 24-hour care.

She seemed at ease there. Danny picked her up and took her to church on Sundays, then brought her home for dinner before returning her to the home.

Danny was witness to the merciless effects of Alzheimer's. Ermine continued to deteriorate. After a year at the home, she was taken to Tri-City Nursing Home.

It was an uneasy time. Danny felt a heavy guilt when he did not visit his mother. When he did visit her, she did not respond. She wore diapers and groaned constantly. When, at last, she died, it was a relief to all of the Pratt siblings. The great, heavy millstone of guilt had been lifted. To watch her in the last stages of her life had worn heavily on them all.

It was a conundrum, a question that was impossible to answer. How could it be considered a humanitarian act to sit by and watch someone carry on and on in obvious pain? But who would be responsible for stopping Ermine Pratt's pain? It certainly wouldn't be a doctor. A doctor would be sued. It made Danny question his humanity. He would expect that if he were in the situation that his mother was in, someone would not allow this seemingly eternal suffering to continue. He had seen dogs and horses put down because they were suffering. But putting your mother down to end her torment was out of the question.

There was no great amount of sorrow at her funeral. To the family, she had left them many years before. It was obvious that none of the Wesleyan Methodists who came to pay their last respects for Ermine Pratt really knew the reclusive woman who had been the wife of their former Sunday School superintendent. She raised her family under the strict rules of the church. No one was really capable of showing grief for Ermine Pratt. Her greatest fear, when she was relatively lucid, was realized. She died in isolation, just as she had lived in isolation for so many years.

• 20 •

OLD SNAKE AND MORNING STAR

"Life is either a daring adventure, or nothing. Security does not exist in nature, nor do the children of men as a whole experience it. Avoiding danger is no safer in the long run than exposure."

~ Helen Keller ~

Nov. 4, 1994
Bay City, Mich.

The sun shown brightly through thin, clear air on an unseasonably cold day for early November. Danny Pratt pulled into the parking lot of Trahan's Funeral Chapel on Madison Avenue. The parking lot was full. He pulled his 1987 Astro minivan into a tight space on the farthest corner of the lot.

He was met in the foyer of the home by a short, portly man in an appropriately black suit, who spoke in a reverent, quiet voice: "Who do you wish to see, sir?"

"Frank Davis," he said, already feeling a tightness in his throat.

He followed the man down a decorative hallway to a large, crowded room. He found Marie Davis sitting next to her youngest daughter, Nancy. Both were weeping. Danny embraced each of them and gave his condolences. Mike Davis stood nearby, his eyes wet and reddened, his face distraught.

"I'm sorry, Mike." Danny embraced his old friend. He hated to cry in public. The pressure would build up to a point that he no longer could hold it back. An emotional dam would break and years of pent up anxiety would come exploding through his eyes. He hated the way his face distorted when he was trying to hold the dam back. He decided to move on before it was too late.

He walked slowly toward the casket, dreading the first look at the old man's dead body. There he was, surrounded by silk and fragrant flowers. He spoke a few words designed mainly to mask his awkward feelings. The corpse looked like Frank Davis, but Danny never had seen his image surrounded by silk and flowers, with his large hands crossed so reverently. He could feel his eyes filling and his throat throbbing. He turned to look for a seat in the crowded room.

He panned the room for an empty chair and saw Jim Davis, Mike's older brother, and Lynn, the oldest sister. He found an empty chair next to Georgina Blue, a childhood friend of Lynn Davis and also a former member of the Wesleyan Methodist Church, which Danny attended when he was young.

The honor guard was there from the American Legion.

As the pastor began the service, Mike's face contorted with pain. Danny's throat continued to constrict. Jim Davis sat straight-backed next to his wife and betrayed no emotion. Jim was now a successful businessman and wore the same determined and stoic expression Danny had seen on the old man's face. The intensity was also there with his erect posture and in the way his head was set firmly on his shoulders. Danny thought Jim looked much like he expected him to look after not seeing him for more than 10 years.

The eulogy was generic, bringing out the positive aspects of the life of Frank Davis. The American Legion Color Guard did a 21-gun salute to the World War II veteran. It was quite a reverent tribute to Frank. Danny recognized a girl from his school days. The former Sue Shatzer was one of the guards. Danny couldn't help but wonder how many of the people in this room today knew what a complex man Frank Davis had been.

───

It all began for Danny Pratt when he met Frank's son in Miss Rhinehart's kindergarten class at Fremont School in Bay City's South End, in the crotch of the thumb of Michigan's Lower

Peninsula. They first met while taking the mandatory afternoon nap on a homemade throw rug on the tile floor of the classroom. Mike was witness to many of the same experiences that Danny was in their early school years.

One morning as Danny walked to school down Broadway Avenue, he found a handful of small change that apparently had dropped in the grass in front of the Broadway Baptist Church. Danny counted 42 cents. The only time Danny ever had that much money was when his Grandma Warren gave all of the kids in his family a dollar bill for Christmas in an envelope with a hole in it that let you see George Washington's face. His mother always held that dollar for "an emergency."

Wow, he thought. This is an opportunity. He could spend his 42 cents on anything he wanted. He ran as fast as he could to Alpern's Corner Store, just kitty-cornered to the school on Broadway. He bought 10 redhots and took them to school in a small, brown paper bag. He put two of the large gum balls in his mouth and was drooling a small stream of red saliva as he walked into the classroom just as the bell was ringing. Mike Davis entered at the same time. Danny handed one of the gum balls to Mike. Mike stuffed it in his pocket.

Miss Rhinehart was not there that day and was replaced by a substitute, Mr. Zielinski. Mr. Zielinski was a tall man. He looked like a giant to the kindergarten class, but in reality, the man was probably around 6 feet 3 inches tall. His voice and his demeanor were intimidating to Danny.

"What do you have in your mouth, young man?" The huge man was staring at Danny. "Yes. I'm talking to you," he pointed a finger directly at Danny.

Danny thought of swallowing the large wad of gum, but it was just too big.

"Well, since you insist on chewing gum in my class, I'm going to allow you spend some time out. Come here."

Mr. Zielinski had Danny spit out the gum. He then stuck the gum to the end of Danny's nose and stuck his nose against the chalkboard. "Now, you stay right there and look at your gum for a while. I want you to remember that you never chew gum in school."

Danny was humiliated but never again chewed gum in school.

In the fourth grade, Danny and Mike were fellow students of

Miss Dulong, a short, round, long-suffering woman. Once a week, Miss Dulong would wheel an ancient, portable pump organ into the classroom for some sing-along music. They sang from a book of American folk songs like "The Arkansas Traveler," "Oh, Susanna" and "She'll Be Comin' 'Round the Mountain." Miss Dulong's head sometimes would get lost behind the old organ as she pumped away on squeaky pedals. Danny's older brother, Peter, was also a student of Miss Dulong 12 years earlier.

Every Friday Miss Dulong would announce show and tell, a chance for anyone to get up in front of the class and sing, dance, tell jokes — whatever they wanted to do to hold the kids' attention for a few moments. Mike danced on one particular day. He did some shuffling movements in his pegged pants. Danny knew little about dancing, but he thought Mike had a lot of guts getting up in front of everyone and moving like that. He got some applause and a "Thank you, Michael" from Miss Dulong.

Danny always told jokes and stories when they had show and tell. He would wave his hand frantically to be called upon. He would tell stories that were mostly made up, stories of traveling around the world and relating to adventures he had experienced only in his mind.

Miss Dulong sometimes would comment on the content of Danny's talk, which she always had to cut short for lack of time. "My goodness, Daniel, but you have done a lot of interesting things for such a young man," she would say.

In reality, Danny lived in a protective and strict environment. Except for his life at Fremont School, he had little contact with people outside of the Wesleyan Methodist Church, an ultra-conservative faith, where, at least in Danny's mind, anything enjoyable was sinful. On the list of sinful activities was going to movies, swearing, drinking alcohol, smoking, any kind of physical activity on Sundays, dancing, lustful thoughts and overindulgence in anything. The list of sins that could send you to hell seemed endless.

According to Danny's mother, Ermine, the most important rule for her youngest son was: "Never go near the Saginaw River, which was about the length of a football field away from the front door of their home at 206 24th St. His earliest memories were of sitting on the front porch during warm summer days watching the giant Great Lakes freighters move up and down the river and the steam locomotives, running on tracks that snaked along parallel to the river on Water Street. Danny's interest in the river peaked each time his mother spoke of the dangers of the river where old Bull Block drowned. Danny vaguely remembered the time his mother had snatched him from his playpen on the front porch and had run down to the green river to watch the flashing lights of the police cars as they pulled Block's bloated body from the murky waters near the foot of the Lafayette Street Bridge.

As Danny grew up, the Saginaw River became the center of his daily activity. He became skilled at doing and saying the correct things to his mother to get away from the house for the day in the company of his neighbor and mentor, Bobby Antcliff. Bobby lived next door to the Pratts. He had graduated from high school when Danny first began to visit Bobby in his garage, the same year Danny started first grade. Bobby always seemed to be working on something. He introduced Danny to many things that were forbidden by the his religious upbringing. Bobby showed Danny pictures from a book of female body parts and explained how babies were made. Bobby always had a cold Pepsi whenever he visited. He gave Danny an occasional Winston cigarette. But the most important thing Bobby did for Danny was to teach him how to swim in the Saginaw River. This opened up a whole new world to Danny at the age of 6. He became well-versed in things pertaining to the Saginaw River but had little knowledge as to how other people outside of his faith lived.

One day after school, Mike invited Danny over to his house. They walked the 1 1/2 blocks from Fremont School to the Davis residence. Danny was amazed by the freedom that Mike enjoyed. It was the opposite at his home. He followed Mike into the rear entrance into the kitchen. Mike stopped at the cookie jar, grabbed a treat, then poured himself a glass of milk. This was unheard of in the Pratt home. Milk was rationed to one glass per meal. The siblings never helped themselves to anything. This is not to say that the Pratt children weren't well-fed. They got what they needed but little else. Thus was the life of many Americans who married during the Great Depression. The frugality didn't end there.

Mike's mother, Marie, was kind, soft-spoken, friendly and doted on her children, much like the mother on "Leave It to Beaver," a popular TV show. There were four siblings in the family, Jim, the oldest; Lynn, Mike, and Nancy, the youngest.

Marie always would stop whatever she was doing to attend to Mike's needs. She seemed happy to see him and interested in whatever he had to say. Mike had a self-assurance unusual for someone so young.

Mike and Danny became close friends when Danny discovered that Mike's grandparents, Frank and Mable Van Zale, lived just a few blocks away. Mike would spend weekends and much of the summer months at his grandparents' home, where he was doted upon just like at home. Mable Van Zale was a typical-looking grandma, with gray hair done up in a bun and her grandma dress with the ruffled apron.

She also was kind to Danny's older brother, Peter, who was the Van Zale's paperboy. One year at Christmas time, she gave Peter an entire homemade apple pie for being a good paperboy. Peter brought the pie home for the family to eat, since he was a diabetic. He was quite proud of that.

Frank Van Zale, Mike's grandpa, was the most laid-back person Danny had met. He moved slowly and spoke slowly with the same gentle kindness of Mike's mother. Mike called him Pal. Pal was an ardent Detroit Tigers fan. The first thing he always said, after greeting Danny by his first name, was: "How about those Tigers?" Pal also greeted Mike with kindness and respect that was unseen in Danny's experience.

Mike confided in Danny in later years that his Grandma Van Zale was a closet alcoholic and that she occasionally lost her temper when she had been drinking heavily. It became a habit of Mable's, when drunk, to throw one of the cast iron burner plates from the gas stove at Pal, breaking the brittle metal to pieces and embedding some in the plaster walls. Pal simply would wait for his wife to calm down, then go get a new cast iron burner from a box he kept in the basement.

The South End of eastern Bay City in those days was peaceful for the most part. There was little serious crime, at least in Danny's neighborhood. They seldom locked the doors. Part of the thinking may have been that they had very little anyone would take the trouble to steal. Besides, Mrs. Beach and Mrs. Wendt were the neighborhood watchdogs. Between the two old widows, little happened in the area that they did not witness.

Many of the side streets in those days were gravel and tar. Every summer, a fresh layer of hot tar was spread on the dirt roads. It showed up everywhere — on the sidewalks, porches and rugs and stuck to shoes.

———

The summers were always good, and Danny loved them. When he was 10, his parents bought him a J.C. Higgins bike from Sears and Roebuck. He could go anywhere on his bicycle, and he did. Danny would ride from his house to Frenchy's Dock or Whitey's Dock, near the mouth of the Saginaw River. He carried his fishing gear on the bike and a woven stringer for fish. There was a 25-cent charge for fishing. Pop, snacks and live bait were sold in a small store there.

In the evenings, when the winds came from the southwest, they brought the scent of burning trash from the municipal dump in the Middlegrounds. There was little, if any, regulation on what could be dumped on the little island in the middle of the river. Whatever couldn't be burned in a 50-gallon drum in the backyard had to be hauled to the dump in a little trailer Harold Pratt kept in his side yard near the alley. Literally, everything that could be thrown out ended up in the dump. This great tonic leeched into the Saginaw River.

———

From Mike's grandparents' home on Wilson Street, Mike had the freedom to visit Danny's house more frequently. Up to this point, Mike never had gone for a swim in the Saginaw River. Like Danny, Mike was intimidated by the murky depth of the green river. Danny took Mike to an old sunken ship named Gumshoes, where Bobby Antcliff had taught him to swim. The real name of the sunken ship was the Marquis Roen. The boys also swam from the rusty barges at Meagher Dredging Co.

It was impractical to sneak a suit out of the house whenever they wanted to swim, so the boys just skinny-dipped at different points along the eastern shore of the river. They also swam in a small pond next to the municipal dump, appropriately named the B.A.B., or Bare Ass Beach.

There was little small-boat traffic on the river during the late '50s. It was considered a dangerous place for a kid to be. None of the boys who swam in the river did it with their parents' consent. But there was great fun in the adventure of doing something that other boys the same age were too scared to do.

It was around the age of 10 that the two boys began smoking. Danny had smoked before. Bobby Antcliff would give him an occasional filtered cigarette before he left to join the Army. First, the boys just smoked old cattail reeds that grew along the shore of the river. Then Mike began raiding his dad's ashtrays for butts. They played on the giant sand and gravel hills at the city lot along the river, then smoked whatever butts they could salvage.

On a warm summer night, Danny was riding his bike, no-handed, down 25th Street, thinking of impressing the Retzloff girls, when he heard guitar music. He turned to find Mike Davis sitting on a steel garden chair playing a six-string. Danny stopped and listened for a while. He was impressed with the way Mike moved from cord to cord so effortlessly, the harmony of the six strings hanging in the air. The Retzloff girls were sitting on their back porch across the street listening.

• 21 •

Looking Back
1964

In Danny's sophomore year at Central High School, he took up playing the drums. He had played the snare drum in Mr. Burnhart's music class at MacGregor School in the South End. He discovered that he had a sense of rhythm and enjoyed the experience, but he never had applied himself to learning the rudiments of drumming or reading percussion music. He simply kept the beat and passed the classes. He needed one more elective to fill his schedule for his sophomore year. He chose band class, under the tutelage of Walter "Doc" Cramer, the esteemed director of the Central High School marching band.

Danny had much to learn. He bought a pair of drumsticks at Herter Music Center and began practicing on any hard surface available. He would drum out the marching cadences on his thighs or the kitchen counter. He brought one of the older snare drums home from school and practiced in the basement until his parents ordered him to quit.

One day, Danny visited Mike Davis while Mike and his older brother, Jim, played guitars in their second-floor bedroom. Mike played lead guitar and Jim played rhythm guitar. They played music by The Ventures, a popular instrumental group. "Walk, Don't Run" was one song they played well. Danny mentioned that he played the drums. The next day, Danny brought the borrowed marching snare drum from school and kept time with a solid rock 'n' roll beat. They liked the music they made together and began playing on a regular basis.

Danny came across an ancient set of drums in the want ads in the Bay City Times for $25. The set included a snare drum, a bass drum, a high-hat with two smaller cymbals and a tinny-sounding crash cymbal. The bass and snare drums crudely were painted bright red. They were battered and beaten, but Danny was proud to have them.

One afternoon during the summer, the boys were practicing in the upstairs room when Mike's dad, Frank, showed up outside the bedroom door. Since Frank rarely smiled, Danny had the impression that they would be chastised for making so much noise. Frank was holding a sculpted piece of wood in his hands. He handed the wood to Mike.

"Maybe just a little thinner in the neck," Mike said, as he fingered what would be the fret board on an electric guitar Frank was making.

One month later, Frank presented Mike with the first of two guitars he was making for the boys. It was a beautiful piece of workmanship and looked like a Fender Stratocaster.

Danny was amazed that Frank had the ability and gumption to create such a fine instrument. Frank was not a person who displayed any kind of affection.

Danny learned from Mike that his dad had been a fine craftsman for many years. He had built the rolled and pleated pilot seats for many of the unlimited hydroplanes that designer and builder Les Staudacher had produced.

In the following year, Frank got the boys a few gigs at a Klein Brother's company birthday party and a small party in Saginaw. The group did little after that and disbanded after a year.

In the '60s, there was a Gulf gas station on the corner of Union and Henry streets owned by Marty Friedel. Marty had once worked for Consumers Power. He was a Utility Workers Union steward at a time when Frank Davis was becoming a strong influence in the union. Frank mentored Marty in union law and could answer virtually any questions about the current union contract with Consumers. Marty left Consumers feeling indebted to Frank Davis. He also was intimidated by the man.

Marty had a successful business and did small repairs in his two-stall garage. He didn't allow anyone to buy on credit.

One day, Frank Davis stopped by. Marty was under a '59 Chevy changing oil when Frank walked into the garage.

"Friedel, you got any quality tires here? I don't want any cheap shit."

Marty was startled by the loud voice in the quiet garage. "Frank. Good to see ya. What are you driving?"

"That Chevy," said Frank, pointing to the car.

"Oh, sure, Frank." He began wiping his hands on a rag and walked to one of the tire racks at the front of the station. I can give you a good price on a set of these. You can't buy a better tire. ..."

"Fine. I'll bring my car by tomorrow around 3 p.m. You put a set of those on. I'll only have about 30 minutes between meetings. You can do the job in 30 minutes?"

"Of course."

"Good. Three tomorrow afternoon it is." Frank left abruptly.

The next day, Frank showed up at Friedel's Gulf station at 3. Marty dropped the hoist and backed out the car he was working on and had Frank pull his Chevy onto the hoist. Marty mounted the new tires, balanced them, then lowered the hoist.

"We're all set, Frank."

By that time, Frank was behind the wheel of his car. He turned to Marty as he backed out of the garage.

"What's that come to Friedel? I need to get to my meeting."

"Give me just a minute, and I'll figure it up."

"Don't have time. Figure it all up, and I'll come by next week and give you a payment." Frank backed up and turned south on Henry.

As the years passed, Mike and Danny went their separate ways. Danny graduated from high school in 1966, knowing that he soon would be drafted as the war in Vietnam escalated. Because Danny had become "unmanageable," his parents sent him to live with his brother in the tiny town of Hanfield, Ind. Danny's mother had hoped he would stay with his brother indefinitely. But Danny returned to

Bay City that September and found a job at Kuhlman Electric Co. in Bay City.

In March of 1967, Danny left his job as a production line worker at Kuhlman Electric to start a four-year commitment to the U.S. Air Force. He had passed his draft physical, and since he had no plans to go back to school, he was sure he would be drafted. He thought he would have a better chance at getting into a career field he wanted if he enlisted. He served four years in the Air Force, working as an artist/illustrator for a pilot training school at Hurlburt Field in Florida. During this period, he met and married a captivating, level-headed, young nurse named Betty Knight. Betty gave birth to a son, Derick Martin, just before Danny was discharged in 1971.

After spending the summer in Detroit, Danny, his wife and new son packed all of their belongings in a U-Haul and moved to Denver, Colo., where Danny entered classes at the Colorado Institute of Art. On an icy, sub-zero December day, a daughter, Marcy Gwen, was born.

It would be seven years before Danny again saw his old friend, Mike Davis. Mike also married and had one son. It took several years for the two men to rekindle their old friendship. They would see each other when the two couples would play Michigan rummy while the growing children played. Mike took classes at GM Tech and was working as a certified mechanic at the Dunlop Pontiac Dealership in downtown Bay City.

Over the course of several years, Danny learned from Mike that his dad, Frank, had become a force to be reckoned with as an arbitrator for the Utility Workers Union. Then Frank became president of the union for the state of Michigan. Frank was the only UWU to become state president without ever having been a local union president.

He moved into an office at union headquarters in Jackson, Mich. Since it would have been a 140-mile commute, he co-rented an apartment in Jackson and came home to Bay City on weekends.

Frank "Snake" Davis was head of the union during the days of the state-wide strike in 1968. There had been a bitter fight between the union and Consumers Power. Coal train tracks allegedly were sabotaged. There were arrest warrants out for all high union officials, including Frank. It sounded to Danny like a made-for-TV drama.

It was interesting to be acquainted with a union boss. He could see his friend's dad as a chair-throwing, intimidating union negotiator.

———

One icy, wintry day in January, Mike called Danny to invite him to a Saginaw Gears hockey game. The Saginaw Gears was a Minor League team. His dad had some free tickets from one of his union associates, and Mike suggested they give the extra ticket to Danny. Danny had little interest in hockey in those days, mostly because he never had taken the time to understand the game. But he jumped at the chance to see his first game.

Frank, dressed in a tailored business suit and brown topcoat, picked up Mike and Danny. Danny never had seen Frank dressed up like that. Danny remembered the man from when he worked at Consumers Power and wore the familiar working-man's blue uniform with a dark-blue Tigers baseball cap. He had not seen Frank Davis in nine years.

Frank exuded confidence. The swagger, which had always been there, was a bit more pronounced.

He had a crease in the middle of his brow, which gave the impression that he was eternally angry. He looked like a union boss.

"How you doing, Mr. Davis?" Danny asked. He felt like he hardly knew the man.

He looked at Danny under the light on Mike's front porch.

"Pratt." Frank gave Danny a look. "Let's go."

They jumped into Frank's Chevy and headed out River Road toward the Saginaw Civic Center. Danny sat in back. Frank seemed in a hurry as he passed several cars on the narrow road, going well over the speed limit.

Danny was impressed with Frank's demeanor and the importance of his union job and the tailored suit.

"So, Mr. Davis, are you in good with the Italians?" Danny laughed at his joke, but no one seemed to hear it.

———

Frank and Mike knew many of the players on the Saginaw Gears team by number and name. The energy at the game was contagious. Mike explained some of the complexities of the game to Danny and gave some of the team history. The Gears won.

Danny was pumped on the way back to Bay City. Frank's expression had not changed throughout the night.

Mike and Danny went to several other Gears games that winter and began listening to the games on the radio. Danny also became a fan of the Detroit Red Wings.

• 22 •

CATCHING THE WIND

It was a warm and comfortable evening in mid-June. Just after supper, Mike Davis called, to invite Danny Pratt for a short sail on his dad's boat, Morning Star.

Mike was not an enthusiastic sailor. Snake, as Frank was called, was a demanding captain on his boat. It was difficult for Mike to say no to his dad when he would call at a moment's notice wanting Mike to take a sail on Saginaw Bay.

Mike had been divorced for several years by this time and had custody of his two boys, Aaron and Neil. He was a good dad. He made sure his kids always had clean clothes, and he did his best to provide what the boys needed. Lately, when Mike sailed with Snake, he brought the two active boys along. Mike told Danny that he never really felt relaxed when Aaron and Neil were there. Mike had asked Danny to take some of the pressure off him by sailing with Frank more often. Danny was happy to do so.

Frank Davis was in the process of retiring as Utility Workers Union president. At Snake's retirement party in Jackson, he was given a plaque with a broken chair leg mounted to it. He had been in a heated argument with one of the union members when he picked up his chair, broke one of the legs off and threw it at the man. Depending on where they sat at a conference table, people either loved Snake Davis or hated him.

———————

Sunset Marina was busy as Mike drove the meandering road that skirted the slips where a variety of boats were docked in the protected harbor. One sailboat Danny noticed had a deep-blue hull with the name Dolphin written across the stern. Mike explained that it was a racing boat owned by one of the Ruhlands, owners of the Made Rite Potato Chip Co. in Bay City.

As Mike pulled into a parking spot near his dad's boat, he pointed to the Morning Star, Frank's 27-footer. "It's the boat with the gold mast," he said. Snake was there tidying the ship.

Danny followed Mike out on the dock then stepped aboard.

"Hey, Frank. You must be the captain," Danny said with a wide grin.

"Hey, Pratt," Frank said without looking up from his chores. "We've got some wind. Should be a good day for a sail."

"Can you get this rig going fast enough to water ski?" Danny joked.

Snake gave him a venomous stare. "Get that cover off the mainsail, Pratt."

"Aye, aye, sir." Danny gave snake a military salute.

Mike was already at work, pulling the jib sail from below deck through the forward hatch. Snake lowered the 15-horse Johnson outboard into the water. He squeezed the bulb on the fuel tank several times. The starter cranked for a few seconds, and the motor putted to life quietly.

Mike loosened the dock lines and shoved off. They putted slowly through the marina.

Danny liked this already. There was a variety of fishing boats, cabin cruisers and sailboats of every description and style. These people were proud of their boats, lining the gangplanks with potted plants, chaise lounges, barbecue grills, everything needed to live at sea. With the electrical hookups, some looked as though they never intended to leave the dock.

A young family was busy putting provisions away for an extended stay in the double-decked, wooden-hulled, 40-foot Chris-Craft. The old boat was maintained immaculately. Danny could sense the excitement that the two young boys felt as they jumped with glee as their mother pushed off from the dock. The deep, guttural tones of a large engine growled as the big boat pulled out just ahead of the Morning Star. They followed the cruiser out of the harbor and onto the Saginaw River.

From Sunset Marina north to the mouth of Saginaw Bay was a no-wake zone. The river and the bay bustled with activity. They watched as the cabin cruiser reached the end of the no-wake zone, just 50 feet ahead. The bow raised as the stern dug in. The engine roared, creating 3-foot waves in the translucent-green water. There were many sailboats in the vastness of the bay. One magnificent red-and-yellow spinnaker billowed like a prized orchid against a deep-blue sky.

Dozens of fishing boats were anchored along the outer perimeters of the shipping channel, which was marked by red buoys on the left and green on the right. Mike explained that there were two markers every half-mile to the end of the designated shipping channel, 8 miles out from the mouth of the river.

"Tis a grand night we be 'avin' 'ere, captain," Danny said with an exaggerated pirate accent. Mike and Snake were busy checking the wind speed indicator on the top of the mast.

"We've got good wind here, Mikey," said Snake.

Snake guided the boat to the west edge of the channel, past the giant range light, where he took a northwesterly tack.

"Pull up the main, Mikey," Snake ordered. Mike had been standing by waiting for the order and quickly raised the mainsail.

"Pratt. Pull up the jib sail," Frank ordered, pointing to the correct rope. Mike came over and helped Danny secure the sail, then they returned to the stern and took their seats.

Snake steered the ship to 60 degrees off-wind.

"Always watch your head when you come about or while correcting your course," Mike said, as the boom shot across overhead with surprising force, hitting the vang and cupping the wind as the main and the jib billowed. Morning Star sprang to life like an eager stallion. Snake cut the engine and raised the motor from the water. The boat keeled to the wind as all three of the men moved to the high side of the ship. Danny felt a nervous exhilaration.

"What ya think of that, Pratt?" said Frank, with a slight smile.

"It's better than sex," Danny said, with a wide grin. "Of course, that would depend on your partner."

Snake muttered something, then turned away.

Danny had been on a sailboat only one other time. It was on the Gulf of Mexico when he was stationed in Florida while he was in the Air Force during the Vietnam War. The sailboat was small with a removable keel. There was little wind that day, and Danny was not impressed with sailing at the time.

He felt a rush of adrenaline as a rogue wave broke on the bow, wetting the crew.

"Yahoo," Danny yelled.

To the northeast, another sailboat appeared. The boat seemed to be about the same size as the Morning Star. The boat was ahead of the Morning Star by half a football field and seemed to be on a converging tack.

"Let's catch 'em," Snake yelled. "Tighten up the main, Mikey. Let's see if we can catch some more wind."

Snake adjusted the course until the red threads on the tailing edge of the mainsail stood out straight.

As they moved closer to the other boat, they could see the bustle of activity.

"It's a Hunter," Snake said. It's like the Chevrolet of sailboats. They sell them at Brennan Marine. It's too bulky in the beam to out-sail the Morning Star."

Danny grabbed the binoculars and scanned the deck of the Hunter, which was now just 50 feet away.

"I know those people," Danny yelled. "It's Ray and Lucy Grills." He stood and waved to the couple on deck. There was a look of recognition on the man's face. He raised his right hand slightly in a half-hearted greeting, then anxiously adjusted the sail and checked his tack. Lucy raised a large jib, much larger than the one on the Morning Star. Both boats were keeling to the wind, cutting through the waves and sending explosions of spray over the decks. Ray Grills rushed about his boat nervously while Lucy took the helm. He desperately tried to coax more speed from the Hunter.

"Ha! We're doin' 12 knots," Snake yelled with excitement.

It was obvious that the Morning Star soon would overtake the Hunter. Just as she was about to surge ahead, the Hunter came about, giving up the race.

"Yahoo," Danny yelled out his exuberance in an accidental falsetto.

Snake, Mike and Danny all stood and raised their hands in triumph. Ray gave a nervous glance as the Hunter moved off to the east. Danny said that it would be an embarrassment for Ray and Lucy to lose a race. He would be sure to rub it in when he saw them again. Lucy had been an RN at Bay Medical Center during the time Danny worked there.

"Just take a look at the lines of the Hunter. She's not a bad boat. But there's no comparison when you look at the sleek line of the O'Day sailboat. The Hunter is just too wide in the beam. And her curve to the bow is too severe to cut cleanly through the water," Snake said, the pride showing on his face.

"I dated a girl once that was a little wide in the beam. It didn't slow us down much though," Danny said. He could see that Snake was getting a little irritated with his attempts at humor.

They toured the bay, changing tack frequently. An enormous freighter appeared on the horizon, seemingly out of nowhere, moving in the marked shipping channel leading to the mouth of the river. The great bulk seemed to be moving silently through the water.

Danny cautioned himself about giving Snake the one-liners every time he said something. But Danny couldn't seem to stop. He listened as Mike called him Snake.

"Is Snake a reference to your sexual prowess or does it just describe your personality?"

Snake stared directly at Danny and snarled: "What the hell are you, some kind of cheap comedian?"

This really tickled Danny's funny bone. He laughed so loud, he began to snort. Snake just scowled and looked away. Mike smiled to himself and paid attention to the tiller. They returned to the marina. Frank was pleased with his boat and the sail they had experienced.

"It isn't always this good, Pratt. Sometimes there's no wind. You are always at the mercy of the wind. You might as well leave your watch at home. If you're a sailor, you can't be in a hurry.

The sun set when they finished stowing the gear and covering the sails. The sky glowed in bright orange hues.

Danny thanked Snake for the sail, thinking he would not be invited back, since he had been so irritating to Frank.

The silence and grace of harnessing the wind was inspiring to him. He told BJ and his kids about the sailing. He could think of little else; he had found a new passion.

It was only two days later that Snake called Danny. "We've got some wind. Let's go for a turn on the bay."

And so, the adventure began. The two men sailed whenever Danny's schedule permitted.

———

Snake was retired and enjoyed the pace of retirement. He was getting old. His knee hurt like hell, and he couldn't move quickly anymore. Breathing attacks were frequent. Sailing by himself wasn't in the cards any longer. Danny Pratt might just lengthen his sailing days. He was young and strong. If he would can the smart-ass wise-cracking, he would make a good companion. He also was self-employed and could pretty much make up his own schedule.

———

Danny made the most of his yearly income as an artist during the summer months. He attended a juried art show almost every weekend, traveling to Royal Oak, Grand Haven, South Haven, Saugatuck, Flint, Glen Arbor, Midland, Birmingham and the Summer Art Fair in Bay City, among others. If he made a good showing and sold a lot of his work, he would have to work that much harder for the following show. Danny worked mostly with drawing mediums, pastels, colored pencil and pen and ink.

If he was to make a living at art, he would need to start making prints of some of his pen-and-ink drawings.

Through the summer, he worked at matting, framing, drawing and driving to shows on weekends. When he sailed with Snake, it usually was during the week.

BJ traveled with Danny to only every other show, due to scheduling at Bay Medical Care Facility, where she was a nursing supervisor. She was good company. On the weekends when BJ worked, Danny brought along their youngest son, Lucas (Luke.)

There were days that the rains came. At one outdoor art fair in Paris, Mich., it rained buckets and ruined more than 300 of Danny's prints.

Other days were sometimes spent in the baking heat. There was always a lot of loading and unloading of displays that sometimes had to be carried a long distance. The art business was proving to be demanding. Danny and BJ would return home exhausted, usually on Sunday in late afternoon or evening. BJ's mom, Wilma Knight, said when she first heard that Danny was getting into the art show business: "Well, that sounds like an easy way to make a living."

Danny worked up a group of drawings depicting humorous situations. A half-dozen were aimed at the University of Michigan market. One was a pen-and-ink of a small man with a U of M T-shirt on. Around the little guy were some large, hostile-looking men wearing Ohio State shirts. The caption was "Hostile Territory."

Another was of a middle-aged man in his attic trying on his old U of M, sweater. The sweater was not big enough to cover his exposed navel. In the background are two framed pictures, one of his wife in her cheerleader uniform and the other of the man in his football uniform, a tough and able young athlete. The caption read: "Still Fits."

He made other drawings by whimsy, or whatever showed up in his head when he was just sketching. Several works were made into prints.

They were numbered, usually from one to 250, then signed in pencil. He matted and framed some of the prints and wrapped others in plastic. He also hand-colored some of the prints with Prismacolor pencil. He also worked through the winters creating original pastel and colored pencil drawings.

During the summer, any sailing Danny did with Snake was on weekdays between shows. Danny tended to get anxious over his ability to produce enough art to sell. He somehow found days when he was able to sail with Snake, sometimes on a two- or three-day trip to Tawas or Au Gres.

Snake became Danny's sailing mentor. He showed him how to tie a variety of sailor's knots — the reef knot, sheet bend, bowline, figure-8 and the clove hitch. He learned to reef the mainsail, trim the sheets, to steer the boat 60 degrees off-wind to attain maximum hull speed. They practiced coming about, working on the timing so as not to lose the momentum of the wind as they reversed directions. Snake taught him what sails to use in differing wind speeds.

————

On one of their first evening sails, Danny learned something about Snake that even his family didn't know. Snake liked his Jim Beam and Squirt. He cautioned Danny not to let his wife know that he drank alcohol. Snake's wife, Marie saw her mother, Mable Van Zale, become a closet alcoholic. She was vehement when it came to Snake drinking any type of alcoholic beverage. Danny couldn't help thinking how peculiar it was that a timid woman like Marie Davis could have so much influence over a head-strong man like Frank.

Snake would pour 8 ounces of Jim Beam into a 24-ounce plastic tumbler, then fill the rest of the cup with Squirt and ice. Danny dubbed it a "union drink." Since Danny had been a beer drinker most of his adult life, the hard alcohol went straight to his head.

————

Danny loved sailing. He had felt a similar euphoria when he was on his first-ever flight in 1967 to Lackland Air Force Base, Texas, to begin basic training. He never had seen the Earth from above. It was a spiritual awakening, an enlightenment. There was an unexplainable force at work, which told him all things were somehow connected. It was a feeling that in later years he referred to as "an instant of purity," a microsecond of crystal clarity. Humans were so tiny, almost insignificant. It took some of the weight off his shoulders to believe that humans were central to all life, that humans alone were the reason for creation.

————

As Snake had predicted, there were days when sailing was not an adventure. They took several trips that first summer to the state docks in Au Gres and East Tawas. There were times when the sun baked the skin, and the wind did not blow.

In August, black flies were a menace. Frank sometimes would wait for hours in the sun as they bit hunks of skin before he started the engine on windless days and motored to their destination.

————

It seemed at first that Danny and Snake had little in common besides the love of sailing. Danny began bringing cassette tapes along on overnight sailing trips. He played some of his favorite classical music as they just sat back and relaxed while the autopilot kept the Morning Star on course. They found they could be comfortable without constant dialog. They would sometimes sit for hours just listening to music and gazing at the stars.

And there was always the Tigers. In the summer of 1984, they followed the Tigers on the radio of the ship's stereo system. They had become good friends and both seemed to have the ability to enjoy themselves no matter what the conditions. Danny found that beneath the crusty exterior, Snake was a decent man who expected much from himself and those he befriended.

During the winter months, Snake stored the Morning Star at Brennan Marine on the Saginaw River in Bay City. The boat was pulled from the water and placed in a cradle in the fenced yard along Water Street. Snake managed to hook up to an illegal electrical supply. He had a small heater that took the edge off cold winter days as they shared a few union drinks below deck and planned for the next season of sailing.

At one of these meetings, Danny mentioned a video tape he recently rented.

"Have you seen "On Golden Pond"?

"Isn't that the one with Jane Fonda?"

"Yes."

"I wouldn't pay to see one of her movies. I hate that woman and her politics," Snake said, waving his hand to dismiss the subject.

"It's too bad you've closed your mind. It's really a good movie. Jane Fonda bought the rights to the movie as a tribute to her dying dad. It's won several Academy Awards," Danny said.

Snake made no comment.

Danny thought on that for a moment. "Do you mean to say that if you don't like somebody's politics, you just shut the door on anything they might have to say?"

"That's just the way the world works. You pay attention to the people you admire or share the same ideas with and disregard the rest."

"I agree that Jane Fonda did a lot of harm as far as her methods of disputing the righteousness of the fighting in Vietnam. But she didn't write "On Golden Pond." She bought the rights to the movie and played the daughter of an old, retired professor, and Henry

SNAKE AND MORNING STAR

Fonda played that role; Katherine Hepburn played the professor's wife. They are all great actors. It's a feel-good movie about growing old."

"There's a lot about getting old that doesn't feel good," said Frank.

The subject eventually was dropped.

One day that same winter, Snake bought lunch at State Lunch in downtown Bay City. After eating catfish specials, Snake took Danny for a ride over to Columbus Avenue near Bay Medical Center.

"Where we going?" asked Danny.

"I just wanted to show you something," he said, as he turned into a graveyard on Trumbull and Columbus. He pulled into an open area and parked the S-10 pickup.

"This is where Marie and I will be buried," he said, pointing to a shaded area beneath a large maple tree.

From the graveyard, Snake drove to Brennan's for a drink at the Morning Star. Danny noticed that Snake was a little more somber than normal. Snake unlocked the main hatch, and they went below deck and started the heater. Snake mixed two union drinks and handed one to Danny. They sat at the small galley table.

"I rented that movie," Snake said, as he propped his feet on his toolbox.

" 'On Golden Pond'?"

"Scared the hell out of me. In the beginning, when they first arrive at the cottage to spend the summer season, the old man goes out into the woods to pick some berries and gets lost. All of a sudden, nothing looked familiar to him. I turned off the machine at that point. The idea of dying doesn't bother me as much as losing control of my mind. I wouldn't watch any more after that." Snake looked forlorn.

"You missed the best parts. There was one scene where Henry collapses on the front porch of the cottage. When he gets over the dizziness, his wife says: "I thought you were dead."

" 'How did I look?' says Henry. 'Not bad,' says Katherine. It's just a very good movie about two people in their 80s who have come to terms with their own mortality. Henry won an Academy Award for best actor, and Katherine won for best actress. Jane Fonda bought the rights to the movie because her relationship with her dad was similar to one she had with her dad in the movie."

"Are you religious? Do you believe in God?"

"Yes. I believe that Jesus Christ is the son of God, and that he died for our sins," said Frank.

"That sounded more like a commercial endorsement than a profession of faith," Danny grinned, "but you don't attend any church meetings, right?"

"No."

"Do you believe there is a heaven?"

"Yup."

"How about hell?"

"Yes."

"Hell doesn't make any sense to me. Why would God create us, equip us with a free will, then if we don't live by some extremely nebulous rules, we burn forever in a lake of fire. If you really believe that there is a hell, if you really believe that you will go there if you don't follow the rules, then you must be following the rules. Right?"

"No, not even close. I don't want to be a hypocrite. I've lived my life as I chose to live it. Now that I'm old, I'm not going to change just before I die, repenting as I take my last breath. I'd feel like a phony."

"But, you can't be taking hell seriously. There is nothing in your life that would prepare you for burning forever, always feeling the terrible pain. I think you are like me and a lot of others who are afraid not to believe."

Nature was becoming Danny's church. Sailing on the Morning Star with Snake and experiencing Lake Huron was more of a spiritual experience than attending a church meeting where the same uninspired message was repeated over and over. The priests, the Jimmy Swaggarts, all of the play-acting, holier-than-thou-posturing in the name of religion; they were all perpetrating a fraud that people were afraid to expose. He had never heard a minister say: "I'm just not feeling that spiritual today," or "I really don't know the answer to that question." Danny always became impassioned when he talked about religion. He had a hard time believing that the God of love, as described in the New Testament, was the same God of wrath that was personified in the Old Testament.

"Do you believe that human life is the only reason that life exists?"

"Yes, I suppose I do. It says in the Good Book that God made man in his likeness so he would have company."

"I know this is going to sound a little off the subject but stick with me for a moment. Have you ever known anyone who lived to be 100 years old?"

"Yes. Several in fact. It's not that uncommon, really."

"OK. Suppose a man reached his 100th, birthday, then died. On the very day that he died, another man was born who also lived until his 100th birthday, then he died and so on. Do you know that it would take 21 people to take you back to someone who was alive during the time of Christ?"

"I've never really thought about such things. But it is thought-provoking. What's your point?" Snake asked.

"My point is that the universe is measured in light years — millions of light years. The Earth is supposed to be more than 4 billion years old. The time that humans have inhabited the Earth is figured to be anywhere from 10,000 to 1 million years, depending on what you call the first human. If the Earth was indeed made just for humans, why did it take so long, and why make so many stars and planets if the only space we occupy is one tiny, sub-microscopic speck?"

Danny spent an hour pouring out his feelings and misgivings about religion as Snake listened and made an occasional comment.

When Danny finished what he had to say, he just sat there drinking his Beam and Squirt and looked at Frank.

"Well. Ginka dat," he said, using an expression he had picked up from his grandkids.

<hr />

On a mild spring day that year, Danny and Snake took a break on the deck of the Morning Star. She had just been taken from her cradle and placed into the Saginaw. The ice was mostly gone. All the necessary, yearly maintenance had been done. The hull had been scraped and repainted with anti-fouling paint, the antifreeze had been removed from the tanks and all that had to be done was to motor out to Sunset Marina, where the boat would be kept for the sailing season ahead.

Frank made coffee, and they sat watching some of the other sailors who were scurrying about on their boats. Dr. Tim Patterson was in the dock slip to the south of them. Danny and Tim had played in the Central High School marching band together back in the '60s.

Tim played the tuba. Snake also knew the doctor from seeing him at various docks around the state. They exchanged pleasantries and sailing yarns. They were all excited about the sailing season that was to begin soon.

―――――

After Tim shoved off to sail up the river to Saginaw Bay, Snake and Danny sat for a time and just talked.

The topic of discussion was labor unions. Danny had strong feelings about the United Auto Workers. Snake, of course, a past president of the Utility Workers Union, also had some strong feelings.

Danny told Snake about a guy he had known when he worked at Mercy Hospital before it became part of Bay Medical Center. The man was a friend of a ward clerk Danny worked with on 1-F, an all-male floor. The man worked for General Motors on the night shift. He bragged to Danny about playing euchre for six hours a shift, then working for two hours.

"I think the unions have become too strong. They continue to make demands of GM and Ford with no thought of how high the prices of autos are. They constantly want more pay for less work. That's what happened in the early '70s. I owned a Vega. What a piece of junk. It was poorly engineered with troughs on either side of the hood that held water and rusted through after a year or two. If you owned one for a while, you had the pleasure of watching both fenders rust and fall off. The best thing that ever happened to the American auto companies was when Japan started making better cars at a lower price. Then, out of necessity, we began making better quality cars. I really think the labor unions have outlived their usefulness, to everyone's detriment."

"The company has to share equal responsibility if you're going to be pointing fingers. The auto companies could have just refused to raise wages or increase benefits," said Snake.

"And just let the union go out on strike?"

"Ya. Let me tell you the basic philosophy of a union: A day's pay for a day's work."

"That may be a union philosophy, but any UAW workers I have met don't give a hoot about the company they work for. The union can be like a giant leech that sucks the blood out of the host until there is no more blood. The average line worker makes more money per hour than a psychologist I worked with in the mental health unit at Bay Med."

"It'll all work itself out eventually. Look at the cars now. American cars are much better than they were. Checks and balances govern prosperity. The pendulum will swing back again, and business will make the necessary adjustments."

Danny found it inspiring to have these little discussions with Frank. His opinions always were well thought out. At times, it was difficult to determine whether he was arguing a point he really believed in, or if he was just getting a knee-jerk reaction from someone who was accustomed to defending a union member as an arbitrator, whether he believed him or not.

• 23 •

A WEE BIT TOO MUCH

It all started innocently enough, with two men simply enjoying themselves in the middle of Lake Huron. Snake and Danny were in a better-than-average mood. They left Bay City around 9 that morning. The wind was good, around 11 knots out of the southwest. The temperature was 75 degrees. And the Tigers were ahead of other teams in their division by 12 games.

It was a great day for a weekend sail with predictions of clear sailing for the next two days, at least. The livin' was easy, the fish were jumpin', and somewhere, the cotton was high. Danny was in La La Land. They started drinking union drinks just after lunch, and Danny was having a hard time with his sea legs. He watched Snake as they neared the state dock in Au Gres.

"What in hell are ya watching me for; grab the dock," Snake yelled.

They hit the dock with moderate force, as Frank revved the engine in reverse, trying to lessen the impact of the collision. Danny reached for a piling that was no longer there, nearly falling overboard. Snake rammed the engine lever forward. This time, Danny grabbed the piling with both arms and hung on. He looked around to see that they were pretty much the center of attention around the marina.

The stern of the boat began to drift away from the dock. Snake grabbed the telescopic boat hook and caught a cleat on the dock. He gave a mighty tug on the boat hook, losing his grip. The boat hook fell into the water, then sank from sight.

"Those goddamn boat hooks are supposed to float. Wait 'til I see Pat Brennan," Snake said, with mock anger.

Danny was beginning to sense that they soon would be in trouble. They eventually got the Morning Star secured. Snake stepped from the boat and stumbled slightly on the dock. They walked slowly to the harbor master's office. Danny was amazed. He knew the state that he was in, and his partner had just as much Jim Beam and Squirt as he had. To the casual observer, Snake was just an old guy with a slight limp.

"Frank," Danny caught up to him. "Maybe it would be a good idea if we stayed away from people for a while, at least until we sober up some."

"Ah," Snake said, making a face of mock disgust and dismissed Danny with a wave of the hand, opened the door and walked into the harbor master's office. No one was there. Frank walked behind the cluttered desk and sat down heavily in the desk chair, which rolled back a few feet.

Danny was getting nervous. Then came the worst-case scenario. The harbor master returned. The surprise was written on his weathered face when he saw the man sitting at his desk.

"Where in hell do you eat around here?" Frank demanded, before the man could speak.

"W-well, there's Lutz's across the road," said the harbor master.

"Been there. I want something different."

"H&H Bakery and Restaurant. ..."

"Been there."

The man looked puzzled and anxious.

"How about the Au Gres Hotel on the point," he said, with a hopeful smile, pointing toward its location.

"How would you expect a sailor to get there from here?"

"I'll call them for you, sir. They'll be glad to send a car to pick you up."

"All right. While I'm here, you'd better sign us in to the slip we're parked in. Have them pick us up at 6, after we've cleaned up a bit." Snake could see that he was in control now.

"I'll do that, sir."

They did the necessary paperwork. Danny and Snake slowly walked back to the Morning Star.

"Holy shit, Frank. I can't believe it. We're both three sheets to the wind, and you had the harbor master eating out of your hand."

"Ginka dat," said Snake.

———

They showered at the state dock facility, changed from dungarees and work clothes to slacks and sport shirts.

Danny was surprised to see Frank when he returned from the shower. "You know, Frank, you don't clean up too bad for an old guy."

"Ha," Snake yelled, with a wide smile.

The car from Point Au Gres Hotel pulled up near the slip where the Morning Star was docked at 5:50. The young lady who picked them up was friendly, and the 5-mile trip out to Point Au Gres was pleasant.

They ate a bountiful and delicious meal. Snake insisted on paying. Danny said he liked that idea. After a few drinks, the same young woman returned them to the Morning Star. Frank gave the girl a substantial tip.

They both crashed early, done in by the night of overindulgence, and slept soundly.

They took a late breakfast at Lutz's. They lingered on for a while over an extra cup of coffee.

"You know, Frank, I seriously thought you and I were going to end up in the local slammer yesterday. I think my blood alcohol was 40-proof."

"Ahh, bullshit," he made a dismissive gesture. "That guy works for us."

Danny laughed.

"What? You think I'm kidding?" Snake went on with his reasoning.

Danny just shook his head and smiled.

• 23 •

The Faded, Red Coat

*There is no such thing as death,
In nature, nothing dies:
From each sad moment of decay
Some form of life arises.*

~ Charles McKay ~

Danny was thrown off balance and brought back from his daydream. A large cruiser passed at full throttle, leaving a huge wake. The autopilot buzzed and corrected for the wake. The mainsail flapped from the disturbance. Danny and Snake were headed for Tawas on the Morning Star. It was a cool and pleasant day with moderate wind.

Snake leaned against the bulkhead and looked through the binoculars as Danny watched in silence. Frank reminded him of his dad. They had a similar build. Danny's dad was bigger, but they both had broad shoulders and strong arms. They had similar postures, the ramrod-straight back, the chin down, giving them a sturdy, determined, almost military appearance. Danny's dad would be 10 to 12 years Snake's senior had he lived.

It was only the week before that Danny was cleaning out the clothes closet in his home on Ninth Street. He came upon his dad's old hunting jacket. He opened the jacket and found the old, insulated hunting pants that once matched the jacket. It was obvious the jacket had been exposed to the elements many more times than the pants. The sleeves were worn and thread-bare. The pants still retained some of the red color they had when his dad bought them back in 1958.

———————

On a Friday in December,1974, Danny and his brother, Peter, went to their dad's home on 24th Street in Bay City. They had planned a rabbit hunt on the following morning. Danny was concerned when repeated calls to his dad's house were unanswered. Danny called Peter, and they went together to their parents' house.

The house was dark when they arrived. Harold's Oldsmobile was parked in the alleyway. There was a terrible sense of apprehension. They entered the house through the rear entrance. The lights were out, and they had to make their way from memory, up the stairs to the kitchen doorway. Inside the kitchen, Danny felt along the wall for the light switch. There was a dark form on the kitchen floor. He found the light and flicked it on. Harold Pratt lay there on the floor, his arms stretched out, his right foot under his left knee and his radio next to his outstretched right hand.

The blood had pooled in his neck. His skin was cold.

"He's dead. Dad's dead," Danny said, as he stared in disbelief.

Danny picked up the phone mounted on the kitchen wall, where it had been since he left home, and called Gephart Funeral Home. He began reporting that his dad was dead when Peter spoke up.

"You don't want Gephart's. You need to call Penzien Funeral Home, or we'll have some family problems," Peter said.

Danny called Penzien's, which was partly owned by a cousin, Mary Ellen and her husband, Bard Penzien. The police were called.

The police and two men from Penzien's arrived at the same time. Some other family members also had arrived, and they were asked to wait in a front bedroom while the body was removed.

Much of the rest of that night was blurred for Danny. He remembered watching his mother at his home in Alpine Village, while BJ and the kids were at Peter's house making arrangements for the funeral. Danny's mother, Ermine, had advanced Alzheimer's and no longer recognized any of the family. Harold evidently had died the night before, and she had been stepping over her husband's body for the past 24 hours.

Danny called Mike Davis. His voice cracked as he told his friend of his dad's death. He explained that he was watching his mother while the family made arrangements.

"Do you want me to come over and keep you company?"

Danny thought for a moment. "Yes. That would be good."

So Mike came over and sat while Danny talked. He needed to talk to someone. This was a side to Mike that he had not seen before. He was a friend.

The next day, Danny met the family at the old home on 24th. The one thing they had in common was the old homestead, where they had grown up. Danny had felt numb when he woke up that morning and began moving through the day with little energy. Now, as they met at the house, reality was demanding attention. It was now about things. Harold Pratt's 61 years of life had come to an end. And the only traces of his life would be disbursed through the family.

Danny walked out the kitchen door and down the too-narrow steps to the basement. It was quiet but for the hushed conversations taking place on the floor above. He walked to the far side of the basement, near the old coal bin and the converted oil furnace, to a small, movable closet where the hunting gear was stored. The old closet looked just like it did in 1962, when Danny first hunted rabbits with his dad and his prized beagle hounds. There was a silver whistle, tied to a red cord that Harold had used to call his dogs when they ventured too far for them to respond to his voice.

He began to cry. He hadn't allowed himself to cry since the death of his best friend, Ray Bock, three years earlier in a car crash. It was as if something had burst inside of him, and all the suppressed guilt held for so many years suddenly gushed from his eyes and ran down his cheeks. He had been a difficult child to raise. He had not set out to be a problem for his parents. He didn't want to be a bad son, but he seemed powerless to stop it.

The sound of footsteps came down the stairs. Quickly drying his eyes, he tried to collect himself, but he couldn't stop sobbing. Danny's brother-in-law, Ron, noticed that he had been crying. He reached out and pulled Danny to his chest, wrapping his arms around him. Danny was extremely uncomfortable in this situation but could find no way to get out of it gracefully. So he waited for it to end.

There was much sorrow at the funeral. The minister gave a generic eulogy that could have been a fill-in-the-blanks sermon for anyone. Danny felt stunned. He listened with tears in his eyes as one of the church regulars sang "My Heavenly Father Watches Over Me," his dad's favorite hymn.

The funeral was held at the Penzien Funeral Home. Mary Ellen Penzien was a cousin, and she had not had any social contact with the Pratt family since she married Bard Penzien years earlier. She was conspicuous about her comparative wealth. She attended none of the family funerals unless they were held at Penzien's. Danny felt no obligation to add to his cousin's wealth by having his dad's funeral there, but Peter didn't feel the same vindictiveness as Danny, and he was now head of the family. So, the choice was Penzien.

Since the family was giving her some business, Mary Ellen Penzien did show up at her uncle's funeral. She was friendly and sociable.

How condescending of her, Danny thought.

Danny grieved for several years after his dad's death. He felt unfinished. He had not proven himself to his dad. In fact, his dad didn't even know him. He wore Harold's faded, red hunting jacket whenever he hunted with Peter, even though it was several sizes too small. His appearance became shabby. He would later look at pictures of himself in the jacket and realize he had been wearing it because it belonged to his dad. He didn't want to let him go.

Danny looked through the pockets of the insulated pants he had not worn because the waist was too big and the legs too short. There was a dried, brittle piece of Beechnut Peppermint gum in one of the front pockets. The pants had not been worn since his dad died in 1974. As long as Danny could remember, Harold had chewed Beechnut Peppermint, and he would give a stick to Danny when he was just a toddler sitting in church in his lap.

It was while hunting with his dad and his prized beagles that a bond was created between Harold and his son. There was an emptiness that overwhelmed him and a morbid feeling that he already had failed. With help from BJ, Danny survived those years of morbidity and now was putting his life back together.

He sat for a long while, lost in thought, looking at the tattered, faded coat, remembering the feelings of inadequacy that haunted him for the past 20 years since his dad died. His dad never could validate Danny from the grave. These feelings would go on forever unless he stopped it now.

In his thoughts, Danny gave his dad a silent homage, a personal good-bye.

Danny wrote his dad's epitaph in his head:

> *Harold Pratt was not wealthy or famous. He was not a hero in the public sense. He worked hard every day of his 61 years and did not expect to have anything beyond what he already had. He displayed true Christian virtue. He was a good, honest and humble man. He was deeply loved.*
>
> *Good-bye, Dad.*

With some reluctance, Danny took his dad's hunting outfit, folded it, wrapped it in a plastic bag and placed it respectfully in a trash can. The tattered, faded, red jacket was a metaphor for a tattered life. He would move on.

A rogue wave brought Danny back to the present. Snake was sitting there with the binoculars. Looking at Frank Davis, it would be easy to make comparisons between his dad and Snake. They were both hardened and crusty, demanding much of themselves. But Harold Pratt never would have shared a drink with Danny. He never would have repeated an off-color joke. He never would have cussed the way Snake did. Frank Davis was a liberated Harold Pratt. Danny enjoyed old Snake's company and his approval.

Several years later, Danny was sitting in his backyard contemplating the stars and the vastness of space. A train horn sounded off in the distant darkness. He thought of his dad and felt a deep loneliness. That night, he wrote:

Tracks
by
Danny Pratt

The distant train sings a mournful song,
And not a soul has seen it pass,
Pass into the blackest depths
Of doleful paths beyond
Beyond the realm of conscious dreams,
And depths of loneliness

• 25 •

DRY DOCKED

After the autumn leaves fell and began to decompose when the temperature dropped and ice began forming on Saginaw Bay and the Saginaw River, Danny and Snake made the trip up the river to store the Morning Star for the long, cold winter at Brennan Marine. A large crane with two straps pulled the Morning Star from the green water and set her on a cradle near a fence that ran along Water Street.

Once the Morning Star was in her cradle, Snake ran a power cord from the ship to an electrical box attached to one of the power poles. Danny stood watching Frank trying to pinpoint exactly where they were on the shore of the river.

Danny grew up just a block from there. There was a sunken and partially burned remains of a boat that sat with its prow stuck heavily in the sand. Mike Davis and Danny swam from the boat many years ago. They called the boat Gumshoes. The real name of the boat was the Marquis Roen. Brennan Cruiser Sales at that time was near the end of Fremont Avenue. Since that time, Brennan's grew to own a mile of property from the Lafayette Street Bridge to the foundation of the old Cass Avenue Bridge. Danny figured that it had to be one of the largest marinas in the state.

Frank Davis was well-known at Brennan Marine. During the winter months, Snake visited his boat almost daily. He always seemed to find a reason to visit Brennan's to look for a part or just see what was new. Everyone seemed to be respectful of the old man. Some of the workers called him Mr. Davis. Pat Brennan called him Frank.

Something about Snake made people want to please him. Maybe it was his loud bark when he was displeased, or maybe it was his piercing eyes and the furrow between his brows that showed his intensity. Snake could be an intimidating man.

Pat Brennan, son of one of the original three Brennan brothers, ran the parts department. He knew that Frank's bark was indeed loud. But he never had seen the old man bite anyone. Pat kept a good humor when Frank was around. Snake asked a lot of questions if Pat wasn't too busy, testing his knowledge. Pat always lived up the challenge.

One cold winter day, Danny accompanied Snake to the Sears service and repair store behind Fashion Square Mall in Saginaw. Frank had a Craftsman router he bought a year or two before that day. The motor had burned up, and he wanted the router either fixed or replaced. They arrived at the repair shop just before noon in Snake's S-10 pickup.

There was a line at the service desk. They waited 20 minutes and finally got the attention of an abrupt woman in her mid-30s.

"Good morning. How can I help you?" the woman said, without looking up. You got the impression that she wanted to be somewhere else.

"I want this fixed. The motor burned up," said Snake, in a soft voice. He adjusted his stance, as if getting ready to defend himself.

"Do you have a maintenance agreement?"

"I don't need a damned maintenance agreement. I've been a loyal customer of Sears Roebuck for 40 years. If you don't stand behind your products, I will not ever cast a shadow in this place again." Frank was loud and menacing. He had turned every head in the place. The clerk backed from the counter.

"Where the hell is your manager?"

"Right here, sir." A balding man appeared from behind a cubicle.

Frank began a tirade that left no room for compromise. He used his right index finger for emphasis and to direct his anger. He had a rhythm going, and the words rolled from his mouth so fast and sure that Danny wondered how he was able to breathe.

The manager held up both hands in surrender. He called Snake sir a half-dozen times.

"Sir. We'll gladly replace your router."

There was silence. Everyone in the building was looking at Frank and the manager. The manager's face was a bright pink. There was sweat beading on the top of his hairless dome. He looked to have been running a long distance.

"Fine," Snake said, finally taking time to breathe.

Several people became involved in getting Frank Davis on his way. The manager returned with the necessary papers for the transaction. One of the office workers took a voucher over to the Sears store in Fashion Square Mall and quickly returned with a new router. The necessary papers were signed, and Frank and Danny turned to leave.

"God bless you, sir," said an older black woman, who had been standing in line. "I don't like them agreement contracts either."

On the trip back to Bay City in the S-10, Danny finally spoke. "You've got one enormous set of Winnebegos."

"Is that the same thing as testiculars?"

"Ya. Testiculars," Danny laughed.

• 26 •

The Pratt Frame Company

A year later, on the first day of December, Danny opened the doors of the Pratt Frame Co. on Columbus and Washington avenues. He had gone through a difficult year with his art business.

His last show of the season was the Royal Oak Art Fair in a park on Woodward Avenue. He sold little of his art that day. He stood at a distance and critiqued his display and his art. He had lost his inspiration. It was evident. He had become more interested in making money in the high-pressured world of original art and lost the uniqueness of his work. He became disillusioned with his life and his lack of passion for his art.

Once he excepted the fact that his art would not have purpose until he again became inspired, he began to look for some kind of work that would help keep food on the table for his family. These were dark days for Danny. He worked at Meijer's on Center Avenue. He would see old schoolmates while he was stocking shelves and want to be somewhere else. He could see that he was becoming too prideful.

He sent a slide portfolio to the Detroit News art department, addressed to the art director. He met with the art director a week later and did several illustrations for the Sunday supplement, Michigan Magazine.

He sent samples of his older, inspired work to Playboy magazine. They held the slides of Danny's work and sent a letter stating they liked his work, telling him to keep them up to date on his art portfolio until they could find something suitable for his illustration style.

It did stroke his ego a bit after receiving the letter from Playboy with the rabbit-embossed logo on the stationary.

But ego-stroking puts no food on the table. Since he had been matting and framing his art for many years, it seemed like a logical step to get into the custom framing business.

———

Peter, Danny's brother, helped clean up and paint the small space that would be the Pratt Frame Co. in downtown Bay City. In just three days, they remodeled the place. They made pegboard panels to mount the hundreds of frame samples that would be displayed in the front of the shop. The back of the office was where all of the work would be done. Danny made a crude workbench from a sheet of ¾-inch plywood.

Two days before he planned to open, Danny took a trip to Saginaw to a framing supply wholesaler called E.A. Boehm Co. He filled out the necessary paperwork to become a wholesale customer, bought frame and mat samples, then purchased a frame chopper and a wall-mounted glass cutter.

That afternoon, his new sign was delivered and was hung from a pre-existing sign frame, which stood atop a 20-foot steel post on Columbus Avenue.

On the seventh day after renting the workshop, the Pratt Frame Co. opened to the public. Within a week, Danny was getting all of the business he could handle. It was getting close to Christmas, and many of the framing projects were expected to be delivered before the holiday. It proved to be a learn-as-you-go situation. For example, he never had framed or matted needlepoint work. But through trial and many errors, he learned.

———

Danny was busy with work in the back of his shop when he heard the front door open, wiggling the little brass bell that was attached to the door jam. He walked to the front.

"Not too bad." It was Snake. "Do you know how to do all of this?"

"What I don't know, I can learn," Danny said.

Frank grabbed a cup of coffee and watched as Danny joined two halves of a frame in a corner vice on his improvised table.

"You work bending over like that, you're going to have one hell of a back ache," Frank commented. "Your table needs to be higher so you don't have to bend over." He walked over to Danny.

"Stand up straight." He measured the distance from the floor to Danny's waist, then added a few inches. "How big would you want your table to be?"

Danny paced off an area, then measured it. He then measured the depth he would need to accommodate his vises, large frames and the mat cutter. Frank took notes.

"I'll make you a real worktable. Just pay me for the materials."

"That would be great," said Danny.

Only three days later, Snake pulled up to the front of the shop with a load in his pickup. He walked in the front door. "Give me a hand," he said.

They carried in the parts for the new worktable. Frank set about assembling it, while Danny waited on a customer. When he returned to the shop area, there it was. It was much nicer than he could have imagined, fitting perfectly in the spot it was designed for and just the right height.

"Wow, Frank. That's a beautiful piece of work. I don't know what to say."

"Don't say anything. Just pay me for the materials."

"I'll buy your lunch, too," said Danny.

During the cold, winter months that year, Danny noticed he hadn't seen his friend Snake for some time. He normally would come to the frame shop a couple days a week, and they would have lunch at the Market Restaurant or at State Lunch on Saginaw Street.

Danny called Snake's house. His wife, Marie, answered the phone. She explained that Frank was a patient at Bay Medical Center. He had an attack of emphysema and had been in the hospital for two days. Danny had seen patients with emphysema when he worked at the hospital years earlier and knew what a devastating disease it could be, the choking and gasping for air. Frank had worked with asbestos during his laboring years with Consumers Power. He also smoked heavily for many years.

———

Danny went to see Frank that afternoon. He was restricted to his bed and was tubed and wired with oxygen, IVs and monitors. The rails were up on both sides of his hospital bed. He was in good spirits and was eager to talk about the coming sailing season. A nurse brought in his dinner tray and placed it on his bedside table.

"You can take everything but the coffee and the juice," Snake said, with a dismissive gesture.

"Mr. Davis, you know you need to eat something. I'll leave your tray, just in case you change your mind," she said.

"No appetite?" asked Danny.

"I don't want to use the bedpan," he whispered.

He had not eaten a thing since his admission to the hospital two days earlier.

Danny was surprised at how vulnerable his sailing partner was.

• 27 •

SEAGULL ISLE

It was crowded and noisy for a Thursday night. The Bell Bar was well-lit for a Bay City bar. Bay windows and a glass door gave an open look of the street, letting daylight flow in. At night, ambulance activity on Columbus Avenue, going to and from Bay Medical Center, could be seen. Tuthill's was just across the street.

The regular patrons know the Bell Bar owners, the Borkowski family, by name since all of them had worked here at one time. Cribbage, euchre and pool tournaments completely fill the bar on designated days, giving the bar an old-time tavern atmosphere.

Bay City, it is said, has more bars per capita than any other town in Michigan. Out of the 120-something bars in the city, Danny and his friends had chosen the Bell Bar to meet weekly because it was a brightly lit, friendly place, and the price of beer fit into the average man's budget.

Danny met some of his friends here every Thursday evening. It was a convenient location for most of them, and there were no scheduled activities that night. It was a pleasant ritual that had gone on for years. Danny liked to call the gathering at the Bell "choir practice." He had been disillusioned with church of any kind. These meetings with five or more outspoken opinions on any subject were much more inspiring than any church service. So, if anyone should happen to ask what he was doing on a given Thursday, he would say: "I'll be at choir practice."

Mike Davis, Tom Doerr, Mark Michalak, Dan Robinson and Darin Scott were the regular attendees. The group would grow as the night progressed. The discussions were always passionate. Everyone seemed to feel free to argue any point.

Davis was working for the city as a mechanic. He was heavily involved in the union, as might be expected. Mike liked to argue and had the same iron determination of his dad.

Doerr was a friend from the days when Danny worked at the old General Hospital. They had been getting together over a beer for many years when they frequented Denny's Green Hut with the hospital crowd when the 3 to 11 shift came there. Tom was now a nurse anesthetist at Midland Hospital. He had the ability to remember names and places and always brought an educated, well thought-out opinion to the group.

Michalak was now a registered nurse and was working at a hospital in Saginaw.

Robinson owned Robby's Hobbys, just down Columbus Avenue to the west. He was a technical, computer person. Dan had been part of the group in the days when they frequented Denny's Green Hut. He was a Pepsi delivery man for many years when he decided to open a hobby store. Dan played Pac Man like no one else. Denny Hayes, owner of the Hut, owed Dan so many 12-packs of beer for high weekly score on the game that Denny had to discontinue prizes.

Daren Scott was an accomplished musician. Darin seemed like a shy, unassuming sort of guy. He sometimes stuttered, and his laugh was spontaneous. But Daren had been around. He had played backup guitar for Eddy Money and frequently played for Broadway productions in Saginaw at the Civic Center. He was a graduate of the Hollywood Guitar Academy. He taught guitar in a studio above Herter Music Center in Bay City.

Danny was owner of Pratt Frame Co., a one-man operation.

The night normally would end around midnight. But on this particular night, someone who sat with them had a birthday, and shots of whiskey were passed around several times. Not one for leaving the table without consuming whatever was placed before him (a Pratt family rule) Danny drank way more than usual. Dan gave Danny a ride home.

Danny awoke with a punishing headache. It took him a moment to recall the reason he felt so terrible. He remembered the gathering at the Bell but could not remember how he had gotten home and into his bed.

He was awakened by the phone. He waited for someone downstairs to pick up, but no one did. The caller was annoyingly persistent. Danny's mouth felt like the bottom of a dirty ashtray. His heart mercilessly pounded blood to his swelling brain. He obviously had forgotten to take the customary two aspirin before going to bed. The phone rang and rang and rang. Whoever was calling was extremely rude or maybe it was some kind of emergency. He bounded from bed, got dizzy from getting up too fast and fell into the closet, then fell again, slipping on the carpeted stairs. When he finally reached the phone, he was out of breath and severely nauseated.

"Hey, Danny. What are you up to today?"

It was Snake. Danny's brain was full of cotton. He needed to think fast or he would be expected to go sailing. Nothing came to mind.

"It doesn't sound like you're real busy. Let's take a turn on the bay."

"I have some things I really need to do today. How long will you be out?" Danny knew from experience that he already had lost the argument.

"Just a few hours. I'll pick you up in 30 minutes."

An hour later, they sat in the too-hot sun, sails hanging limp, not a wave in sight. Snake made instant coffee and brought Danny a cup. He still felt terrible. The aspirin he had taken had not kicked in, and he was in need of something to drink. Anything wet would do. He already had at least a quart of water and guzzled a large glass of milk.

"You look like you've been hit by a truck," Snake said.

"I was," Danny replied.

Danny was grateful for the lack of conversation as he sat there, smoking his cigarette and drinking his coffee. He had quit smoking many times. He didn't have the heart to smoke around BJ. She thought her husband had given up the bad habit. She had been after him to quit for years, and he had quit for a time. But now he was a closet smoker, ashamed of his lack of willpower. He was back to smoking one to two packs a day.

Snake rigged a tarp over the boom to shade them from the burning sun.

The shipping channel was dotted with sport boats, mainly along the edges of the channel where the depth dropped off to at least 28 feet. Danny grabbed the binoculars to see if anyone was catching any perch. It was difficult to tell. Some of the people were intent on their fishing poles with great expectations. Others were just enjoying the leisurely pace of a hot summer day on the water, sitting in deck chairs on sailboats or enormous cabin cruisers.

A light gust of air caught Snake's attention. "Hey look at that," he pointed to the wind speed indicator.

Danny looked as the wind moved the indicator for a half-dozen revolutions at the top of the mast.

Then nothing again. They drifted with no breeze for another hour before Snake started the little engine on the Morning Star.

They headed in the general direction of the small island near the mouth of the Saginaw River.

"What's the name of that island?" Danny asked, as they neared the dock on the island that was used by dredging barges as they dumped their loads from the bottom of the Saginaw River.

"I don't know if it even has a name," said Snake.

They decided to tie up to the dock and check out the island. They secured the Morning Star. Danny climbed the huge boulders to the top of a rise that overlooked the holding pond. Thousands of seagulls were everywhere. There were fuzzy chick heads between nearly every rock crevice. The noise made by the raucous birds was deafening. Adult gulls filled the air.

"Holy crap, Frank. You should see this," Danny yelled. "Unbelievable."

"I'm too damn old to be climbing rocks."

Danny returned to the dock and told Snake what he had seen.

"I dub this island Seagull Isle," Danny said with an overdone English accent. He was beginning to shake his hangover, and his mouth no longer tasted horrible.

• 28 •

PERFECT SAIL

*"If it were somehow possible to condense the universe
to a scale that could be comprehended,
our solar system would be so tiny as to not be visible,
even through an electron microscope."*

~ D.A. Boggdweller ~

Danny looked up at the air speed indicator at the top of the mast on Morning Star. They were on their way to Au Gres. The main sail and the big jenny were raised. The slight breeze was gone. No wind.

The black flies were blood-thirsty fiends. Snake and Danny took turns with the fly swatter. They piled the dead flies in a neat mound on the deck. Between the two, they killed 120 of the biting pests. The afternoon sun made the calm bay feel like a giant slow-cooker. Danny could not imagine how all of those flies could come out of sight of any land and find the Morning Star in the middle of Lake Huron.

"What's the plural of carcass?" Snake asked.

Danny thought for a moment. "Carcasses doesn't sound right. Maybe it's carcai."

"Look at all the carcai," Snake said. They chuckled.

"After a leisurely supper of grilled cheese sandwiches, Snake made a dodger out of a small canvas to shield them from the hot sun while they sat in the midst of the stillness of Lake Huron. Frank told of his adventures in WWII in the South Pacific. He had been diagnosed with malaria. He spent several months at a Naval hospital in California, recuperating from an episode. He played baseball for an Army team and did some amateur boxing.

Danny watched Snake as he relived his war experiences. He enjoyed the stories, though he already had heard most of them more than once. Frank was an excellent companion. He was intelligent and articulate. And Frank didn't seem to have the need to compete with Danny.

Competition was crucial in the younger days of a man's life — part of his survival. But, Danny was not a young man any longer. He enjoyed the extended sails and the solitude of the great lake. He no longer felt the need to compete with anyone. Snake was much the same. There had been times when they just sat for an hour or more in silence, knowing there really wasn't anything that needed to be said.

There were times when Snake thought of himself as the father figure, as if he had to present himself as he would to one of his sons. Danny had an uneasy relationship with his dad. The best times as his father's son were while they hunted or fished. He could not imagine himself enjoying a union drink in the middle of Lake Huron with his dad. But he would have welcomed the experience.

———

"You smile too easily," Snake said, breaking into Danny's daydream. "People think you are simple-minded or naive or too eager to please when you smile too easily."

Danny thought for a moment. He had been smiling and was still smiling.

"What do you think?"

"I don't think you're simple-minded. Maybe a little naive about some things. You generally are eager to please other people."

"Then, is there a problem?"

"Ha." Snake slapped his knees and chuckled. "Ginka dat." He grabbed Danny's empty plastic tumbler and went below to mix more drinks.

Just as Snake came from below deck, the mainsail ruffled.

"Hey, we've got wind," Snake announced. He set the autopilot on a course for Au Gres, while Danny found the Tigers game on the radio.

The air cooled as the sun nestled in the west in a golden sky.

"Now this is what life is all about. 'Tis a grand night," Danny said, in a simulated Irish accent. "A good breeze, a Tiger game, a good drink, a good friend and no place that you have to be. How can it possibly get any better than that? Here's to you, Captain Snake, and here's to the Morning Star." Danny held out his plastic tumbler and touched Snake's drink.

"This is one hell of a boat and one hell of a night," Snake agreed.

It was a leisurely sail, and the wind was timid. The Morning Star held at a steady four knots. The stars made a show of the night. The Milky Way was a source of illumination. Danny turned on the running lights. He had brought a few cassettes along. He put Mozart into the ship stereo system. The ship, the night and the music were in concert.

They sat quietly, enjoying the grandeur of a clear, sparkling sky and the gentle swaying of the boat. Snake sat at the tiller. Danny leaned back against the bulkhead with his feet on the bench. He still felt a buzz from the drinks they had earlier. He followed the expanse of the Milky Way across the sky from Cassiopeia, through countless points of light. He then noticed a luminous shape, high in the stratosphere. It had an almost human shape that was constantly shifting and changing form. Danny called to Snake, then pointed to the sky. The vaporous specter had taken on an angelic form, with a long, flowing, filmy frock trailing behind it. It was moving across the sky at a good clip.

Snake glanced briefly at the apparition, then refused to look again or even acknowledge it was there. Danny thought he saw Snake shudder. But it was difficult to be sure when the night is only illuminated by starlight and heavenly images.

An hour later, they were zeroing in on the mouth of the Au Gres River. The red and green lights could be seen. Snake brought out Big Max, his million-candle power search light to help guide them to the correct angle to enter the river. The huge boulders that formed the jetties on either side of the river easily could sink a ship. Danny lowered the jenny and stowed it below deck through the forward hatch, then he lowered the main sail. Frank lowered the outboard and started it with no difficulty. Once inside the protection of the jetty, the Au Gres River was mirror-calm, the slight hum of the engine the only sound on the quiet river.

Spots of illumination from mercury vapor lamps made the homes along the river look like vacant stages, the actors sleeping quietly within.

Frank seemed in a daze. He had to admire Snake's tenacity. He couldn't think of anyone else in their 70s who would be out sailing at 3 a.m.

They were fortunate enough to find an empty slip at the state dock. They hooked up the electricity, tidied up the ship and slept the sleep of tired men.

———

The smell of instant coffee woke up Danny. He did not want to move, but he looked to the front berth, and Frank was not there. He got up.

He found Snake on deck with a plastic cup of instant coffee, checking out the other boats at the docks. He pointed to a two-masted schooner.

"Have you ever heard the expression: 'A boat is a hole in the water that you fill with money?' "

"No. Can't say as I have," Danny laughed.

"That schooner over there is all teak wood above deck. A 60-footer. She's a beauty. It would cost the guy who owns it more than you and I would make in a lifetime."

Danny caught the aroma of frying potatoes floating through the air from some of the other boats. Even at this early hour, the marina was bustling with activity. Boaters were everywhere, walking to or from the showers, cooking breakfasts out on the decks, some quietly visiting.

They ate breakfast at Lutz's across the road from the marina. Snake was in a jolly mood. The breakfast buffet was varied and good. Danny bought two long-johns from the bakery and brought them back to the boat to have with coffee later. They took a tour of the marina, looking at different boats. Snake would comment on the sailboats and how they compared to the Morning Star. Usually the Morning Star was the superior boat in one way or another.

———

Snake had a vast amount of knowledge about sailing, which he was happy to share with Danny.

Some of the yachts were more like luxury homes than boats, with all the latest accouterments. An old couple waved from a two-decked cruiser. Two small motor scooters were aboard. The couple dropped a ramp and rode them off to explore the area. Danny noticed a gallon bottle of Cutty Sark in the cabin window of the cruiser and two large, potted geraniums on either side of the boarding ramp.

The morning was spent talking to other boaters and sampling confections and an occasional drink offered by the festive boaters. Some had come to party and would not leave the dock until they returned home. Others would stay long enough to eat and shower before they continued on their journey. Snake and Danny enjoyed the art of sailing and talking to others who liked catching the wind.

Danny, being comparatively new to the sailing sport, did his best to add to the conversation. But he was learning that he had much to learn. He spoke to one of the old sailors about a recent sail he and Snake had taken when they were dead in the water for several hours. He used the words "in chains" to describe the lack of wind. He noticed a look of puzzlement on several faces and a smirk on Snake's. Snake explained later that the term for being dead in the water was "in irons" rather than in chains.

They ate a heavy lunch at H&H Bakery and Restaurant, just down the road from the marina.

When they returned, Snake set up a sun shield on the deck. They spent a leisurely afternoon just enjoying the fact that they had no appointments to keep. They had no plans until the next morning, when they would make the return sail to Bay City. Both men took a nap on deck during the heat of the day, enjoying an occasional light breeze that brought some comfort. Frank showed Danny how to splice a line and how to tie some of the knots he had yet to master.

After dinner, Snake turned the ship's radio on to hear the marine forecast. The forecast was for scattered thunder showers for the entire southern and central regions of Lake Huron, with 25- to 30-knot winds.

"Just right for a sail," Snake said casually. He looked at Danny and immediately read his thoughts. "You don't want to leave tonight, do you?"

Danny grinned. They set to work. Snake rigged a storm jib, and Danny took the cover off the main sail.

In 15 minutes, they were pushing away from the dock and waving goodbye to the folks they had met.

"It could get nasty out there," yelled one of the sailors.

"He's just envious," said Danny.

There were giant, ominous cumulus clouds piled high on the northwest horizon as they motored out the Au Gres River. The air was heavy with moisture. The temperature was 86 degrees, according to the marine forecast. They would not have to wait long before they experienced bad weather. The thunder squall was not large but intense and moving swiftly toward them. The energy boiled in the darkness of its core. Lightning flashed wildly, a warning of what was to come. Deep rumbles of jarring thunder reverberated across the vast lake. Danny felt fear and exhilaration.

Snake told Danny to take a southwesterly tack, hoping to move from the path of the storm, but it was too late. There was a definable line at the leading edge of the storm — one side calm, the other white-capped and blown.

Frank disappeared below deck. Danny's bright-yellow rain gear landed on the deck in front of him.

"Get those on. I'll take the tiller," said Snake, as he emerged from below deck in his rain gear.

There was a blinding flash and a simultaneous bone-quaking bang that caused both men to flinch. Lightening hit something nearby, probably one of the channel markers, not 50 feet from the boat. Snake had installed a brass plate to the hull of the Morning Star that was wired to the mast. If lightening did strike the mast, the charge would go directly to the brass plate and harmlessly into the water.

Snake closed both hatch doors to prepare for the coming deluge.

Then the rain came with a fury, and the wind whipped hard and cold into their faces. Snake looked humble in his bright-yellow rain hat as the rain drenched everything in sight. Snake was saying something Danny could not hear over the roaring thunder, the wind and rain. Danny pointed to his ears and shook his head. The powerful little storm came and went in less than three minutes. The dark, unfriendly curtain of energy moved off into the lake to ravage other boats in other places.

The sun broke through, and a beautiful, clear blue sky appeared.

What an incredible display of energy, Danny thought.

Snake had kept an eye on the wind-speed indicator. The wind had built up to 44 knots during the squall. Now, there was no wind at all.

"Pull up the main," Snake yelled.

"Aye, aye, Cap'n."

"Ginka dat. We're in chains," Snake laughed.

Danny raised the mainsail, just in case the wind began to blow. It only flopped from the wake of a passing speed boat. The air-speed indicator was not moving.

Snake threw the rain gear over a halyard to dry. "You know, we might as well head back to the marina and leave tomorrow morning. I doubt we'll get any more wind tonight. I don't want to motor all the way back to Bay City."

Danny was just then finding the Tigers game on the radio.

"We'll give it another half-hour," said Snake.

A few minutes later, Ernie Harwell was announcing that Kirk Gibson's hit was "long gone," when the mainsail suddenly flapped and the air-speed indicator began to spin. Frank grabbed the tiller and headed on the correct course to Bay City. The knot meter read 4 knots, then 8 knots. Soon they were going the maximum hull speed of 12 knots. Snake was ecstatic.

It was hard to imagine their luck of being dead in the water, then picking up a strong wind that propelled, full speed on a perfect tack to destination. But that is exactly what happened once they cleared Point Au Gres.

Snake set the autopilot, then went below to fix union drinks.

It was a grand night. The two men sat and listened to the last four innings of the game. The Tigers won, 7 to 3. They had led the division from the beginning of the season and were expected to win the pennant.

Frank told stories from his union days. He explained in detail some of the arbitrations he engineered. The night was invigorating.

The sunset was a magnificent display in reds, oranges and yellows in a cloud bank that skirted the western horizon behind an indigo shoreline.

"What a great night," said Danny.

Darkness came. After turning on the running lights, Danny returned to his seat to enjoy the gushing of the waves, the absence of the hum of a motor and the warm breeze. It was another beautiful, starry night, the air swept clean by the steady 18-knot winds.

Danny grabbed Snake's binoculars he kept hanging on a wooden peg below deck. He focused on a random area of the Milky Way that stretched from horizon to horizon.

"Wow," Danny repeated the word several times.

"What're you looking at?"

"The Milky Way. I wonder if anyone has ever tried to count the stars in the Milky Way." He handed the binoculars to the old man.

Snake gave Danny the tiller while he looked. "Ain't that somethin'?"

"It makes you feel a little insignificant when you contemplate how tiny we are and how enormous the universe must be."

"Ain't that something?" Snake said again. "This is one of the best sails I've ever had. Perfect wind on a perfect tack, perfect weather. ..."

"And some pretty good union drinks," Danny added, as he held out his tumbler for a toast.

They listened to "Ride of the Valkyries" by Wagner on the ship stereo. The rhythm of wind and wave kept perfect time with the music. A convincing argument could have been made that the music was written under full sail on a night just like this.

Danny went below and found a cassette he found at the Bay City Public Library of songs by Stephen Foster. The music had been performed on instruments that would have been common during the Civil War, when many of them were written. There was a sadness and a longing that transcended the years. "Bygone Days" and "My Old Kentucky Home" took on a deeper meaning as they moved through the night as if in direct communication with those who had lived more than 120 years before. These were the same stars they would have looked at and the same moon.

This was the feeling that young Danny Pratt sought in the Wesleyan Methodist Church of being part of something beyond the human influence and experience, something that fulfilled the promises made in the beautiful hymns of the church. He remembered well the times when he took the leaf from his parents' Formica kitchen table and made a platform that reached out his bedroom window to lie on. He would look up at the countless wonders of space and dream of infinite possibilities while realizing the microbe that he was in comparison to it all.

———

Just as Snake had predicted, they sailed directly into the shipping channel that gave safe passage to the Saginaw River and then home without changing tack.

Danny removed the autopilot once they entered the marked channel. The range light and the blinking lights of the twin stacks of the Consumers plant shown some 8 miles in the distance.

The channel markers gave them a better sense of how fast the Morning Star moved through the water.

"Now there's a sailor," Snake said, pointing behind Danny to the north.

Danny turned to see a catamaran approaching at good speed. They were sharing the channel, and the lighter, more agile boat soon would overtake them. A lone sailor, an older man with a shock of long white hair and beard that shone like silver in the rising moonlight, was at the helm. The boat seemed to be flowing along fluid-like, skillfully in tune with the wind. The man seemed oblivious to the presence of another boat, his silvered hair flowing with the wash of the sail.

"Two ships passing in the night," Danny quoted from a poem he could not name.

Now that the journey was nearing the end, Danny felt the deep fatigue of one who had stayed alert the whole night. Frank was quiet.

They moved past the dock at Seagull Isle. Snake moved to the bow to look for deadheads. The range light moved by when he yelled, "Start the engine." The 15-horse Johnson putted to life.

"Here comes Dodge Island. Move farther to starboard in the channel."

Just around the bend of the river, the searchlight and silhouette of the Dodge Island Dredge came into view, scanning the waters ahead and along the shore. The ship seemed alive and menacing as it moved along almost silently through the rippling water. As the ship came nearer, Snake went below and came back up with the signal horn. The horn was loud enough to be heard by the bridge tenders along the Saginaw River and was powered by a can of compressed air.

"I want to make sure that Dodge Island sees us."

The deafening horn blasted twice, shattering the quiet of the river basin. The dredge found them with the searchlight. The blinding light stayed on them as Danny moved as far to the west side of the channel as possible, coming close to the last buoy. The barge came within 15 feet of the port bow of the Morning Star, when the engine revved, growling violently as she accelerated, creating an enormous wave that completely swamped the forward deck of the Morning Star.

Danny watched helplessly, unable to leave the tiller, as his friend was swept from his feet by the force of the wave. Snake managed to have a good grip on the cable rail and a halyard, which saved him from being washed overboard.

Snake cursed the pilot of Dodge Island in a thunderous voice. Danny was relieved to find that the old man was sopping wet but not injured. Neither of the men had been wearing a life vest.

Both hatches had been open. They had taken on a considerable amount of water below deck.

Ten minutes later, they pulled into the slip at Sunset Shores. They assessed the damage. None of the electronics had been damaged, but the water was a foot deep below deck. The bilge pump was turned on.

Returning the next morning, the hatches were opened, and the Morning Star was aired out. Both agreed they had a great sail, spoiled only by the encounter with the Dodge Island Dredge.

• 29 •

THE LAWYER

*"I do not care to speak ill of a man behind his back,
but I believe the gentleman is an attorney."*

~ Samuel Johnson (1709-1784) ~

In the summer of 1988, Danny's business, Pratt Frame Co., was not doing well. Though he stayed busy, his lack of business skills soon took a toll. He gave too many people too many "good deals." He could save $400 a month by moving his business into his old home on Ninth Street. The house was built in 1901 and was owned by the founders of Trahan Funeral Chapel. It was a large house, with four bedrooms and 9-foot ceilings. In the back of the lot was a small carriage house, which Danny now used as an art studio.

He hired a boyhood friend, Alan Hill, to do some renovating before he made the move. Alan recently had retired from Herter Music Center in downtown Bay City after several decades of moving pianos. He had just ventured into the renovating business. Alan was what you might call a child prodigy, having an exceptional gift for music.

Over a two-week period, Alan put in a new front entrance with a small porch and steps, installed track lighting and turned the former dining room into a new showroom for framing materials. Danny had light-blue commercial indoor/outdoor carpeting installed in the downstairs rooms except for the kitchen and bathroom.

Alan did a wonderful job. The former dining room was now a

much more efficient space for business. The new entrance had a small sign that read: Custom Picture Framing, which easily could be removed if Danny needed to leave the premises. He didn't want to draw too much attention to the fact that he was operating a business in his home. He hoped only to continue servicing the people who already were loyal customers.

As expected, the framing business declined over the next several months in the new location. Danny gave drawing classes in the new room through the winter months. He also taught cartooning and drawing at the Center for the Arts in Midland, Mich. He discovered that he was not a good teacher. He did not have the patience.

On a summer day later that year, Danny was doing some much-needed repairs on his old front porch. He was in the process of tearing out the partially rotted steps on the front entrance when Snake drove up in his S-10 pickup. He tooted his horn and anxiously waved for Danny to come to the truck.

"I've been trying to reach you by phone for the last hour," he said. "We need to take an emergency sail. My old union lawyer is coming to town. I told him I'd take him for a turn on the bay. I need you to be my first mate."

"No. I can't sail today. I told BJ I would rebuild the porch. I can't just leave it."

"Sure you can. I'll come over tomorrow and build your porch." He looked at Danny expectantly. "C'mon. I need to impress this guy and show him a good time. It'll only be for a couple of hours."

Danny tried to form the word "no" with his tongue and lips, but it would not come.

He climbed onto the porch and went in to tell BJ he would be gone for a few hours, then left with Snake. He was really miffed at himself for not standing up to Snake and simply saying: "No, Frank, I have work to do." He saw himself as being weak-willed when it came to asserting himself with Frank Davis.

But Frank loved to sail, and so did Danny. He never seemed capable of staying angry at the old man for long. They stopped at the Ideal Party Store to get supplies, then headed out to Sunset Marina. Frank wanted to get there early to make sure everything was ship-shape.

The air-speed indicator at the top of the main mast was spinning at a rapid clip. The water on the river looked choppy.

"It's going to be a bit rough out there today. Won't be needing the jenny. We'll even reef the main sail just a bit and see how she goes," said Snake.

———

Danny Pratt did not like lawyers. Most of the attorneys he had known were really into the predator versus prey kind of thinking. Morality had nothing to do with the practice of law. The fact that lawyers now advertised on TV seemed unethical. He thought they were ambulance chasers, bottom feeders and carrion eaters. But he had to admit that there was some value in having a lawyer to protect you from another lawyer. It all came down to what was always the bottom line, money.

Tom Doerr, a friend from the days when Danny worked at Bay Medical Center, had a plate on the front of his Mercedes Benz: "He who dies with the most toys, wins." Danny respected Tom's intelligence and his ability to remember names. The quest for unlimited wealth seemed to be the most consuming goal in the lives of too many people. Lawyers were the instrument of that greed. Right and wrong was defined by these people who were motivated only by personal gain.

Snake was respectful of Ted Sachs. The lawyer arrived with no fanfare. He was a small, unassuming sort, with a slight, frail-looking body. Danny looked for signs of conspicuous consumption but found none. He wore an old, gold watch, probably a Bulova, not a Rolex. Wearing a sport shirt and denims and a pair of deck shoes, he looked more like an accountant than he did a lawyer.

Ted's law firm had been on retainer for the Utility Workers Union for decades. He had worked closely with Snake during union negotiations. Snake was respectful of this small, unpretentious lawyer.

Sachs looked a little apprehensive as they left the dock at Sunset Marina, then headed out the mouth of the Saginaw River. The river was choppy. The Saginaw Bay showed white-caps and 3- to 4-foot, rolling waves. The sky was a steely gray, with fast-moving low clouds rushing southeast.

Once they passed the Consumers Power plant, Frank took a tack to the northwest. He nodded to Danny to raise the main sail. The Morning Star keeled to the port side, leaving Sachs on the high starboard. He looked concerned as he held tight to the steel cable rail with white knuckles.

"Take the tiller," Frank said to Danny. He went below and brought out three life jackets, handing the smaller of the three to Ted. "You need to put this on," he said.

Ted was reluctant to remove his death-grip on the cable rail. He managed to get the jacket fastened. His face had paled to an ashen gray.

With great difficulty, Ted managed to put his head over the rail. He vomited the full contents of his stomach, then wretched several times before returning to his seat. Danny went below and brought back a plastic cup filled with water for the lawyer to rinse his mouth.

The tour of the bay was cut short that day. It was obvious that Mr. Sachs was not enjoying himself. Once they returned to the calmer waters of the marina, Ted was able to regain control over whatever remained in his stomach.

They sat for a time on the deck of the Morning Star, remembering the days when they both represented the Utility Workers Union. It didn't take long for Danny to get to like Ted. He already had shown his human side when he puked over the side of the ship. He was a ponderous, deep-thinking sort of man.

It was when Frank went below that Danny asked Ted what it was like to work with Frank Davis.

"I've yet to work with anyone who was better prepared for negotiation than Frank Davis. He was tough, passionate in his beliefs. He had a way of putting his point across that could be menacing to the company lawyers. He knew the union contract, and he knew the laws that affect it. I have a good deal of respect for his ability. He didn't let the fact that he had little formal education slow him down. He researched everything thoroughly. He held his own. He could have been a fine lawyer if that would have been his chosen profession."

"I talked with a guy named Charley Mark not long ago at the Green Hut Bar in Bay City, telling him I had been sailing with a guy who had been a Utility Workers Union president. Since Charley had worked for Consumers for decades, I knew it would spark some interest. He asked for his name. 'Frank Davis,' I said. 'Oh, that old son-of-a-bitch,' he says. 'He's got a reputation for being a mean bastard.' I told Charley that Frank was a friend and that I really enjoyed sailing with him."

"Yes. He could be menacing. Did you know that Frank was the first Utility Workers president that had not been elected by his local union first?"

———

"Anyone for more coffee," Snake yelled from below deck.

"None for me, Frank," Ted said. "My stomach won't be settled for a while."

They talked for another hour of the current labor agreement. Ted was impressive with his knowledge, and his demeanor was not in the least bit haughty, as Danny had expected.

Snake was very much the gentleman that day during the visit of Ted Sachs to the Morning Star. Though the weather was not ideal, it turned out to be an interesting day. Ted left to prepare for a meeting with the newest union president later on that day in Jackson.

Frank was true to his word and was at Danny's front door at 8:30 the next morning to begin replacing his front porch. Danny had been in the habit of doing his own repairs on his century-old home on Ninth Street. He did not profess to being an accomplished carpenter, but for the sake of thrift, he got by as best he could.

Once they removed the old porch, they found it was in worse repair than they had anticipated. By the time they finished tearing the rotted boards out, there was nothing left of the old porch except the roof.

Snake took charge from that point. While Danny picked up the rotted materials and raked the area, Frank calculated what they would need in materials and how the new porch would be built.

It was noon by then. Frank thought they should take a break for lunch.

Danny suggested he fix lunch since Frank never had tasted his cooking. "We had a roasted chicken for supper yesterday. I'll fix you some of the best chicken soup you've ever tasted."

"Sounds good," Frank said. "I'll figure up what we need in materials and make some final measurements while you fix lunch."

Danny washed up and set about making his favorite chicken and rice soup. When he went to the refrigerator, all he could find of the left-over chicken were two small wings. He would not let this minor setback stop him from making his gourmet soup. He found some chicken bouillon, boiled the two chicken wings to get whatever broth he could get from them, added some finely chopped carrots, onion, garlic and sage, then removed the tiny bit of meat from the wing bones. To give the impression of more meat, he dropped in some egg white as the broth boiled. He made two Colby and mayo sandwiches from homemade bread, then called Frank in for lunch.

As Frank washed up, Danny ladled out the steaming soup and set it on the dining room table with the sandwiches. Frank walked in and sat opposite Danny at the table. He looked at the steamy soup.

"What the hell is this? It looks like a chicken walked through some hot water with waders on."

Danny laughed, bringing a slight smile to Frank's face. "My kids got to the left-over chicken before I did. All that was left were two chicken wings. Sorry, Frank."

The soup was eaten, and Danny made more sandwiches. Frank took the whole chicken episode with humor.

That afternoon as they began framing in the new porch. Tom Hickner, who was the local state representative and lived directly across the street from Danny, came by. Danny's daughter, Marcy, had been their baby-sitter for several years, and Nancy and Tom Hickner treated her like a daughter.

They talked for a time. Frank, knowing that Tom was a state representative, asked him if he could remedy a problem.

"We frequently visit the state docks at Tawas and Au Gres. They don't take credit cards. I don't like to carry a lot of cash. It would be a hell of a lot more convenient if they took Visa or Master Card."

In three days, the new porch was complete. BJ was pleased when she arrived home from work.

"We need to keep the little lady happy," said Snake. "We want to do some sailing in the next several months."

Snake gave Danny with a bill for the lumber and other materials. Danny gave him a check for the amount, plus a fifth of Jim Beam for their next sail.

Two weeks later, the two men sailed to Tawas and stayed at the state dock there. They found an empty slip and went to pay for the space at the harbor master's office. There was a sign on the door to the office: Visa and Master Card excepted.

"Well, I'll be damned. Hickner must have given them the word," said Frank.

• 30 •

THE BIRTH OF D.A. BOGGDWELLER

One fall day, Danny watched the TV-5 News while eating his dinner with BJ and the kids. He was outraged that one story was even told on the local news. He wrote to the People's Forum in the Bay City Times complaining about what he thought was bad journalism:

Bogus News

Voice: Danny Pratt, Bay City

I grew up in Bay City and have depended on TV-5 for local news since Virgil O'Dell and Captain Muddy Waters were around.

I watched the 6 p.m. news on Sept. 2. There was a segment on the program about a young boy who rode the bus to MacGregor Elementary School in the South End. He had cut his head in transit. The cut apparently required several stitches, but there was no major trauma.

There was speculation by the "journalist" that the injury occurred when the bus driver suddenly hit the brake – causing the boy to lose his balance. There was an interview with the

*boy's mother, who intends to file a lawsuit against (I assume,)
the board of education for the pain and suffering that her boy
suffered.*

*I wanted to ask this lady if she would have preferred that
the driver run a stop sign or hit a tree. They also interviewed
some of the other parents of children on the bus. One lady said
while she was sorry the boy was injured, it wasn't worthy of all
the attention it was getting.*

*What kind of wimps are we turning into? When I was in
the process of growing up in the South End of Bay City in the
'50s and '60s, we took our lumps, bumps and cuts in stride. We
didn't whine or turn around and sue someone.*

Why is this story newsworthy?

*Why has our No. 1 source of news for this area stooped to
such inflammatory, sensationalistic stories?*

*Are they oblivious to the fact that they are not only
condoning frivolous law suits, but they are giving these people a
soapbox to help promote them?*

*I am not a bulimic, but I had a very strong urge to run to
the toilet with my finger down my throat.*

*This is an age of terrorism. People are fighting and dying
to preserve our liberties. Pain and suffering are a part of every
one's life. The woman who plans to sue over her son's pain and
suffering must be living in a bubble.*

*I would be surprised if she doesn't get a deluge of phone calls
from opportunistic ambulance chasers.*

*I would ask TV-5 to either become more responsible with
its "news" stories, or leave the news to others who know news
from frivolity.*

When Danny saw his opinion printed in the Bay City Times, it
gave him the enthusiasm to write about his experiences.

He began to read the Forum daily. It felt good to have a voice,
a voice that said what was important to him. He really began to see
what his values were. And he was happy with what he found.

While getting groceries with BJ one Thursday, Danny found
himself standing next to a neighbor who lived just a half-dozen
doors down from his home on State Street. He didn't recall the
man's name.

"Hey, you're Danny Pratt. I read your piece in the Forum. Good job. Frivolous law suits tie up the courts with ambulance chasers every day. I've been tempted to do the same thing. But I just haven't had the ambition to do it."

"I just couldn't believe that news report," Danny said. "The news reporter was giving this woman, this opportunist, a soapbox so she could tell the whole state how her boy had been injured on a public school bus."

Danny felt a boost in his ego after talking to the man.

In the next year, Danny sent the People's Forum eight opinions, and three were published. He enjoyed the occasional responses to his opinions, even if someone disagreed.

Danny and his family had been attending church at the North Euclid Church of God. He was witness to the church being torn apart by selfishness and politics. He was angered by the way it all came about. He decided to express his feelings through an alter ego. He wrote his feelings down as D.A. Boggdweller, a pen name he created to somehow express his family's ancestral origins:

Words With the Pastor
by
D.A. Boggdweller

"The faith that stands on authority is not faith. The reliance on authority measures the decline of religion, the withdrawal of the soul."

~ Ralph Waldo Emerson (1803-1882) ~

Norman Fletcher was well-versed in the topic of religion. He had struggled with it since his growing years in an ultra-conservative church. He scrutinized other religions, hoping to find something that was tangible and not just a ritual or oft-repeated hope of something intangible.

Now in his mid-40s, he still was filled with doubts about his place in the Grand Scheme. Religion seemed to be fertile ground for the Jimmy Swaggarts and the Jim Bakkers, televangelists who reaped millions from naive Christians who gave their faith and their meager savings to put air conditioning in Bakker's doghouses and to finance Jimmy Swaggart's liaisons with local prostitutes. It was easy to find people who want to believe in something and like taking candy from a baby to exploit them.

Norman was angry because there seemed to be no one to look up to for guidance in politics or religion. He stewed over simple things and was not conscious of where the anger originated. He also was saddened that his artistic career had taken a plunge lately. His beer drinking had increased, and he was looking for someone to knock the chip off his shoulder.

If Norman had believed in such things, he would have thought the planets had aligned themselves, a perfect time for a conversation with Pastor Donald Brown.

———

Early on a Friday morning, Norman was sitting alone at the Bay Cafe, enjoying a good cup of coffee and focusing his attention on the new day that was just dawning. He was comfortable in the small cafe, where the food was good, the faces familiar and friendly. Sherry, the waitress, was out-going, with a good sense of humor. Norman was beginning to feel a little optimism about what his future held.

Norman's wife of close to 30 years was in Florida, visiting her sister, Mary.

The first couple of days after Molly's departure, Norman had stayed up late and slept later than usual, enjoying the freedom of only having to think for himself for a few days. But after four days, he missed his wife. Picking his life's companion had proved to be one of the best choices he had made. She said what was on her mind, and once she had stated her opinion, she would let the subject go.

After a disagreement, Norman always had to think about the argument. He realized that he was head-strong and stubborn and often would be more concerned with winning the argument than he was over the validity. Molly was rational and steady and rarely was angered. If he thought her opinion was valid, *he would sometimes concede the argument. He was confident in her love for him, even though in his opinion, he sometimes felt undeserving of her love.*

———

The sun broke over the horizon of houses and trees and filled the cafe with brilliant light. It was a pleasant morning, but a hot and sticky day was predicted. Norman squinted and held his hand up before his eyes. The first rays of the morning sun invigorated him. He partially closed the blinds on both sides of the entrance door to filter out some of the glaring light.

He had just retaken his seat in the padded booth in the no-smoking section, when the front door opened, letting the brilliant sun in again. Even with the sun in his eyes, he knew the silhouette. The Rev. Donald Brown shut the door, removing the brilliant halo of sunlight from around his head.

"Oh shit," he whispered to himself. Norman was not happy to see the pastor.

"Norman! How are you?"

Norman had been pretending not to see the man.

"Just ducky," he said.

He walked over to Norman's booth. "Mind if I join you?"

"I'm not much of a conversationalist at this hour of the morning," he said, trying not to be overly rude.

"I'd really like to talk to you for just a few moments." The pastor had a habit of overemphasizing words for the sake of drama as part of his "I'm-teaching-you-something" demeanor.

Norman shrugged his shoulders and gestured toward the bench opposite him in the booth.

———

He first met the reverend eight years earlier when he was the new pastor of Grace Valley Baptist Church, where Molly was a member. Norman had been a member, years earlier. But there had been a rift in the church, and he could not believe how "brothers and sisters in the Lord" suddenly could become so venomous toward each other. The hate was real in these people. The love was suspect.

The Espy family considered themselves the founding family of the church of around 250 people. When one of the Espy sons,

Samuel, became associate pastor, the will of the Espy family became known. Samuel was not content just being associate pastor. He began throwing the political weight of the Espy family around and challenged Jerry Fowler.

One Sunday morning, just a day after Samuel threw a temper tantrum in an argument with Jerry, Samuel stood in front of the congregation of Grace Valley Baptist Church and gave an impassioned, self-righteous and gooey speech. He was wronged in his opinion and had not been given the chance to lead the church in his personal vision from God or the right direction. Someone should have reminded him that he was the associate pastor, but the congregation was so shocked, they were mute.

He closed his emotional speech with: "I have decided to resign as associate pastor of Grace Valley Baptist, effective immediately." Then, Samuel Espy strutted self-righteously from the podium, down the center aisle and out the far exit, effectively ripping the church apart.

Pastor Fowler was embraced by half of the church and ostracized by the other half. A week later, Jerry Fowler knelt at the altar and requested that he be anointed by the lay people of the church.

When the call was given for the lay people to come to the altar, conspicuously missing was the Espy family and its supporters, who watched the proceedings from the rear seats of the church.

Pastor Fowler's supporters, which included Norman and Molly Fletcher, joined him at the altar in a declaration of support.

The Espy family and company left Grace Valley Baptist Church and joined a church on Frazier Road, where they soon dominated the politics of that church.

Pastor Fowler tended his resignation several weeks after the incident and moved to Little Rock, Ark., where his family had roots.

———

Shortly after the church split, those who remained as the congregation of Grace Valley began an earnest search for a new pastor. The Rev. Donald Brown gave a sales pitch in the form *of a sermon one Sunday morning. He was voted in as the new pastor. He wasted no time in laying down his expectations. It should be noted that Grace Valley had been quite liberal in comparison to the new minister's beliefs. He said on his first Sunday as minister that he did not believe anyone who smoked cigarettes should hold a seat on the church council. Several members never returned to the church and voiced their anger that they had been judged as unworthy by a man new to the church. He had several more guidelines he would be enforcing, which pushed even more established saints of the church out the door.*

Pastor Brown had been looking for a home for himself and his four children in the Bay City area. He had no place to stay, and his family was in another state.

Norman and Molly had purchased a late-model Dutchmen 24-foot camper. Molly told Norman she wanted to allow the new pastor to use the camper until he found a place to live.

Norman was raised in a humble and frugal home. Whatever he bought of any value was well cared for. He waxed his car and truck several times a year, and the mechanical maintenance always was done on time. He kept the same Schwinn Super Le Tour for more than 30 years, putting more than 30,000 miles on the old bike. He was reluctant to loan the nice, shiny trailer to a total stranger. But he agreed with Molly that the young family needed somewhere to live.

"You know that I am leaving the church," said pastor Brown, bringing Norman from his distracted thoughts. He nodded.

"I also know you aren't exactly sad to see me leave. I would like to know what I have done to alienate you. We were getting along just fine when I first came to Grace Valley. Then you just quit coming to church. Molly, of course, stayed with us and is now one of the outstanding lay people. Be candid with me. Was I the reason you left the church?"

"Yes. Well, you were part of the reason anyway."

"Could you tell me why?"

Sherry approached, to take the breakfast orders. "I know what you want Norm," she said. "Two eggs, over-easy, hash browns, crisp, with a little onion and whole wheat toast. Right?"

"Right." Norman smiled.

"And what can I get for you, sir?"

"Just coffee," said the pastor.

"Norman picked up where the conversation had stopped: "What difference does it make? You're leaving," he said.

"Since I first stayed with you and Molly in the trailer in your backyard, I liked you both. I respected you for giving an honest opinion on whatever topic we might discuss. Sometimes I agreed with you, and sometimes I didn't. But you always stimulated discussion and allowed me to answer some of the questions I never asked myself."

"Such as. ..."

"Do you remember the night we sat in your backyard at the picnic table. You offered me a beer, knowing that I don't drink alcohol. You gave me a lemonade while you drank your beer. You asked me if I considered myself an honest person. I said that I wouldn't be an ordained minister of God if I thought otherwise. You began to ask questions that you obviously had given some thought to. I was uncomfortable with some of your questions, especially the ones I had no solid answers for."

"What questions were those?" Norman was getting interested in this sudden glimpse of humility in the man.

"You asked why God had a different personality in the New Testament than he did in the Old Testament. In the New Testament, God, in the form of Jesus, is loving, forgiving and compassionate. In the Old Testament, he is fearsome and wrathful, telling the Israelites to kill all the Philistines, even their cattle."

"And you answered that Jesus had come to bring forgiveness for our sins. That seemed like a typical, generic answer."

"Then you said, but isn't Jesus God? Aren't they one and the same? I said something, but I recall that even to me it was inadequate. I was on the defensive, feeling that I had to defend my faith."

"And that is the point, how can you possibly say you believe something if you've never asked some tough questions? I have a quote for you pastor. 'Question with boldness, even the existence of God; because even if there be one, he must more approve of the homage of reason than that of blind fear.' Thomas Jefferson said that. If you have a brain to think with, how can you really appreciate the magnitude of God and the universe if you have never asked yourself some really tough questions?'

"I really don't want to get into another religious argument with you, Norman. But I need to know why your heart is filled with venom. What have I done to make you despise me so?" Pastor Brown's eyes were damp and pleading.

"Maybe it isn't just you, Don. It's the clergy in general," Norman said. "You appear to live your life within the rules of the church. You conduct yourself as if you never doubted the church's philosophy. You, Pastor Donald Brown, are pompous, arrogant and manipulative. You can be humble but only when it suits your purpose. You have learned to be a minister. It was taught to you by church doctrine. In order to become ordained, you swore that you believed a large list of church rules and dictates. In other words, you swore never to think for yourself, but to take the rules as stated and believe them. Can you tell me as you look me in the eye, that you don't ever question the church doctrine? When it comes to the real person, the genuine Donald Brown, he doesn't exist. He has become a talking mannequin for the church."

"How would you have me conduct myself, Norman? Should I wear my mood on my shirt sleeves and let everyone know when I don't feel like doing visitations, or when I don't feel like listening to problems, when I don't feel like getting out of bed at 3 in the morning to rush to a person's deathbed to console them in their final hours?" The pitch of the reverend's voice rose with every sentence.

"Wow! You're really ticked aren't you? Listen, Pastor, you make a big deal out of the fact that you have been ordained by God to teach his children and to lead them on the straight and narrow path of righteousness. If you are not another Mother Theresa, quit pretending to be. If your religion comes out of fear instead of inspiration; if you no longer are inspired to do the work, then go sell used cars. People don't really expect a used car salesman to be perfect. If you really want my slant on things, I think you have entirely too much ego to suit my opinion of a clergyman. Try a little Billy Graham and a lot less Oral Roberts. You tell your congregation members they should be Christ-like in their everyday lives, to emulate Jesus. You, Don, *do not emulate Jesus. You emulate the insecurities of a man named Donald Brown. It isn't just you, Don. It's the hypocrisy of religion in general. I grew up with people who pretended to be above it all, who feigned compassion for others and preached the honesty and integrity of the Christian spirit. These people would stand in church on Sunday and testify to being cleansed and forgiven of all sin. They create a comfort zone, surrounding themselves with people who subscribe to the same belief system. But over the years, I have observed that the very same people can change in an instant. Their compassionate feelings turn to bitter hatred when it is found that someone among them might not think the same way. Instead of excepting the sins of others and loving them anyway, as Jesus taught, these "invaders" were shunned and made to feel so much discomfort that they left the church. Those who were thought to not give enough to the church, or if they didn't repeat the right cliches, were perceived as backsliders. People who follow the dictates of the church, giving a tenth of their earnings to God's church would be rewarded with leadership roles in the church and eternal life. I'd be willing to bet, Don, that there are nights when you lie awake, wondering if your life has been a mistake, if there really is a heaven and a hell. I am not an atheist, Pastor. But, it makes me want to vomit when I see "Christians" twisting verses of the Bible, using them out of context to reinforce some self-serving opinion. There is no one more dangerous than the self-righteous and the ambitious, who believe their beliefs are the only keys to paradise. Now we hear about the priest/pedophiles that permeate the Catholic Church; the televangelists who broadcast a holy persona but are merely actors portraying a role that will make them wealthy."*

"There are many things that go on in the church that you are not aware of. ..."

"Wait. Just let me finish what I need to say."

"OK. Good, you are starting to rant," said the pastor.

When you first took over as pastor, my brother, Phillip, was the song leader. He was going away for the weekend. He asked me to take over for him as song leader while he was gone. I had been attending church again, after staying away for several years. My brother has hardly ever asked anything of me. It was something I had not done before. I said I would lead the singing for him. When the time arrived, I was sitting in the church with Molly, waiting for the service to start. You came to me with a list of songs you wanted me to direct, along with the page numbers in the hymnal. I looked at the list of songs and told you I was not familiar with any of them. You said: 'Well, you read music, don't you?' I said no. You said: 'Well, you'd better learn.' Then you walked off."

Norman could feel his anger peaking. *"I tried to lead the singing. But you can't be a tour guide in Paris if you've never been there. I decided I didn't want to follow a spiritual leader who was that mean-spirited. I would like to put you in the same situation. Maybe at the last minute before you deliver your sermon, I could have your notes transcribed into Russian. I didn't have a clue as to how to lead the congregation in songs I hadn't heard. I felt like a complete fool. You could sense I felt that way, and you enjoyed it."* Norman's face was red, and his eyes were narrow and focused.

Pastor Brown sat looking at Norman for a moment, not believing he was finally finished with his tirade.

"Norman, I saw in you as a fledgling Christian who had not reached his full potential. I wanted to help you become a fully realized child of God. Tell me honestly, Norman, do you make any profession of faith?"

"No. Not any longer. I am totally disillusioned with organized religion. Too many contradictions. Too much deception. Too much greed. Too much authoritarian bull crap."

"Norman, listen to yourself. Listen to your arrogance."

"Yes, you bet I'm arrogant. And head-strong."

"Try to get along, you two," Sherry yelled from the back of the cafe.

The pastor seemed derailed by the interruption, pausing for a brief moment. *"But what do you believe, assuming you do have some sort of belief?"*

"I believe that the human race is no different from any other life. We live and we die. I don't believe a God that created heaven also could create a hell. I believe I should live my life to the best of my ability and offer whatever talents I might bring into the mix."

"But God wants us to love him in return. That's why he gives us a choice."

"Please. Save your breath. I already heard that argument. If God is all-powerful and omnipresent, and He loves us as you have said, why can't he just do away with Satan and Hell?"

"Because He wants us to make a choice!" His voice was getting louder.

"Ya, some choice. Do as I command, or you'll burn forever in a lake of fire, the worst possible torture, to never stop burning, never stop feeling the flames. That sounds more like the voice of some power-hungry clergyman than the voice of a loving God. I think the Bible stopped making sense when a divisive cleric got his hands on it. Whatever the Bible originally said inevitably was reinterpreted by the people who had a different inspiration than the original authors. Would you sentence your own children to the same punishment if they misbehaved? Could you say: 'I'm letting you burn forever, because I love you?' "

"I'm not God. I can't second-guess God's ways. God works in mysterious ways, his. ..."

"Please. Don't start quoting the Bible. I'd like to talk to the real Donald Brown. Come out from behind your veneer of righteousness for just a moment."

"I've been ordained by God to be his messenger."

"No. You've been approved by a group of self-righteous men to be a minister of the church. I'd like to see some authorization from a higher authority before you start talking about your hot-line to God. It's far too easy for someone with selfish intentions to pose as a messenger from God. I'm sorry, Pastor, but I don't see God talking when you speak. All I see is someone who is well-versed in theology trying to inflate his own ego. And while we're on the subject, isn't Jimmy Bakker an ordained minister? Isn't Jimmy Swaggart an ordained minister? And the priest/ pedophiles are they not sanctioned by the Catholic Church as leaders and teachers of the church? You need to understand that for those of us who are just mere people, the whole subject is confusing."

"Yes. There have been a few that have fallen through the cracks. But that does not lessen the fact that these people have been forgiven of their sins through the grace of Jesus Christ, and that they have been chosen to lead others to His grace and forgiveness."

"How about taking a polygraph? Would you submit to a lie detector test?"

"For what reason?" There was now a furrow in the pastor's brow.

"To determine your sincerity. To determine whether or not you really believe in what you preach."

"You know, Norman, for someone who is accusing a minister of being self-righteous, you sound quite arrogant yourself."

"Pissed is a better word. I'm not an ordained minister. I'm Norman Fletcher. I can do whatever my conscience feels good about doing. I don't feel the need to be told by a clergyman how to behave or how much of my money to give. I believe the God we talk about shows himself in all life. He has nothing to do with the churches we build."

Norman could feel the frustration surfacing that had been building up over his lifetime. He was scared into submission when he was young. He went to the altar to confess his sins and to be forgiven by God. He had listened to the fire-and-brimstone sermons by a traveling evangelist that literally scared people to the altar to escape the terrible judgment of burning forever in a lake of fire. He was met at the altar by a layman of the church who offered to help him find God. The man, Charley Webcox, had been spending weekends in jail for raping his stepdaughter. That was the point in his young life where the lifelong confusion began. What was God trying to tell him? Was Charley Webcox there to teach him something?

He read the Bible in one year. He tried to live a pure life. But for Norman, that lifestyle did not work. He witnessed the breakup of two churches he had been involved with. He found the people of the churches he belonged to were Christians because they were afraid of their own mortality. They were afraid not to believe in the dictates of the church. They would rely on their pastor, who may or may not, have honorable intentions. They stopped reasoning things out for themselves and concentrated on doing "good" so they would not suffer the flames of hell after death.

"OK. Since you brought up the subject of death, how do you feel about your own inevitable demise, Norman? You've had several life-threatening situations just recently. Your wife Molly was stricken with cancer two years ago. How did that make you feel?"

"Of course, I was afraid of the possibility of losing her to breast cancer. Whether she was bedridden the rest of her life, she died, or she came out of the surgery fine, I was prepared to deal with the situation to the best of my ability. As for my own death, I no longer fear the ravages of hell fire. A God of love would not allow the existence of a hell or a heaven. I believe that hell and heaven were introduced by the church as a behavior modifier. That explains why the Bible has so many versions. It has been altered over the years to adapt to different interpretations."

"So now it seems that you are on a crusade of your own," the pastor smirked.

"I know that remark was meant to be sarcastic. I don't feel the need to change others. If I could do any convincing at all, it would be to give some decent people, who have led good and decent lives, the knowledge that they will not suffer eternal pain from a hell that does not exist. I don't believe the vast universe was created for humans alone. Our solar system is microscopic in comparison to the cosmos. I don't believe that if you ask yourself some honest questions and give some honest answers, you can belong to any organized religion without compromising your own beliefs. I don't pretend to know all the answers. I try not to pretend at all. You may see that as arrogance; you may see that as being rebellious; you may see that any way you wish. God gave us a brain to think. I don't believe it is sinful to follow what your conscience tells you is right."

Reverend Brown was looking into his empty coffee cup. "I could quote some scripture to you, but I'm sure you wouldn't be open to what I have to say. The scriptures are written in such a way that is somewhat nebulous if you do not have the spiritual guidance to understand the meaning. I really do believe in what I am doing. My faith is real. It is not contrived. I would like to leave this place today, knowing that you and I have made peace."

"Why is my opinion so important to you? Do you need my validation?"

"Yes. I suppose I do."

"Well then, I have a certain amount of power over you, don't I?"

"Yes, you do."

"By the power vested in me, I now pronounce you forgiven." Norman smiled broadly.

"You're so smug. Now, you're making me angry."

"Good. That's a start."

"I have to go. We're in the process of moving to Kansas. I have a million things to do. I'm glad I had this talk with you before I left Bay City. I want you to know that God still loves you, and I do also. I'll be praying for you, Norman."

"Thanks. I certainly have no qualms about that."

The pastor slid out of the booth, and they both stood.

"God bless you, Norman."

"God bless you also, Don."

The pastor held out his hand then decided to embrace Norman, patting his back.

"Don't get gooey with me now, Don. I don't like you enough to leave you anything in my will. I'll tell you what. I'll let you buy breakfast."

"You've got to be kidding. On my pay, you want me to buy breakfast?"

"It would show that you are sincere," Norman said, with a broad smile.

"You'll just have to take my word on faith. Give my love to Molly." He reached into his pockets to pay for his coffee.

"I'll get the coffee, Don."

———

Danny gave Snake a copy of the story. He read through it as Danny took the tiller on the Morning Star on a crisp spring afternoon sail on Saginaw Bay.

Snake read the story then went below to get some coffee. He returned, handing Danny a cup.

"Pretty strong stuff."

Danny looked at his coffee.

"Not the coffee. I'm talking about your story. You've got some pretty hard-nosed opinions there. You damn well better hope there's no hell."

"You know the old saying: 'God hates a coward.' That probably was written by a Marine."

"Or someone in combat," said Snake.

• 31 •

LAKE HURON
TESTING THE METTLE

1984

It was a suffocatingly hot afternoon. Snake and Danny motored out the Saginaw, planning to end up in East Tawas at the state dock there. The wind was light. Frank recently had bought a dinghy from Boat U.S. near Detroit. They towed the little boat 5 yards behind the Morning Star.

They left the shipping channel just north of Seagull Isle, raised the main and the big jenny. The sails just hung there listlessly.

The two men would not let the lack of wind ruin the evening. Snake mixed union drinks. They sat back and waited for a breeze.

Danny thought about Snake being a good companion. They could sail for hours in the middle of Lake Huron without feeling the need to speak. Sailing was soothing. Danny was a hyperactive kid before they invented the term. The tempo of sailing, the long periods with no other stimuli but the wind and water and Snake's drinks were a combination that always let his mind settle. These were short periods when, just for a moment, things were perfect in Danny's mind. There was time to ponder life and to really feel a part of the flowing energy of the wind.

Snake was never in a hurry, now that retirement had set him

free of schedules. The way he walked, slowly and deliberately but with an uncommon self-assurance, said Snake Davis was either an important man or he carried a gun.

The two men had pretty much decided that sailing all the way to East Tawas was questionable after sitting still in the water for more than an hour. The sun sank behind the trees that lined the western shoreline. Snake was nailing down a point that he had made in a union arbitration when the main sail suddenly flopped. Then the big jenny began to flutter. Then, to their great delight, both sails filled with air. The Morning Star sprang to life. Danny grabbed the tiller, which they had left unattended, and directed the boat in the correct direction to merge into the shipping channel. They were now heading for East Tawas.

"Yahoo," came a yell from another sailboat.

Danny looked to the east. A man on a two-masted, wooden ship gripped a halyard in one hand and waved the other. Danny waved and yahooed back to the man, feeling the exhilaration of the sudden speed of the wind. "This is great," he yelled over the wind.

"That's a 60-footer," Snake said. "Look at those lines and the way she sits in the water. You could sail anywhere in the world in a boat like that. She's a beauty. But the maintenance on that thing would cost more that you and I could ever afford."

"Why would you want anything that big? I think the Morning Star is a fine boat," said Danny, with a wide smile.

"Ha! You bet." Snake slapped his knees. "Look at that wind."

The wind was coming from the south, directly behind the Morning Star. The waves were cresting at around 5 feet. The big jenny was taken down.

As the 27-foot O'Day flew past the last lighted buoy in the marked channel, the skies were dark and stars were beginning to pop out of the clear sky. Danny thought it odd that the wind could be blowing as hard as it was, and there wasn't a cloud to be seen. The wind speed continued to increase.

Danny stayed with the tiller as Snake went below and tossed up Danny's life jacket. "Put that on," he yelled. "We're taking too much wind. Too much pressure on the mast. We need to reef the main. Just make sure you don't let us go sideways in a trough."

Snake reefed the mainsail to the last tie, giving the Morning Star only a small triangle of mainsail. "I'll take the tiller, you hook up the storm jib."

Danny went below and placed the small storm jib, then climbed up through the hatch while still hanging onto the storm jib. The ship pitched and rolled, dipping and rolling in every direction. It was a real challenge to rig the sail then hoist it while balancing on the pitching deck. He rigged the storm jib to the port side of the ship opposite of the mainsail.

"We're wingin' it," Frank yelled.

Once the ambient light vanished, the night sky became ink-black, highlighting the most dazzling display of stars.

It was difficult to hear conversation over the rush of the heavy wind and the rushing water. They were pushed through the night by an unstoppable force of wind and water.

Danny's pulse was racing. He could feel his heart pounding in his chest. I'm in a fight or flight response, Danny thought. The adrenaline was flowing. He felt alert and alive.

Snake approached him. "I don't know exactly where we are. We're moving so fast with heavy wind. I'm going below to check the charts."

The waves were moving faster than the boat. Each time a wave overtook them, there was a hesitation before the stern fell back and into the next trough.

It was difficult to imagine a scenario that would get them into a safe harbor. The ship was in the willful grasp of enormous waves and heavy wind. To tack in any direction except the one they were on would put them sideways between two giant waves.

This was a genuine adventure. Life or death. At first, Danny had been nervous and unsure. Then he began to feel the exhilaration of the moment. He could see by looking at Snake in the light of the map table that he was feeling the same. His eyes were wide with excitement as he was tossed about below deck.

Manning the tiller was getting to be hard work. Danny wondered if his old friend was up to the task. Snake always had been a fighter, a pit bull. He was getting on in years now, and he certainly wasn't physically fit. His diet was terrible. He ate whatever pleased him. He had a large abdominal hernia, which made his work pants stick out in an unusual way. He had smoked for decades, though he now had quit. He had emphysema and shrapnel wounds from World War II. He had been advised by his doctor to get a knee replacement. But Snake wouldn't have it. He didn't want any surgery that would have a long rehabilitation.

An unusually large wave overtook them from the stern. Danny watched as Snake was thrown violently across the galley and into the cupboards.

"Frank, are you OK?"

No answer.

Danny could not leave the tiller but stretched as far as he could to see Frank as he rolled with the motion of the boat, still on the floor.

Danny faced the possibility of piloting the boat into safe harbor to get Frank to seek some medical help.

"Frank," he yelled as loud as he could.

"Ya. I'm OK." Snake appeared in the hatch. His forehead was bleeding. "I just bumped my head. I would have broken a few ribs if it wasn't for this life vest. It just knocked the wind out of me for a minute."

"You scared the hell out of me," Danny said.

Snake came above board and stared into the darkness, trying to find anything familiar. Lake Huron seemed to take on the temperament of Lake Superior, raw and unforgiving of any mistakes made at sea.

Danny tried to imagine what it would have been like for the early explorers sailing toward a place they never had seen, fearful of falling off the edge of the Earth. How brave they must have been.

Snake pointed to a blinking light ahead. Danny caught a faint sound. It became louder by the moment. It was an ominous, mournful, moaning sound, which caught the mind by surprise and awakened a foreboding deep in the gut. Danny could feel the goose flesh oh his arms. He looked at Snake for an explanation.

"It can't be Gravelly Shoals. We couldn't have come that far. Not yet." Snake checked his watch by the light of the compass.

The rotating beacon could be seen at the top of the high tower, warning of the rocks nearby.

"Ho-ly shit. That's Gravelly Shoals. We've come all the way from Bay City to the Shoals in three hours."

Snake had Danny take a tack that would avoid the rocks around the treacherous shoal. Neither of them had heard the Gravelly Shoals horn before. It had an eerie sound somewhere between a wounded wolf and a soul in torment.

Passing by Point Lookout to the west, the Morning Star was closer to land. They could get an idea of how fast they were traveling by the lights along the shore from docks and private homes. As Danny held the tiller, the thought crossed his mind that the situation they were in was very much like being in a large and unruly crowd that was moving uncontrollably toward an unknown destination. There was no way to slow down, and there was no way to escape the crowd that swelled around them.

The adrenaline was pumping hard through his body. He felt a longing for his three kids and his wife, BJ. There were things he needed to say to them. He needed to tell BJ she was what had held his life together for the past 25 years. She was special, an excellent wife and mother. She was always the one who brought sanity into any situation. She supplied the nurturing their three kids needed. She supplied the compassion. He had been the disciplinarian, the enforcer, just as his dad had been and his dad before him. It was a new world, where the lines between male and female were blurred, neither gender knowing what was expected, and kids did pretty much as they pleased.

At the moment, his future was in doubt as they raced through the night, in the control of a willful wind and enormous waves. He had the urge to make a deal with God, that if he and Snake made it through this adventure, he would be a better dad and a better husband. But Danny was unsure of what God really was, whether as a tiny human on a tiny planet in the vastness of the universe, he could even be seen. He became aware of his thought process. He was trying to bargain, as he had done when he was young, attending his parents' church.

Whether they survived or not, the reality was that he was on a boat called Morning Star with a man called Snake, and they were going to do their best to make it to East Tawas.

"I'll take the tiller for a while," Snake yelled. "You get up there on the bow and make sure we don't hit anything."

Danny moved to the bow, clinging tightly to the cable rail. His glasses were getting drenched, but he could see nothing without them. He found the bottom of his T-shirt and wiped the glasses off between waves. Snake closed the main hatch to avoid taking more water below.

The huge conveyor and loading dock in Alabaster were well-lit. It was a familiar landmark. The conveyor brought gypsum from an enormous pit mine just west of the highway. The reflected light from the loading dock gave a glimpse of how deep the trough between the waves really was and how fast they were moving.

The passage of time was difficult to measure. Danny rode the prow like a bucking horse, completely drenched from the spray.

———

They had not seen a single boat since the two-masted one at the mouth of the Saginaw River. Danny wondered if they were the only sailors crazy enough to be out on Lake Huron in the raging wind.

A searchlight flashed in the distance. Larger concentrations of lights along the shore meant that the dock in East Tawas was getting closer. The searchlight had to be the lighthouse on Tawas Point.

Danny's attention was drawn to a group of lights that seemed to be extending a distance from the shoreline. The evenly spaced lights were being foreshortened as they grew nearer.

"We're going to hit the pier," Danny yelled at full volume.

They came about with the precision of a military maneuver.

"Comin' about."

Danny had joined Snake in the stern by this time, having to duck to miss the deadly force of the boom as it swung across the ship, catching the wind on the opposite side. The boom hit the vang with terrible force. The little engine did its job, taking a few seconds to make headway against the enormous waves and away from the steel and concrete structure of the dock. By the time they reversed direction, the prop from the Johnson 15-horse motor was but 10 feet from the pier. The huge waves smashing against the breakwater told what their fate would have been had they waited another second to come about.

Danny lowered the fully reefed mainsail and tightened the vang as they rounded the Tawas dock and headed into the relative calm of the harbor.

The dock slips were filled to capacity. They moored a distance from the central dock, greatly relieved to be out of danger.

The harbor was choppy with smaller waves. Snake checked the two anchors to make sure they were spaced correctly and would keep the Morning Star from drifting into the dock or another boat.

The last thing Danny remembered was the clanging of the steel cable against the mast in the wind.

———

When Danny woke up to the smell of Snake's instant coffee, Lake Huron had calmed but was still choppy, the sky and water, gray. He made himself a coffee. Danny was feeling good about the adventure they experienced. They had out-maneuvered the reaper. Danny found Snake kneeling on a cushion and leaning on the cable rail.

"Well, if it ain't old Cap'n Snake," said Danny, as he joined him at the rail. "That was one hell of a bit of sailing we did last night, Frank. It's no stretch to realize that if we hadn't come about when we did, there was just no way we would have survived."

"That was a dandy piece of work. We came about perfectly. We both did what we had to do and did it right."

"Check this out." Danny pointed to a sailboat being towed in by a power boat. The deck of the racing boat was covered by sails and snarls of cable, the mast laying across its length.

"De-masted," said Snake. "There's another one along the shore and one on the far side of the dock. This is the same weekend as the Port Huron to Mackinaw Race. Most of these boats are racing boats. I'm thinking that these boats have dropped out."

After finishing their coffee, Snake moved the Morning Star over to the main dock when an open slip became available. He walked down to the harbor master's office on the dock closer to shore, paid the necessary fees, then returned to the sailboat. As they sat on the deck of the boat, talking over the plans for the day, Snake noticed that a familiar boat was in a slip to the east. It was the Dolphin, owned by Dave Ruhland. To the west was another racer with long, sleek lines and furled Mylar sails and two beautiful young ladies in string bikinis lying on their bellies with their halters untied. The lack of sunshine on this gray day didn't seem to concern them. Danny talked with a young, fit man in his early 20s later that morning and found that the boat owner hired girls out of Detroit every year as a bonus for his sailing crew. The long, sleek ship had been damaged in a collision with another boat, but the damage wasn't evident on the hull.

They spent several hours that morning talking to the other sailors who had been out on Lake Huron during the high winds. From what they were able to learn, no one had been seriously injured. Snake told and retold the adventure of sailing from Bay City to Tawas. He praised the Morning Star. "She's a fine boat," he said.

Snake's version of the story was slightly different from Danny's. They talked with a group of veteran sailors that crewed one of the sleek, state-of-the-art sailboats. As he told the story, Danny was at the tiller, and he was on the bow as lookout, yelling to come about. He referred to Danny as "my buddy, Danny." He was happy that Frank thought of him as a friend, and he really didn't mind that the story had been changed.

On the return trip to Bay City, Snake brought up the fact that he had revised the story of their adventure. "Don't tell my wife that it was you who spotted the dock. She worries about me too much when we're sailing. She wouldn't want me to sail if she thought I couldn't see any better than that."

Danny agreed not to tell her.

It was a year later that Danny wrote a poem about the night he and Snake sailed the Morning Star to Tawas:

Old Snake and Morning Star
by
Danny Pratt

One steamy night in August
We started on our way.
Old Snake Davis and myself
In his 27-foot O'Day
A sturdy ship, a seasoned vet
Through many storms had sailed.
Stood high and proud through raging seas
And scarcely wet her rails.
The toughest test was yet to come
The toughest test by far
For two men far away from shore
In a ship called Morning Star.

If good winds blew, away we'd sail
We'd sail all through the night.
Then, sometime in late morning
The Tawas pier we'd site.

We motored out the Saginaw
The dinghy brought in tow.
We'd pass the dock at Seagull Isle
Where offshore breezes blow.
Prepared, we thought, for anything
Come rain, come wind, come sleet.
Snake turned our bow into the wind
While I pulled in the sheets.

The 12-knot wind we'd hoped for
We simply could not find.
The jib, the main flopped listlessly.
Of wake there was no sign.

While Saginaw Bay lay tranquil
Our glasses we did raise.
Snake told of South Sea battles
And bygone union days.
Time was at a stand-still
Good friends with time to spare.
We sat there for an hour or more.
Life held not a care.

A setting sun sent golden clouds
Cascading in the west.
When the sun sank from our sight
'Twas then began the test.
Many a tale there has been told
Of deadly, angry gale.
From Huron waters, mountains grow
That cause stout hearts to wail.

A chilling breeze filled all the sails
And sent us on our way.
Where placid, mirrored seas had been
A towering torrent swayed.
Then blackness fell upon the sky
A million stars shown out.
The wind kept building up in strength
And battered us about.

The knot meter we buried
While surfing down the swell.
We pulled the jib and reefed the main
And still we flew like hell.
We flew wearily into the night
'Til passing Gravelly Shoals
Whose siren song in mournful horn
Could shake the bravest soul.
"How can it be, we've come this far?"
Snake yelled above the blast.
"We've been gone but three short hours
Now Gravelly Shoals we've passed."

'Twas then I felt the fervor
Of sailors long since dead.
Who caught the wind and challenged seas
With grandeur in their heads.
Who wandered far from safety's shore
The heavens for their guide.
Whose tattered, wind-blown faces
From danger would not hide.

The fear of what we faced that night
Suddenly was gone.
Courage welled within the breast
A sailor I'd become.

We sailed on and on with zeal that night
'Til Tawas light grew near.
'Twas then that Snake yelled from the bow
"We're going to hit the pier."
I guess 'twas mainly instinct
That took control just then.
We came about with lightening speed
And turned into the wind.
The boom shot by just overhead
With deadly cannon force.
We tacked beyond the breakwater.
Again we changed our course.

We sailed around the protective wall
A citadel against the blow.
We moored a distance from the docks
Our dinghy still in tow.
Then, exhausted, fell asleep
Awoke with morning glare.
When upon the deck we stood
We could do naught but stare.

The many ships surrounding us
Most the ships we saw
Had left Port Huron day before
And raced toward Mackinaw.
Several ships had lost their masts
Some had lost much more
One racing ship, while being towed
Sank quite near the shore.

Tales were told about that night
When waves as big as masts
Had sent the veteran sailor
Retreating from the blast.

Old Snake and I were proud that day
Proud we'd come so far.
And braved the raging seas once more
In a ship called Morning Star.

Danny typed the poem on his word processor. He did a drawing of Snake, his sparse hair blowing in the wind, in colored pencil from an old photograph. Then he framed the poem and the portrait and presented them to Snake. Snake hung them in the hallway next to his bedroom at the top of the stairs.

• 32 •

Butting Heads

"It is important to our friends to believe that we are unreservedly frank with them, and important to a friendship that we are not."

~ Moliere ~

One day that summer, Snake and Danny got into a heated argument in the back room of the frame shop. As he was listening to Snake, Danny realized he was not making any headway in his argument with Frank Davis, the union president and arbitrator.

"Do you ever look at things objectively? Do you really believe in your argument or are you the union arbitrator, arguing a point that you don't even believe in yourself? I can't argue with someone who never makes concessions, a professional arguer," Danny said, a little louder than he intended.

"That's the biggest pile of horse shit I've ever heard."

Frank walked briskly out of the Pratt Frame Co. He did not return, and after two weeks, Danny started wondering why this was happening.

Danny valued Frank's friendship. Even though they argued frequently, he was intelligent and full of enthusiasm. He sent Frank a note requesting a "cease-fire."

Snake came by the frame shop the day he received the note and took Danny out for lunch.

In addition to the framing business, Danny also had gotten into the shirt business. He found a printer in Freeland that could print his artwork on T-shirts and sweat shirts. The art was exclusively black, pen-and-ink drawings on white shirts. He designed a logo, using the name Pratt in cursive, which was embroidered on the white sweat shirts on the right sleeve near the cuff. There were 10 designs printed. The designs began to sell well. Ford's Mens Store and Lady Ford's in downtown Bay City bought several designs and displayed them in a window on Washington Avenue. He soon was taking orders for his shirts in Charlevoix, Cadillac and Traverse City. A women's fashion store in the Amway Grand Hotel complex also began to take orders for his shirts.

The printer in Freeland was being kept busy. When picking up some shirts for Lady Ford's, the printer approached Danny, telling him that he would need to pay for his shirts when he delivered them from that point forward. Danny had been given 30 days prior to that date so he could collect the payment from his customers. It was a potential problem.

The next time Danny sailed with Snake on the Morning Star, they had several union drinks. Danny mentioned to his friend that he was having some cash-flow problems with his shirts.

"I'd be glad to loan you the money," Snake said.

"Thanks for the offer. I won't have problems as long as all of my customers pay me on time."

"Well, I think you're good for it. How much money are we talking about?"

"The job I have at the printers now is going to come to around $1,500. But I would only need the loan for a week at most ... hopefully. But borrowing money can make fast enemies."

"Ahh," Snake said, waving a dismissive hand.

They sailed to Au Gres that day and spent the night at the state dock before returning to Bay City. The winds were not favorable. They had to change tack a half-dozen times. It was close to midnight when they finally motored into Sunset Marina. Both were tired and cranky.

Early the next morning, the printer called from Freeland, a small town 20 miles from Bay City, to tell Danny his shirt order was ready and would he please pick it up as soon as possible. The bill for printing the shirts was $1,500. Danny would not have the cash for the shirts for at least one week.

Danny thought of the offer Snake had made concerning a loan. It couldn't hurt anything, Danny thought. He said he would be "glad" to loan him the money. He called Snake to see about a short-term loan. Frank was surly when he answered the phone.

"Hey, Frank. I need to take you up on that short-term loan offer you made." Danny was not comfortable asking for money. But under the circumstances, what harm could it do?

"Shit! God dammit! How much do you want?" Frank obviously was not happy about loaning the money.

"Fifteen hundred."

"Fifteen hundred!" There was an uncomfortable silence. "I suppose if I told you I would loan you the money, I'll have to do it. When do you want it?" Snake was not trying to disguise his anger.

Danny told him he would like to have it that day.

"I'll have to go to the bank and get a cashier's check made out," he said, then hung up the phone.

Danny began to have second thoughts about getting a loan from his friend. Frank wasn't happy to loan him the money as he said he would be. It was out of character for Danny to ask anyone for money. Snake's anger was disturbing. He called Frank again, before he had the time to leave for the bank.

Frank answered on the second ring.

"Never mind the money," Danny told him. "I'll take care of it myself."

It was obvious Frank was relieved. Danny had made a mistake in asking for money. He knew better. Snake had sounded so sincere when he offered help. But, they had been drinking when Snake made that generous offer.

Danny found the whole situation unsettling. The next Thursday, Danny got together with the gang at the Bell Bar. He told Mike Davis about what had happened.

"You know, Mike, I love that old man of yours, but I can't get along with him," Danny told him. He explained that he was embarrassed by the whole situation. In retrospect, Danny later would see this as the beginning of a cooling of the friendship with Mike.

Snake called several times in the next couple of weeks, leaving a message on the answering machine to call him back. To Danny, all of this was embarrassing and demeaning. That would be Danny's last contact with Frank Davis.

―――――

During the following year, Frank was diagnosed with mesothelioma from the years of working for Consumers and his contact with asbestos during that time. He sold the Morning Star to a young couple who wanted to buy the boat for several years. The combination of emphysema and the other physical problems he had experienced proved fatal.

―――――

In November of 1994, Mike Davis called Danny. "My dad's dead," Mike said, his voice cracking. Though Danny knew deep down in his guts that it would never happen, the possibility of ever making amends with the old guy was gone now.

Snake Davis had been a good friend and a great sailing companion. They had many great times on the Morning Star. They were two stubborn people who had respect for each other but just could not seem to get along.

He attended the funeral at Trahan's three days later. There was a military color guard there from the American Legion.

―――――

Danny would get together with Mike Davis many times after Snake's death. But the two men, who had been lifelong friends, found they no longer had much in common. The conversations were not the conversations of friends. There was a competitiveness that wasn't there when they were young. Danny tried to understand the sometimes passive/aggressiveness he could see developing.

It all began when Danny told Mike of the argument he had with Snake. Mike was surprised that Snake had offered to loan him any money. Danny tried to understand how he would feel in Mike's situation. He remembered the look on Mike's face when he told him: "I love the old guy, but I just can't get along with him." Danny would not have been happy if his dad hunted and fished with Mike Davis and they had become friends.

But there was no way to heal the damage that had been done. They were different people now, and Snake was gone. Mike probably would suffer the same anxiety Danny experienced when his dad died.

Snake was a dynamic person. Danny thought he was a better person for having known the man. Frank Davis was a person you either loved or hated. Danny loved that old man. He just couldn't get along with him.

• 33 •

Sept. 11, 2001

Danny was busy in his workshop. He was making a video out of old photographs he had taken of his daughter, Marcy. She was to be married later that month. It was a tedious job, having to tape the still photos on the wall against a white background, focus and shoot. He was nearly finished with the project, having shot almost 300 photos after trying to put them in some sort of chronological order. Over the years, he had taken thousands of pictures. Many of the earliest pictures of his daughter were lost when their U-Haul trailer caught fire while they were traveling through Texas.

He only had a few photos left when he heard on public radio that a plane had crashed into the World Trade Center in New York City. No one knew yet what kind of plane it was. Danny had thoughts of the old King Kong movie, where the giant gorilla is swiping at the small biplanes as they circle overhead.

He finished shooting, shut down the floodlights and turned off the lights in his workshop. It was lunch time. BJ recently had returned to work after taking time off after her breast cancer. The house was empty. He made a sandwich, took it into the living room and turned on the TV.

Breaking news streamed across the bottom of the screen. A plane had crashed into the Pentagon in Washington, D.C. Plumes of black smoke came from the damaged building and the plane wreckage. It was an airliner filled with people.

"The United States is under attack," came the voice of a newsman.

"Holy shit," he yelled. He could not take his eyes from the TV.

The screen divided, showing a live feed of the World Trade Center, a giant cloud of smoke billowing up from one of the towers. Then someone yelled, "Oh my God!" as an airliner crashed into the second tower.

How could this be happening?

There also was a report that another airliner had crashed in Pennsylvania. Some of the passengers had been in contact via cellphone with relatives and found out what had taken place at the World Trade Center and the Pentagon. The plane had deviated from the intended course and was headed for Washington. They overpowered the pilot, killing themselves and all those aboard to avoid an even greater catastrophe.

Then the first tower that had been hit began to implode, crushing debris and filling the air with smoke. People were running desperately trying to escape the heavy wall of dust that was pursuing them. It seemed like a terrible nightmare. A panoramic view of the island of Manhattan showed how great the devastation really was.

Hundreds of firefighters were entering the second tower. Danny was awed by the bravery of these men as they showed them in full battle gear climbing the stairs inside the second tower. Surely they had to know that the second tower would collapse just as the first tower had. These would be the last pictures taken of these men.

The gravity of what was taking place flashed before his eyes of the lives already lost, the lives that were yet to be lost.

• 34 •

Hard Times

The Bay City Mall was crowded. Gray-haired seniors were going through their daily walking exercise. Some were limited by arthritis; others were spry as teenagers.

The morning was windy, damp and chilly enough that Danny wished he had worn a heavier jacket.

BJ had gone to Saginaw for a doctor's appointment. She had found a new lump in her left breast and was concerned enough that she was having a biopsy done, just to be safe. Each new lump had to be mapped, just to keep track of them all. She would stop at Sam's Club on the way home to get some bulk items.

She found the new lump just a week before in a self-exam. She immediately called Dr. Guisinger to schedule a mammogram. The doctor ordered the exam but cautioned her that it might not be paid for by the insurance since it had been less than six months since her last mammogram. BJ told the doctor she wanted it done anyway, even if she had to pay for it.

The mammogram showed a suspicious lump that had grown quickly.

Danny was home alone and restless. It was too cold to bike, so he came to the mall to get a brisk walk in before BJ returned from

Saginaw. He stashed his jacket in a 25-cent locker at the south end of the mall and started out at a brisk pace. He was striding along, feeling more energetic than he had for a while when two ladies, both old enough to be his mother, passed him with seemingly little effort.

Danny considered himself to be in fairly good condition for someone in his 50s. Maybe he wasn't getting enough aerobic exercise. He noticed there were many more elderly women walking in the mall than men. He wondered if there were fewer men because of attrition, or if women were just more energetic in their later years.

He circled the mall twice and found that he was getting tired. He reasoned that it was probably because he had a full calendar the day before. He was now a certified massage therapist and was working out of his home. BJ and Danny had gotten to know many of the clients personally and became friends with many of them.

Danny wrote a monthly newsletter called "Feelin' Fine," which featured healthy tips, quotes and stories he had written about growing up in Bay City. He and BJ were content with their lives.

He was rounding the corner in front of the Target store when he heard a voice behind him.

"I thought I saw an old and familiar head."

Danny turned to see Bruce Sherbeck. Bruce had been a first-chair drummer in the high school band back in the '60s when Danny played the bass drum in the marching band. Bruce also played drums for the Counterpoints, with Dave Garcia, Bob Delaney and Alan Hill. Bruce was a good drummer, but Danny would never tell him that.

"So, how have you been? I haven't seen you in years," Bruce said, with a slight smirk on his face.

"I'm doing good. Are you still teaching?"

"Yes, I'm still teaching in Saginaw."

Danny never really got along that well with Bruce. During concert band rehearsal one afternoon back in 1966, Danny and Bruce were doing a little verbal fencing, when Bruce threw a tympani mallet at Danny, then ran behind the heavy stage curtain. Danny watched as a form moved alone behind the curtain. Sure that it was Bruce, he gave the bulge in the curtain a healthy whack. There was some cursing and some frantic movement as the form searched for an opening. It was Doc Cramer, the esteemed band director.

"I should have known it was you, Pratt. Sit down there and try to act your age."

Doc Cramer rubbed his sore shoulder while Bruce Sherbeck made a hasty exit.

Danny's antagonistic relationship with Bruce seemed to pick up where it had left off 30-some years ago.

———

When Danny reached his home on State Street Road, he saw his wife's VW Golf in the driveway. He entered through the back door, where he found BJ fixing a cup of herbal tea.

"How'd it go?" Danny asked.

"I won't know until the biopsy results come back from the lab," she said.

One week later, BJ received a call from Doctor Tschirhart's office. The nurse would give no information over the phone. They set up an appointment for the next afternoon.

Danny and BJ were optimistic as they drove to Saginaw the next day. This was not the first time they had been through this routine. Danny chose to stay in the waiting room while BJ went in to see the doctor.

Several minutes later, Danny was summoned by the nurse to join BJ in the exam room. As Danny entered the room, BJ was sitting on the table, naked to the waist. Another doctor was in attendance along with the nurse. BJ was weeping.

"Please be seated," said the doctor.

"The biopsy was positive. Your wife has cancer," he said, showing no emotion. He paused to let his comment sink in.

Large teardrops dripped from BJ's cheeks.

Danny could think of nothing to say. It was something he really had not considered. BJ always had gone about her life in a practical way. She ate well, she never drank alcohol or smoked cigarettes. The fact that she now had cancer caught Danny completely by surprise. He already had rationalized that there was no justice as far as sickness and health were concerned. There was no one to blame. Death came to everything that lived. His throat constricted as he watched his wife weeping silently. He would be strong. But he felt helpless. He watched in silence as the doctor explained what would be done to prolong BJ's life. He realized how very much he loved her. He could not speak for all the thoughts that were racing through his head.

Dr. Tschirhart had been through this identical scenario countless times. Neither he nor his associate betrayed any emotion as BJ absorbed what she would be facing.

"I want to do a lumpectomy. We'll remove all of the cancer that we can, as well as some of the surrounding healthy tissue. After that, it will be chemotherapy or radiation therapy.

BJ was somber and introspective on the quiet ride back to Bay City. Danny did not want to start a conversation that would get emotional while he was driving. Yet he felt a strong urge to reach out to her. He patted her shoulder, just to connect for a moment.

When they arrived home, BJ rested. She was emotionally exhausted. Danny called one of BJ's church friends, Jan Eyre, and requested that she be put on the prayer chain. He called BJ's parents, Harmon and Wilma Knight. His mother-in-law asked Danny if he was scared.

"Yes," he said, without hesitation.

Danny called as many friends and relatives as he could think of.

While BJ rested, Danny opened a beer and went out to sit on the steps of the deck and watch the declining sun. A large gathering of starlings surrounded the house, their black bodies filling the trees and the grass in the field. Their singing filled the air. Then, as if by some unseen signal, they all took flight, forming a tight group as they circled then spread out into a continuous stream that did not seem to stop.

There was a metaphor. Life must continue. He would try his best to give her some strength to get through whatever they were about to experience.

That evening, BJ showed Danny the cancerous lump. He touched it lightly, not wanting to cause her pain. He could feel the heat from the ominous, pea-sized predator. It had a different consistency than the cystic lumps in her breast. She laid her head on Danny's lap and fell asleep as they watched the evening news.

BJ always found solace in her religious beliefs. While Danny had left the church, being totally disillusioned with organized religion, BJ remained a strong supporter. She was not a saint, but she seemed to embody all the virtues of a person who practices what she believes..

The day of the surgery, Danny kissed BJ and squeezed her hand as she was wheeled to the operating room. She received what she referred to as her "I don't care shot" and was calm and relaxed as they moved her down the hall with her catheter and IV pole in tow.

The staff was efficient at St. Mary's Hospital. They had seen so many operations that it was a daily routine to them. But this time, they were operating on his wife. All Danny could do was offer passive submission to their fate.

The waiting room was quiet. Danny took a seat on one of the cushioned chairs near the TV mounted high on a wall in the corner. NBC was showing the process of counting the paper ballots for the presidential election in Florida. Danny never had heard the word "chad" until one of the election officials in a Florida precinct held up a paper ballot with a tiny piece of paper dangling from it. It seemed so inconsequential that a tiny piece of paper could mean the election for either Al Gore or George W. Bush. At the moment, everything seemed inconsequential to Danny.

There was a tiny, old lady who had slipped into the room unnoticed. She sat two chairs away on the same bank of seats. She looked to be in her mid- to late 80s and had a calm demeanor.

"Do you have a relative or friend in surgery?" Danny asked.

"It's my husband. He has cancer. Cancer of the prostate. At least that's what they suspect." She seemed resigned to whatever might happen.

The lady took off her coat and put it on the chair next to her. She sat quietly for a time, watching TV.

"He isn't going to live much longer," she said, without turning her head. "He's lost so much weight, and he's been in terrible pain. He's 90 years old and says he's ready to go. I hope the good Lord takes him. I just hate seeing him suffer."

Danny wanted to console her but could think of nothing to say.

"My wife has breast cancer. They are giving her a lumpectomy."

"Are you afraid for her?"

"Yes." He paused. "But I think she'll be fine. She's strong-minded and is healthy most of the time."

"It's good to keep your chin up. All of us eventually run out of time. It really isn't all that scary. Billy, my husband, has picked out a blue suit he wants to be buried in. It's blue plaid with a yellow shirt and a blue tie. Billy has terrible taste in clothes, always has. I told him I would see to it that he looked his Sunday best. He told me he would be looking back from the casket, and he didn't want me to be looking sad. He said to smile at him as he lay there with his hands folded across his stomach. That was his way of knowing that he could be at peace and that I would be all right. I plan to do that very thing."

A stocky man in his mid-40s entered the room, wearing surgical green with a cap and a mask that had been untied and was dangling from his neck.

"Mrs. Houghton?" he asked. His expression was not cheerful. "Please come with me." He lead the tiny lady into the hallway.

"Don't be afraid," she said as she left.

Danny was impressed with the little lady showing such grace in a time that would devastate many people. Their conversation had left Danny feeling much more hopeful.

Danny sat in the waiting room for another two hours. His anxiety had eased. He was daydreaming while looking out the window when Dr. Tschirhart walked into the room. He explained that BJ was doing fine and that they would need to look at the removed tissue before they knew for certain they had gotten all of cancer. He also removed four lymph nodes under her left arm as a precaution. Since the tumor they removed was not hormone sensitive, he would order 30 radiation therapy sessions at Seton Cancer Center at St. Mary's Hospital.

Two days later, BJ was discharged. Danny was pleased to dote on her for a change. He cooked meals and saw to her needs.

The radiation treatments started that same week. Seton Cancer Center was a model of efficiency and compassion. The staff was aware of the anxiety experienced by the patients and their families. Danny became acquainted with some of these people as he waited for BJ during her daily therapy. The social barriers that were normally there were dropped. They had cancer in common.

Two of the patients there each day were terminally ill. They found comfort in the social interaction, talking freely and openly about their illness. Danny and BJ were grateful for this place and the comfort of new-found friendships.

A month after the radiation therapy was completed, BJ was told that there was no sign of any remaining cancer.

• 35 •

A DIFFERENT PERSPECTIVE

*"You carry with you the poison of comparisons
and you spend your days waiting for something
you have already had and will never come again."*

~ Romain Gary ~

Winter, 2004

The wind whipped and flexed the great wall of windows. Danny Pratt held his fingertips on the glass as the icy air moved over the tarmac, swirling powdered snow. A maintenance crew sprayed de-icer over the wing of a 707 from the tops of two cherry pickers. The pressured spray caused large chunks to fall from the plane. Visibility was 30 feet at most. The crew members wore heavy parkas and ski masks under a spotlight that created an island of light in the darkness.

A female voice came over the intercom: "Your attention, please. Due to the current weather conditions, all scheduled departing flights have been canceled until further notice. We thank you for your patience."

"Crap," Danny said.

It was warm and comfortable inside the terminal at Flint's Bishop Airport. There was a massive storm moving through the southern half of the Lower Peninsula of Michigan at a fast pace. The southern-most tip of the storm reached all the way to Texas.

BJ sat reading, oblivious to the delay in their departure. Danny was annoyed and at the same time, envious of her ability to detach herself completely from all other stimuli while reading a book, making Danny what he called a book widower. Until she completed the thick tome she was reading, she would be somewhere else.

Danny liked to think he had the same capability to turn off the outside world and focus. But he really couldn't remember the last time he was able to do that, at least in his adult life. He had been plagued with the anxiety that if he didn't pay attention to everything going on around him, he would miss something vital. He hadn't liked himself. Never had. He found that his expectations had been much too high. His art had become lifeless and plain. Whatever the spark was that once had driven him to inspiration fizzled and died.

It took a few shake-ups for Danny to finally decide what was really important. BJ's breast cancer was a harrowing experience. Seeing her break down in tears caused him to pull his attention from himself and focus on his wife. It made him realize he would do whatever was required. He realized how very much he loved her.

Danny eventually forgave himself for his imperfectness. He forgave his mother, now in her grave, for her hatefulness while in the terrible grips of Alzheimer's disease.

He determined what his beliefs really were by asking questions and coming up with honest answers that were supported by his own rational thinking.

He was getting better with the self-loathing. Though not completely gone, it had improved to Danny's betterment.

The airport TV was playing the same old garbage. He and BJ were paying a large amount of money for cable TV, something that really held no interest for him at all. He liked to think he was detached from the world of television. Though he did enjoy watching the NFL games, the Tigers and occasional boxing match, TV was the scourge of modern life. The media had the ability to twist whatever mind it held captive. To him, life was what happened before your eyes. Anything else was an abstraction.

BJ had been talking to her niece, Kristine, this past summer at a family funeral and told her she would like to get away from

Michigan for a week or so during the winter months. Kristine told BJ she had a proposition.

She and her husband of 15 years, Harrison, were planning to take a Windjammer Cruise in the Bahamas. They were leaving their two sons, Truman, a feisty 10-year-old; Dunc, the 12-year-old; and their Doberman, Shredder; at their home in Brownsville, Texas. She wondered if BJ would consider living in their home for two weeks at no charge, in return for watching the two boys and the dog. "Just see to their needs," she had said. "They aren't bad kids, just full of energy and mischief. Like we were."

Danny heard BJ chuckling on the phone to Kristine and knew something was in the wind by the sound of his wife's voice.

"She's letting us use her house for two weeks, at no charge. It would be like a two-week vacation," she said.

Danny did not react to what she said but sat there staring, waiting for her to get to the part where she told what was expected of them. She did not volunteer that information.

"So, what is expected of us while we use her house? Are the two boys going with them to the Bahamas?"

"No. All we need to do is see to their needs."

"What about Shredder, that likes to eat people?"

"Yes. We'll be caring for him, too."

Danny remembered the two boys from the funeral that summer. Truman was hyper. Dunc was showing early signs of rebellion. He had spiked his Mohawk and painted it blue. He was a real stand-out at the funeral of BJ's conservative, Southern aunt. The boy bragged that he wanted to get his eyebrows and his navel pierced, then described the tattoo he was planning to get of a Megadeth cover illustration he had seen on one of the group's albums. Danny found it disturbing just to look at Dunc. Everything about the young boy was screaming: "Look at me, damn it!"

"Did you tell Cousin Kristine we would do it?"

"No. I said I would talk to you about it."

"But you were looking self-confident when you hung up the phone. You're thinking that you can talk me into this aren't you?"

"Well, I know that you love me."

And that was that. Now here he was at Bishop Airport, getting ready to board a jet to head full-speed into the unknown in Brownsville, Texas.

Danny had been a strict disciplinarian to his children. He didn't know anymore how he would react when the boys challenged or ignored his authority. The "old Danny" would have lost his temper and asserted his demands just as his dad and his dad's dad had done. He no longer thought he could control his children. He no longer wanted to. He only wished for them to make themselves into someone people would admire.

The old ways of intimidation and corporal punishment were gone. The world had made so many drastic changes in a short period of time. His grandkids streaked around in his peripheral vision like pin balls between video games. This is what life is to young people now, he thought. Complete isolation, like BJ, whenever she reads a book. Sitting in his son, Derick's, living room and watching his son and his boys playing video games, he had seen how focused their young brains were and the incredible hand-eye coordination they possessed with the video controls. He could see portions of the brain being developed as they stretched their capabilities somewhere in cyberspace.

There were perhaps 80 to 100 people waiting for the same flight, plus another 200 waiting for flights at the other gates. Some of them found a place to take a nap on the padded seats. Others used carry-on bags for pillows, stretching out on the floor. One nervous young man paced like a lion in a cage.

Two young girls who looked to be in their early 20s talked loudly, gesturing with their hands, using "Valley Girl" phrases, which was the current, cool way for young, rebellious girls to talk. One of them had spiked hair with points that stuck out like an alarmed blow fish. The other girl had shaved her hair except for a braided ponytail that seemed to be glued to the back of her head. Both girls were pierced repeatedly in the lips, ears and eyebrows, with gold and silver rings protruding from the wounds.

These kids can't be poor, he thought. They must have a pound of gold on their sickly, anorexic bodies. What would these kids do if they were caught outside in the blowing snow? The blow fish couldn't possibly put a hood or a hat on. The gold and silver hardware on the abused young bodies would make the Michigan winter seem even colder.

What a blatant exhibition of the willingness to mate. He didn't remember anyone who was that radical when he was the same age.

"Here I am. Come mate with me." There was no pursuit to speak of. But he had to admit it was his generation that started the "free love" concept. It was quite a stretch to think that these people evolved from his generation, the offspring of flower children.

He sat down next to BJ.

"Look at what will inherit the Earth," he said to BJ. But BJ was only half through her chick book. "Well, I can see what I'll be doing for the next several hours, talking to myself. I'm going to the bar for a cold beer." BJ gave no response. He walked over behind her chair, putting his lips close to her ear: "I'm going to the bar to have a beer," he whispered.

"OK," she said, giving him a dismissive gesture with her right hand.

The small bar was crowded and smoky. He checked out the smoke-eaters to see if they were functioning. He found the only available seat at the bar and ordered a Busch Light. There was some pleasant music playing. It was Tony Bennett's "I Left My Heart in San Francisco." At least the entire world hadn't gone to the dogs. He was feeling a little surly. Not seeing anyone that he recognized, he decided to sit here, listen to the music and get a little buzzed. He would be here for some time. His wife would be reading that damn book until she finished it. Why not?

The middle-aged woman tending bar seemed a little stressed. She was the only one working, and the bar was filled to capacity.

"Where you headed?" asked a husky, female voice to his right.

"Straight to Hades," Danny replied, only half-joking. He turned to see a woman who was close to his age, maybe a little older. Her expression was flat. The muscles in her face completely had given in to gravity.

"Sounds more exciting than where I'm going." She made a dismissive gesture and exhaled a cloud of smoke.

Her frail arm and hand supported her chin as she leaned heavily on the bar. The bartender brought her another mixed drink. She took a sip and left a print of her lips in bright red on the glass. A half-dozen cigarette butts in the ashtray were printed with the same color. She looked depressed and drunk. Danny did not want to sit here for the next few hours and listen to this poor creature complain. He had problems of his own. He decided to contribute nothing more to the conversation.

The woman waited for a response. "Well, a goodwill ambassador," she said. "Go screw yourself."

Danny was finishing his beer and was going to move on when the woman suddenly turned to him.

"I know you," she said. "You graduated from Bay City Central in '66. You're Danny Pratt."

Danny turned to look at her, trying to find something familiar in her face and her expression. He saw nothing.

"Marilyn Turgel," she said, her face suddenly brighter.

"Bucky?"

"Yes, Bucky. I'd deliberately forgotten that name. I had my teeth filed down and straightened." She bared her near-perfect teeth. "I had these done back in 1980. Some work was done on my jaw also to allow for a different bite. People stopped staring at my mouth and began to see me as someone other than Bucky." She paused for a moment to take a long drag on her Winston. "You look pretty good for being our age. You must have had an easy life," she said, trying not to slur her words.

"Oh, yes. Life has been just a big bowl of un-pitted sour cherries. I suppose you're going to tell me about all of the hardships you have endured and the agony you have felt over the past 40-plus years. Well, Bucky, I have my sad stories, too. Everything that lives can write a story of pain, misfortune and death. I really don't want to listen to a lament."

"Wow! I'm sorry I stepped on your tail. The Danny Pratt I remember was funny and happy most of the time. You were a really nice guy back then."

"I'd much rather be honest than nice. People think you're an idiot when you're happy all of the time. I remember you as being carefree and content yourself. So, which of us is the bigger idiot?" Danny looked at Bucky, suddenly realizing that what he had just said really didn't make a lot of sense. His face cracked, and he smiled. Bucky was staring with wide eyes.

She began laughing, which made Danny laugh. Both laughed as if someone had just pulled a cork and let loose a geyser.

The laughter continued for several minutes, breaking the ice of their reunion after so many years.

They had many mutual acquaintances and gave whatever history they could offer on each of them. Danny was enjoying himself and after a half-dozen beers, he had attained the buzz he wanted.

"You played in the Central marching band. I remember you and your big bass drum," said Bucky.

"You marched in the parade for Terry McDermot, the guy that was the only person from the U.S. who won a Gold Medal in the '64 Olympics. I thought you looked handsome in your uniform."

"I was skinny as a rail then," Danny said, visualizing the scene as the band marched down to Washington and Center, where McDermot greeted the huge crowd. It seems like that was a century ago."

"Remember the Caris Red Lion?"

"Ya. I loved the hot dogs. We hung out there some days. I remember you showing up with a ski mask. You were trying to be mysterious. I knew it was you when you smiled."

"You mean you knew it was me when you saw the teeth. Do you think I was ugly when we were young, Danny?"

He turned and looked at her. "I didn't ever think you were pretty. But, you certainly were attractive. You were a sexy little filly. You always knew how to dress to show off your body. All of the guys I hung around with in the Band Canyon days thought you were "hot." You had a great body and could really dance up a storm. I can still see you in a miniskirt. Ya. You were quite the number back then. "

"The Band Canyon. Wow. That sure takes me back. I loved to go there and just dance for hours and hours. Remember the Counterpoints, with Alan Hill and Dave Garcia, and the Roll-Air Rink, the Battle of the Bands and Skateland?"

"And Crabbe Road, near Indian Town. That was a great place to park in the middle of a cornfield, with a little pond. I'd stop at Leo Stearns' place and get some beer and spend the rest of the day in isolation with my girlfriend.

"Yes. That's where you took me to seduce me. Do you remember that we did it?"

"I didn't need to do much seducing. You were more than willing," said Danny, with a wide smile.

"What did you think about my teeth? I mean everybody called me Bucky."

"That was just who you were. People liked you that way. I did. That's why I didn't recognize you at first. You're not Bucky anymore."

"But do I look better or worse? You're looking at $23,000 worth of ivory." She opened her mouth to show her dental work again.

"Worse. We all look worse than we did in high school. Good grief, it's been what, 40, 45 years since we graduated."

"When you looked at me, what was your first impression after not seeing me for 40-some years?"

"Do you want an honest answer?"

"Yes, but don't be brutal."

"When I first walked in and glanced at you, not knowing who you were, I saw you as a sad, older woman who was feeling sorry for herself. I definitely didn't want to start a conversation with you. Your whole body had succumbed to the force of gravity. You seem like a lot of baby boomers, afraid of getting old, afraid to die, afraid that life is pretty much over."

"Are you going to sit there and tell me that you are optimistic about your future? We're not going to live forever, you know, Danny. Now is not the time to buy a new house on a 30-year mortgage. We don't have that many years left, or even that many days."

"So take the days that you do have left and feel good about it."

"OK, just like that. I flip a switch and change my attitude and change my life."

"Well, if you want to feel better about yourself, you can start with giving up those coffin nails."

"I can't quit. I've tried and tried." She paused for a moment. "Wait just a minute. I distinctly remember you having a Zippo lighter that smelled like English Leather. I asked you for a light many times 'cause I liked the smell of it."

"I quit. Many times in fact. But the last time, I quit for good, and I haven't smoked in 15 years."

"Why were you successful the last time you quit?" She turned her head to cough.

"That right there. The cough. That's what got me to quit. I had chronic bronchitis, and my health was going down hill. I just decided I wanted to live enough that I could quit. You have to want to live."

"You're not going to give me a sermon, are you?"

"Yes, I am. I tend to be a little idealistic. I have no right to preach at you. It's just that you looked so dismal. And you don't have to be. I'm just thinking that you look so much better now that you've smiled."

Bucky smiled again, showing her perfectly aligned teeth. "Do you remember the campfires we used to have in the Alkali, down on the shore of the river across from Skull Island?"

"Yes. We'd get a couple of cases of Pabst Blue Ribbon from Leo Stearns, build a fire and drink 'til the beer was gone. I remember you dancing around the bonfire when you were really raked. You were uninhibited."

"You were at the party in the old golf course behind Kmart about a year after we graduated. I remember you were hanging around with Louie Green, Dave Piechowiak. ..."

"Yup. And Dennis Hutchinson. Wayne Johnson was there. Man, that guy used to be really wild. He really got into being a full-blooded Chippewa. And Larry Bukowski was at that party, and Tommy Theison. What did you do when the cops snuck up on us with their headlights off?"

" I jumped into someone's car. I don't remember whose, and we drove through that tall grass, then back to the main road."

"You were lucky, Danny said. "We came in Dave Piechowiak's '57 Plymouth and cut through the field with the lights off. We ended up in the ditch. Dave wrecked his car."

"Oh, no. I hadn't heard about that. You were lucky."

"Hold that thought. I'll be right back. I want to check up on my wife, BJ. Be right back."

Danny found BJ where he had left her, lost in the pages of the book. He stopped to reflect on how much he loved this woman. All's well, he thought to himself.

"Do you know what people are missing out on these days?" he asked, as he slid onto the high bar stool next to Bucky. "Good, old-fashioned conversation."

The bartender brought Danny another beer. Bucky paid for it, then turned to look square into Danny's eyes. "I'm glad you came back, even though you sometimes have the personality of a snapping turtle."

Danny noticed her mood had elevated, and she was sitting upright in her chair, smiling brightly. She even looked healthier. "Don't go trying to seduce me. I'm not studding you."

"Why, you presumptuous, pompous ass," she said. But the smile on her face showed she was amused. "You can put a governor on that ego of yours and try just a hint of diplomacy once in a while."

"Good grief. You sound just like my wife."

"Well, I was a wife at one time," she paused. "A damn good one, too. You know I was good in the sack."

"Watch out now. I see a twinkle in your eye."

"I'm so glad I ran into you, Danny Pratt."

"No studding."

"Do you really think I'm coming on to you?"

"Gee, I don't know Bucky. I've only seen your technique a few hundred times."

"Does it bother you, that I'm coming on to you, as you say?"

"Not really. But don't expect me to respond to it. I like being friends with you, Bucky, but I really don't want to fool around with anyone."

"I'll be. You turned into a Mr. Goody Two Shoes."

"No. I've been down that road. I don't want to go there again. Ever."

"So, you're saying that you love your wife?"

"Yes. Very much. She has been through a lot on my behalf. Through all of the years we have been married, I never doubted that she loved me. She's just a good, solid person. Plus, she's good-looking, a great cook and incredible mother. ..."

"All right, I get the picture. I'm happy for you, Danny. I think you might be a pretty good catch yourself."

The bartender was just asking Danny if he cared for another Busch Light when a voice on the PA system broke in to announce that the weather was easing and all of the postponed flights soon would be allowed to depart within the next hour.

"I guess I've had enough." Danny stood and removed several $1 bills for a tip.

"Damn it, Danny Pratt, it was great to see you." Marilyn Turgel stood to give Danny a hug and lost her balance.

"Easy, Bucky." Danny kept her from falling. "You've had quite a few tonight. Let me get you some help."

"No. Just let me borrow an arm and get me to my gate."

Danny slowly walked her to the boarding gate and found her an empty chair. She turned to Danny before sitting down.

"It was great seeing you again, Danny. Would your wife mind if I gave you a hug?"

"Of course not."

Danny gave her a warm hug. She seemed to need some kind of verification. So did he.

She sat down. "Have a great life, Danny."

"Thanks, Bucky. You, too."

Her eyes were tearful, as she smiled brightly.

BJ was as she had been for the past several hours, totally engrossed in her book. He sneaked up behind her and kissed her on the neck.

"You've been drinking. I can smell it," she said, matter-of-factly.

"You caught me. You're not going to spank me are you?"

"I just might." She glanced at him, then went back to her book.

Made in the USA
Lexington, KY
16 January 2015